DEATH HULK

The wounded man rose to his feet, cutlass still lodged in his shoulder. Swinging an arm in a wide arc, the man caught Bryant in the chest with a terrible strength, sending the sailor sprawling into Brooks.

Bryant looked up in horror and disgust at the Frenchman's face. Crooked teeth leered at him from a lipless mouth, the man's skin was stretched and sallow, greying as it rotted. Just a few wisps of mangy hair graced the top of his skull but their attention was drawn to his eye sockets. One was empty, a dark pit of blackness that nevertheless seemed very aware of their presence. The remaining eye dangled by a single cord, bouncing on his sunken cheek as he moved.

"Gods!" Struggling to his feet, Bryant eyed his cutlass, still stuck in the man's shoulder. Steeling himself he leapt forward a step and grasped the hilt of the weapon.

An Abaddon Books™ Publication
www.abaddonbooks.com
abaddon@rebellion.co.uk

First published in 2006 by Abaddon Books™, Rebellion Intellectual
Properties Limited, The Studio, Brewer Street, Oxford, OX1 1QN, UK.

Distributed in the US and Canada by SCB Distributors,15608 South
Century New Drive, Gardena, CA 90248, USA.

10 9 8 7 6 5 4 3 2 1

Editor: Jonathan Oliver
Cover: Mark Harrison
Design: Simon Parr & Luke Preece
Series Advisor: Andy Boot
Marketing and PR: Keith Richardson
Creative Director and CEO: Jason Kingsley
Chief Technical Officer: Chris Kingsley

ISBN 13: 978-1-905437-03-0
ISBN 10: 1-905437-03-X
A CIP record for this book is available from the British Library

Printed in the UK by Bookmarque, Surrey

TOMES OF THE DEAD

DEATH HULK

Matthew Sprange

Abaddon
Books

WWW.ABADDONBOOKS.COM

CHAPTER ONE

The crack of rope against skin, punctuated by moans rising in volume with each stroke, ripped across the main deck. High above, a lone gull circled the furled masts of the *HMS Whirlwind*, oblivious to the human misery below. The entire crew of the frigate stood silent, watching their Bosun administer the Captain's discipline under the watchful eyes of the officers standing rigid on the quarterdeck.

After another two strokes, the Bosun, a heavy set man with the weight of years at sea in his posture, gathered his rope and stood straight as he looked up at the impassive officers.

"A dozen all done, Cap'n," he said.

"Very well, Mr Kennedy. Cut him down and take him to the surgeon." Captain James Havelock nodded. He remained on the quarterdeck, hands behind his back, as he watched the crew file away to their duties as the flogged man was helped below decks to have his bleeding back treated. Corbin, First Lieutenant of the *Whirlwind*, glanced at his Captain and noticed a familiar twitch in Havelock's hawkish nose.

"Third this week, Sir," he said quietly.

"Indeed. The inevitable price of keeping men on ship while land is in sight. But we all have our orders and poor discipline can never be tolerated on His Majesty's ships."

Corbin stayed silent as he looked across the calm waters of Spithead towards land. Dozens of warships lay moored between the *Whirlwind* and the coast, an assortment of sloops, frigates and mighty ships of the line. The pride of the King's Navy was gathered here quiet, laden with awesome potential and yet utterly useless as they awaited direction.

"Still no word of orders?" he asked.

Havelock shook his head. "None, Mr Corbin. And I fear Bonaparte will not dare face us openly at sea." He gave a small grin. "I always thought the man a lion on land but a coward on the ocean."

"We may still have our day, Sir."

"I hope and pray." Havelock glanced down the main deck at the crew of the *Whirlwind*. Most had dispersed but a score remained above deck to go about the dozens of tasks required to merely keep a warship afloat and ready for battle. "Have a word with Mr Kennedy. He needs to keep a tighter grip on the crew. It does us no good to go through this display for every minor infraction that gets reported."

"I always had the impression you find flogging distasteful, Sir," said Corbin.

"It is not a case of that though, in truth, I find it a necessary barbarism," said Havelock. "It is as much a part of discipline as the drills we put our men through or the constant work required to keep this ship clean and hygienic. A warship without discipline is a liability to the Crown and its Captain not worthy of the title. But crews have their own mechanisms for dealing with minor crimes and a good bosun knows all of them. I can live with the odd scuffle below deck but a flogging each day will begin to work against the morale of the crew. Instead of the even-handed rule of authority and justice, it becomes something else. The Captain turns into a bully, or worse, a tyrant. No, inform Mr Kennedy that he is to deal with matters where he can and only bring the worst offenders to our attention."

"As you say, Sir."

Corbin left to descend the stairs to the main deck where he quickly disappeared below to find the Bosun. Havelock walked to the railings and stared at the other vessels moored close to his own, knowing each Captain was facing the same problems he had. The *Whirlwind* had been moored at Spithead for less than two weeks and he knew some ships had been here much longer. He did not envy the disciplinary problems they might be facing. Up to now, the Admiralty had seen fit to keep the entire fleet in a state of constant readiness as rumours of a French attempt at invasion rolled across the channel as regularly as the waves. It was plain to every Captain here that the fleet could not remain in this state indefinitely but Havelock was not entirely sure that the decision makers within the Mad House were completely aware of what was happening at Spithead.

Only one remedy could solve the ills of the fleet. Officers and men alike required action. As Havelock had said to his Lieutenant, he could only hope and pray that orders would arrive soon. Either that or Bonaparte decide to invade.

"I swear it's true, right as I'm standin' 'ere!"

"Murphy, you're full of it." The two sailors were shrouded in the darkness of the *Whirlwind's* interior, both slouched across the gun carriage they had been tasked with cleaning. Brush in hand, Bryant leaned over the cannon he and his crew had christened 'Blow Hard' and grinned a toothless smile. "Just how come you heard this anyway?"

"I over 'eard the marines talkin' last night," Murphy said with some conviction, scratching at his thinning hair.

"You trust the words of a lobster? Lord, man, they have less to do than us right now – their mouths are running away with themselves."

"Nah, not this one. 'E's just come on board, not more than a week ago. An' 'e's been talkin' to others in 'is regiment – they've just come back from Spain, see?"

Bryant sighed. "Well, that plain just doesn't make sense in itself. If Boney is on the attack, why are they bringing soldiers back to England?"

"Hey, I don't pretend to know what 'appens in the army. They're odd enough as it is. They gotta come back sometime, right? Like a ship goes back to port for refittin' and stuff."

Pausing, Bryant thought for a moment. "No, you can just send supplies to an army, wherever you are."

"Whatever," Murphy said, refusing to be waylaid. "I 'eard 'em talkin'. Boney has raised the dead and they now fight in 'is army. Our boys are facin' walkin' corpses, sweepin' across Spain, if ya please!"

The two men worked in silence for a few minutes as they laboured over the cannon, each casting a look out of the open gunport towards land from time to time. Murphy caught Bryant's eye as the taller man turned back towards the gun carriage.

"So how long d'ya think they'll keep us 'ere?" he asked.

Bryant shrugged. "All depends on the Lords that run the war. And the French." He smiled. "Still, if you are right about the fighting dead, maybe they'll send us along to the Spanish coast to root them out!"

"Hey, don't joke about it!" Murphy said as he crossed himself. "Them things are real, I swear. I ain't fightin' 'em. Ya can't kill somethin' that is already dead."

Glancing around, Bryant noticed that the conversations

of the other gun crews were becoming subdued and he gave Murphy a warning stare. "Keep it quiet, man. You know the Captain doesn't like this talk."

Murphy was ready to argue his point but had the sense to lean forward and whisper. "Okay, look at it this way," he said. "S'pose we get our orders tomorrow and then set sail for Spain, as you say. What are ya goin' to do when we see a French frigate, close to board with 'er and then see a bunch of zombies swingin' over the rails, cutlass and knife in hand? Ya goin' to stand an' fight?"

Standing straight and rubbing his chin, Bryant considered this. "Can zombies swing from ropes? Aren't they all, like, shambling?"

Bryant's sarcasm was not lost on Murphy and the shorter man gave him a withering stare, which was returned with a smile.

"Look, Murphy, you and I have been on this ship for more than a year a piece. The Captain will see us right. He won't go sailing us into anything we can't handle."

It was Murphy's turn to stop and think. "Well, that is very true, my friend. But a Cap'n is only as good as 'is officers and crew. Ain't none of us 'ere whose faced a zombie before."

"That is because they do not exist," muttered Bryant, though Murphy either did not hear him or chose not to, and continued unabated.

"As for the officers, you know what I think about them."

Bryant looked up sharply. "For the love of God, Murphy, hold your tongue!"

Instead, Murphy leaned further forward and whispered. "Corbin, that new Lieutenant? Money troubles. 'eard it from Jefferies. Signed on to get a big prize – an' ya know what officers who are after the money are like. Might risk anythin' to get it, if there is nothin' for them back at 'ome. An' ya know what..."

A sharp clash resounded across the gun deck as Bryant brought the back of his brush down hard on the rough metal of the cannon, cutting Murphy off. A few curious glances were sent his way but Bryant ignored them.

"Murphy," he said, very seriously. "Imagine all the zombies you want, tell me all the stories you like about the French but never, ever talk about an officer like that. Hell, man, you know what that talk costs!"

Chastened, Murphy went back to work, taking an intense interest in a stain on the side of the gun's carriage.

"And what are you talking to Jefferies for anyway?" Bryant asked. "The man's an out and out thief! And a liar! Take what he says with extreme caution. Better yet, stay away from him! Your life will be easier."

"I s'pose," said Murphy. "Still, ya never answered me. What will ya do when zombies start crawlin' over our deck?"

Bryant sighed. "Well, *if* that happened, I guess we fight. If the Captain tells us to fight, that's what we do. It's what we are all here for." He shook his head. "The Captain won't send us into battle unless he knows we can win. He's too canny for that. The sea is in his blood, you might say."

"Aye, 'e came from the right family alright," Murphy agreed. "Still... hey!"

Murphy was pitched off balance from behind as a large shadow passed through the crowded deck, sending him sprawling beside his cannon. The short man looked up into the twilight of the gun deck.

"Ah, I'm *so* sorry Murphy," said a deep coarse voice that echoed from the wooden walls and ceiling. The work of the nearby gun crews came to a stop as they glanced out of the corner of their eyes towards Murphy and Bryant, anxious to see what was going on and yet not wanting to draw attention to themselves.

"Didn't see you down there. P'raps you should take a bit more care while workin', eh?" The speaker was a large and heavy-set man who, despite the best efforts of the Bosun, looked as if he had not washed for weeks.

"Have a care, Jessop," said Bryant, instinctively lowering his brush to his side where it would not be in immediate view.

"You know," said the newcomer. "I find myself at a loose end. Couldn't 'elp but think that maybe Murphy 'ere would 'ave a few stories about the Frenchies 'e might like to share." He stooped low over the sprawled Murphy. "What about it, eh? What 'ave you 'eard the Frogs are up to this time? Taken over Spain yet, 'ave they? Got some new secret ship that will clobber us good 'an proper?"

Ignoring the few quiet titters from the other gun crews, Bryant moved to the side of his cannon to get Jessop's attention away from Murphy and on to him. Resisting the impulse to push the man's shoulder to get him to turn around, knowing it would likely lead to yet another fight, Bryant instead said "You got nothing better to do, Jessop?"

Jessop adopted a hurt expression. "Hey, no need to come the high an' mighty. I was just askin' Murphy 'ere for a few tales. Nothin' wrong with that."

"If ya lackin' in work, Jessop, I'm certain I can find somethin' for ya to do!" The Bosun's voice lashed across the gun deck like his flogging rope, instantly returning the other gun crews to work. Bryant stood unmoving as Jessop turned round to face the Bosun.

"Ah, Mr Kennedy, I was just on my way when I noticed li'l Murphy 'ere lost 'is balance." He stooped to give a hand to Murphy, who accepted it after a second's hesitation, grinning nervously around the gun deck as he stood.

"On with ya work, Jessop!" ordered Kennedy. "I don't want any slackin' down here, the Cap'n will be down afore sunset for inspection!"

"Right ya are, Sir!" said Jessop, raising a cocked finger to his brow in salute.

He turned to walk calmly back to his own cannon but brushed Bryant with his shoulder as he went, leaning his weight into the blow. Bryant staggered and immediately flushed with anger. Throwing a punch, he caught Jessop in a right hook straight across the chin with his brush, but the big man instantly flicked his head back, grinning. Ignoring the Bosun's cry for order, Jessop grabbed his opponent by the shoulders and brought a knee up into his stomach, causing Bryant to exhale heavily. Winded, Bryant still managed to reach up with his left hand and grasp Jessop's throat in a tight grip. He maintained the hold as Jessop rained down a solid blow that knocked him to the floor.

Pulling Jessop down with him, Bryant again rammed the heavy brush into the man's face who this time rolled with the hit, and the two of them scrambled for purchase on the wooden floor as each sought to gain an advantage over the over. Jessop strained his neck muscles in an attempt to keep air flowing into his lungs, a task that Bryant was having trouble enough doing himself. Jessop managed to pin Bryant's legs to the floor with one of his own but Bryant twisted again before landing another solid blow. Growling in anger, Jessop responded by heaving the full weight of his body, forcing Bryant to the ground and preparing to rain blow after blow on his opponent.

He raised a fist but, before he could sink it into Bryant's

face, his arm was gripped tightly by Kennedy, who dragged him upright and then stood between the two men, bracing them each at arm's length.

"I said that is enough!" he roared.

Jessop's expression was triumphant but Bryant's face showed something close to murderous intent.

"Back to work, Jessop!" Kennedy said. "An' be thankful I don't report ya to the Capt'!" Slouching off, Jessop retreated further down the gun deck where he received a pat on the back from one of his own crew. Shaking his head, Kennedy turned back to Bryant.

"Gods, man, why do ya let 'im provoke ya like that? Ya think I don't 'ave enough trouble down 'ere?"

Rubbing his stomach, Bryant winced. "Sorry, Sir. Won't happen again, Sir."

"Bryant, ya better than this. We all 'ave to deal with bullies like Jessop but ya never, ever throw the first punch. Never! Ya know that if this went before the Cap'n, it would be you for the flogging, not Jessop."

Shame-faced, Bryant just nodded.

"Right. Just reign in that temper. Oh, an' make sure ya do a good job on the gun – I wasn't kiddin' about the Cap'n comin' below later on."

"Kennedy, a moment of your time."

Though he had been aware of high tensions on the far end of the gun deck, Lieutenant Corbin had taken his time climbing down the stairs into the darkness before making his way forward. It was not until the Bosun had passed down the length of the ship, keeping an eye on the working gun crews as he went, that Corbin called out to him.

"Mr Corbin, Sir, what can I do for ya?" Kennedy greeted him.

"More trouble?" Corbin asked, cocking an eye down

the gun deck.

"Nothing serious, Sir. Just steam getting let off."

Corbin took Kennedy's arm, drawing him closer as he lowered his voice. "Word from the Captain, Kennedy. Try to keep things running smoothly down here. All these floggings do the crew no good."

The Bosun frowned. "With respect, I know my job well enough, Sir. A fist fight below decks is part an' parcel with ship life. I only bring the worst offenders to your attention and the Capt'n."

"I see. Anything I should know about?" Corbin asked, gesturing down the gun deck.

"Not this time, Sir. See, I don't mind passions spillin' over about the French, or the food, or who stole what from who. It's just the boredom talkin'. But I won't stand for no back chat or insult toward the Capt' and 'is officers. Those would be floggin' words. Ain't no other way it can be."

"Okay, Kennedy. Keep them straight and we'll get you your action."

"Well, they can't keep us moored here forever, right Sir?"

Corbin returned Kennedy's smile. "I am sure we'll be setting sail soon."

Climbing the stairs back to the main deck and sunlight, Corbin took a deep breath. He had long since become acclimatised to the darkness and the strange, often powerful, odours below the deck of a ship, but it always came as some small relief when he returned to a place where the wind could freely blow. Only the night before, he had heard Captain Havelock describe the conditions of a Spanish frigate he had once boarded. Such ships might only be properly cleaned when they put into port for refitting and even then it might sometimes be missed. Havelock had spoken of refuse slopping about the lower decks and of air in the hold that was actually lethal if a man were to spend more than a minute within. The ships of the French and American navies were apparently treated in much the same way, with their Captains looking at the fastidious cleanliness of the King's Navy as some strange English affectation. His Captain believed that attendance to hygiene was just as important to the running of a good ship as regular gun drills and, given Havelock's record, Corbin was not about to disagree.

Running his hand along the rail as he walked across the main deck, Corbin marched up to the quarterdeck, where he saw his Captain engaged in observation exercises with the *Whirlwind's* two midshipmen, Buxton and Rawlinson. Both were about fifteen years old and still some way from their Lieutenant's exam, but Corbin knew that Havelock had been impressed by their attention to detail and acceptance of shipboard life. He guessed that by having just two midshipmen on board, rather than the usual gaggle of four or five, a healthy rivalry had sprung up between them which drove their studies on. Taking position at the centre of the quarterdeck, Corbin watched the crew go about their duties as he waited for his Captain to finish the lesson.

After several minutes, Havelock noticed Corbin's regular glances in his direction and set the midshipmen a theoretical navigation exercise that would keep them occupied for some time, before joining his Lieutenant.

"Mr Corbin."

"Sir. I spoke with Kennedy and I am satisfied that he is conducting the discipline of the ship as he should. Only the most serious charges are being brought to us."

"And what is Kennedy's criteria for that?" asked Havelock.

"Disputes between crewmen are resolved by himself. Talk aimed at either yourself or the officers is, umm... "

Havelock smiled. "Try not to take such things personally, Mr Corbin. It is a sailor's God-given right to find fault in those above him." Noticing Corbin had given him a strange look, he continued. "But there is always a line and certain things should never be said out loud, no matter what a man is thinking. The Captain has to be the ultimate authority on a ship and nothing can be permitted to undermine that. I will not pass comment on what a man thinks but if he should make remarks that can be construed as mutinous, that is a fire that must be quenched immediately."

"I think we can rely on Kennedy's discretion, Sir."

"Good. However, I still have concerns about the frequency of these floggings. You do not have to go below deck to sense the tension on this ship."

"The men are all looking for action, and soon. Sometimes I think it would be better if the French just started their invasion now."

"Be careful what you wish for, Mr Corbin!" Havelock said, laughing. "God and his mistress the sea have a habit of subverting your desires!"

"That may be true, Sir, but I think the French might take one look at the fleet here and sail back home sharp."

Glancing at the assembled warships once again, Havelock had to agree. "However, that is all it is – a display. There is plenty of action to go round, especially for frigates such as the *Whirlwind*. If the French start moving or raiding our ships, likely as not it will be the frigate captains who receive orders first. Spare pity for the officers onboard the ships of the line. They were the first to be moored here and will be the last to leave, setting sail only when definite action against the French is expected."

"That is one reason I never found any shame in serving onboard a frigate," said Corbin.

"Oh, don't let any of your peers in the Admiralty snub you. For my money, you can keep the glory and prestige of a ship of the line. Frigates, Mr Corbin. They are the true masters of the sea and, without them, the Empire would crumble into oblivion and barbarity. Take a good look at the *Whirlwind*," he gestured towards the bow. "A fine ship with speed of sail and a turn that would humble a vessel half her size. With regular gun drills, she can easily out-shoot a French ship of the line and she is nimble enough to keep an enemy on the back foot. What she lacks in heavier and longer-ranged guns, she more than makes up for in speed and agility."

"She certainly is a fine ship, Sir."

"Wait until you have had a full voyage on board her, and you'll say that with some affection," said Havelock, smiling. "The *Whirlwind* is a fine ship and aptly named. She also has a strong crew and a good selection of officers." He gestured to the two midshipmen who had turned back to back so neither could see the calculations of the other. "Look, we even have two of the best midshipmen in the fleet, both eager and attentive. Not always the most obvious traits in lads so young. I am glad I accepted their fathers' recommendations."

"Sir, on that note, I wanted to thank you personally for accepting my commission on board the *Whirlwind*. I do not believe it could have been an easy choice, especially with Wynton and Hague already on ship," Corbin said, referring to the Second and Third Lieutenants of the *Whirlwind*.

Havelock frowned. "Do not try to second guess me, Mr Corbin. I do not judge men out of hand and every one of us can find mistakes in his past. I go by what a man says and what he does. You will have every opportunity to prove yourself onboard this ship. As for anything else, well, you know and I know, and that is all that needs to be said about it."

Hanging his head for a second, Corbin tugged the lip of his hat in a salute of respect to his Captain. "Right you are, Sir."

"Good," Havelock said. "Well, that has been said. Now, let us see if our young midshipmen have successfully navigated the Cape, or whether they are on their way to Antarctica. Mr Buxton, Mr Rawlinson, I hope you have completed your task by now!"

CHAPTER TWO

Following the regular routine of shipboard life, the men of the *Whirlwind* found themselves engaged in their unrelenting chores early in the morning. Some were in their hammocks below decks, having just completed the previous watch, fighting for sleep amidst the continuous noise of their shipmates at work. A dozen men worked on their hands and knees on the main deck, pushing rough stones across a wet deck in an effort to rub it as smooth and clean as their Captain desired, while in the masts more toiled with heavy sails and ropes as the furled sails were checked and rechecked. Most had already partaken of breakfast but the smell of fresh cooked meat with eggs, the one luxury of being moored so close to port, still floated up from the galley.

Below the main deck, more men worked to wash the hold, deploy windsails that would circulate air within the nether regions of the ship, and inventory stores. Warships such as the *HMS Whirlwind* were the most sophisticated and advanced machines of their time, requiring an almost unimaginable amount of man-hours to keep them afloat and seaworthy every day, even while in port.

"Boat approaching larboard!"

The cry from the lookout high above at the top of the mainmast caused Lieutenant Corbin to glance up in some surprise and he walked to the railings of the quarterdeck, extending his telescope. Through the glass, he saw a small rowboat closing with the *Whirlwind*, a team of eight marines straining at the oars while another, a sergeant he presumed, stood at the prow trying to gain the attention of the frigate. A flicker of hope caused Corbin to smile briefly. Of late, the Admiralty had been employing marines to ferry orders to and from the ships moored at Spithead and maybe, just maybe...

"Mr Wynton," he said, getting the attention of the ship's Second Lieutenant, who had been inspecting the results of the crew cleaning the main deck. "Would you be so good as to greet our visitor?"

Though they kept on working at their assigned tasks, Corbin could see every man above deck had at least half an eye on Wynton as he stood to the railings and ordered a rope ladder down the side of the ship. It was not long before men started rising from below decks, suddenly having found an important job to do within ear shot of the marine sergeant as he clambered up the hull of the *Whirlwind.*

The sergeant, his bright red uniform seeming almost out of place among the dark blues of the *Whirlwind's* officers and the rather more varied clothes of the crew, saluted Wynton sharply and then produced a sealed pouch which he gave to the Lieutenant. He then turned around sharply and disappeared down the side of the ship as quickly as he had arrived, leaving Wynton to approach Corbin, who met him down the stairs from the quarterdeck. The younger Lieutenant had a gleam in his eyes, clearly sharing the same hopes as Corbin.

"Keep the men calm, Mr Wynton," said Corbin in a low voice. "No need to get them excited until we know what is in here."

"Right you are, Mr Corbin," Wynton said before turning to the crew, many of whom had halted their work altogether as curiosity overcame them. "Okay, men, no one told you to stop! Back to it!"

Descending into the darkness below deck, Corbin could

not keep a slight spring from his stride as he hurried to the stern of the ship and the Captain's quarters. He found himself just as eager to discover if they had been given new orders as any of the crew but resolved not to show any outward indications of excitement. There were some things an officer could not be seen to indulge in.

Noticing no one waiting in the small anteroom known as the coach, Corbin passed straight through to the doors of the great cabin and knocked. He was greeted a few seconds later by Havelock's voice bidding him enter.

Inside, the Captain sat at a large oak table before the large seven-paned window through which streamed the bright sun-lit day, causing Corbin to blink after having just got used to the darkness of the rest of the upper deck. Havelock was scribbling another entry in the ship's log, a leatherbound tome sacred to all the ship's officers while the remains of his breakfast lay adrift on the great table. He spoke without looking up at his Lieutenant.

"Yes, Mr Corbin? What can I do for you?"

Corbin could not help but smile as he spoke. "Captain, the marines just arrived bearing a message. Orders?"

Havelock looked up at this news. "Perhaps, Mr Corbin, perhaps. But let us not get ahead of ourselves." Despite the Captain's calmness, Corbin could sense a change in his demeanour as Havelock stood up and walked round the table. He took the offered pouch and broke the seal after a momentary inspection. Corbin had to fight from fidgeting as silence descended on the great cabin while the Captain read the letter, with only the sounds of gulls and the sea lapping against the hull breaking the monotony. Presently, Havelock looked up from the letter and smiled.

"Mr Corbin, our hopes and prayers have been answered!"

"We are to set sail?"

"With the tide on the morrow. And we have a good chance of action – there is a French frigate that the Admiralty needs sinking. Here... " He offered the letter to Corbin who anxiously scanned its contents.

You are hereby required and directed to proceed without loss of time in His Majesty's Ship under your command to the Cape of Good Hope for the purpose of intercepting the French frigate Elita, destroying or taking her as prize.

The Elita has this past three months sunk or captured sixteen merchant vessels sailing around the Cape and has become a liability to the Empire's continued shipping. She is believed to be under the command of a Captain Guillot, formerly of the Boudeuse. Expect no reinforcements in Southern waters.

List of merchant shipping sunk or captured by the Elita proceeds...

"Captain..." he began to ask but Havelock held up a hand.

"There is much to discuss, Mr Corbin, but I believe we would be better off doing that when others are present. If you would be so good as to request the presence of the other officers and midshipmen to my table tonight, all questions can be answered then. In the meantime, make preparations to sail and inform the purser that if he requires anything for the stores, he has precious little time. Ah, and please ask my steward to attend immediately – this will be our last chance to avail ourselves of food from shore and I believe that officer and jack alike will be grateful of a real meal before we start on what we have in the galley."

"Yes, Captain. I'll attend to it."

"Excellent. For my part, I must consult the charts of the Southern oceans and our hunting grounds."

Though Lieutenant Corbin had been careful not to mention any specifics of the *Whirlwind's* new mission, his subsequent orders to the crew and officers left no one in any doubt that the ship was to set sail very soon. Consequently, rumours started to run rampant.

The sceptical were quick to point out that the *Whirlwind*, a single frigate, had been assigned to nothing more than convoy duty, protecting some fat merchants on a lonely piece of the sea that would never see any French flag sailing. The doomsayers scoffed at this, opining that the French had already won the war in Spain and were even now loading up ships ready for an invasion of England. The King's Navy would be outnumbered at least three to one and the entire fleet would be at the bottom of the channel within a week. Some of the more optimistic actually liked this idea, cheered at the thought of mere three-to-one odds, and confident that a single British ship could withstand the battering of a half dozen French vessels and still remain victorious. The excitable predicted that the *Whirlwind* was the lead element in a reconnaissance squadron that would hunt down and locate the French fleet, tying it up with a series of dashing and heroic actions until the main bulk of the King's Navy could be brought to bear.

Then there were those like Murphy, who happily adopted the latest rumour they heard, then embellished it. Fleets of French ships suddenly grew extended holds crammed full of dead men walking, ready to be unleashed on England's green soil. Stories of a coming invasion became tales of French soldiers (and their zombies, of course) already landing in Yorkshire and setting fire to entire towns. Rumours of French soldiers sweeping the British out of Spain became an account of how the whole of Europe was under the sway of Napoleon – who had recently been turned into an ever-living zombie.

Each new rumour was as readily accepted as the last but even those predicting doom began to work doubly hard as the long stay at Spithead drew rapidly to a close. The extra ration of rum at the end of the day, granted by Havelock, went down especially well, and most of the crew gathered in a toast to their Captain, whom they wished good health and good luck in the coming voyage.

In the great cabin, the mood was similarly buoyant, as officers and midshipmen ate pork with fresh vegetables in a feast prepared by the Captain's steward, and enjoyed the free-flowing wine. Havelock sat at the head of the table, listening to his officers talk among themselves but though he had intended to have the orders read aloud at the end of the meal, he could sense the growing anticipation of those around him and presently gave Corbin the nod to pass on the words of the Admiralty. The midshipmen and other two lieutenants hung onto every one of Corbin's words as he read the letter but it did not take long for the questions and comments to come pouring in after he had finished.

"With luck, the French will not expect a warship in the area if their spies in Portsmouth are watching the fleet," said Third Lieutenant Hague.

Havelock smiled. "Do not count on that, Mr Hague. It is always best to imagine that French spies are at least as good as those we have in Spain and France. They'll notice us leave alright."

Hague snorted. "Filthy spies. That is no way to fight a war, buried in Portsmouth while counting masts."

"And what about our British spies in Paris and Calais?" asked the Captain jovially. "Those brave and noble fellows who tell us what Napoleon is up to, as they constantly wait for a knife in the back?"

"That's different," Hague sniffed, causing everyone at the table to laugh.

"What do we know of the *Elita*?" asked Corbin. "Have you seen her before, Captain?"

"Once," Havelock said. "While she was in port at Brest. A two-decker, likely very fast. Fourth-rater by our standards. Fifty guns, at least."

The table was silent for a few seconds as they digested this information. According to their Captain, the *Elita* was larger than the *Whirlwind*, with more than half as many cannon again and possibly three times the crew.

"The Frogs are building more ships that way," said Hague. "Able to turn sharply with the wind behind them while carrying enough guns to worry a third-rater. When I was last in London I heard tales of the Admiralty commissioning the design of similar ships. Give it a few years and all frigates will be built that way."

"Are they copying the Americans?" Midshipman Rawlinson asked, his round and youthful face fired by the prospect of action and not at all daunted by the news of their quarry's size.

"In concept, yes," said Havelock. "They are what the Americans call super-frigates, only slightly larger than a ship like the *Whirlwind* and yet packed to the gills with cannon and men. The hull and mast design will be all French though, and so should be respected. Hull and masts are what will keep the *Elita* nimble, rather than having all that extra weight robbing her of agility. Such ships are actually quite impressive."

"But are British ships not superior to those of the French?" Rawlinson asked. "Or those of any other nation?"

Havelock sipped his wine before answering but all eyes were on him. "No. Our crews are better trained and better disciplined. Our ships are kept in better working order – and that makes all the difference. However, ship for ship, you have to assume the French and Americans, even the Spanish, are at least our equals. They have some very clever naval architects overseas." He noticed that not all around the table had been convinced by his words. "Look at it this way. If we capture the *Elita*, she will join the King's Navy – you might even get a chance to serve on her later in your careers!"

This comment, at least, was joined with smiles as each man considered his future after this mission. If it succeeded, their careers were guaranteed for at least a while.

"What about this Guillot, the *Elita's* Captain. Do you know the man?" Corbin asked.

"No. That means he is either new and inexperienced, or he has been away from France for a long time, in which case he might be immensely wise in the ways of the sea." Havelock smiled at his officers. "Take your pick. Of course, it might just be that I do not know of every captain out there flying under the Tricolore!"

"Well, in the coming fight, I would rather be here, on the *Whirlwind*, serving under you, Captain, than this Guillot," said Hague.

"Flattery will only get you so far," said Havelock with a grin. "Still, French captains should have our respect every bit as much as their ships do. You should always go into battle assuming your enemy is at least as smart as you are. The difference between he and I will be marked in our crews. Even though we still use press-gangs, our crews are far more disciplined. Every man knows exactly what to do when the cannon start firing and the wood starts splintering. The same cannot be said for those who serve under a French captain. If you ever find yourself wondering why I have ordered one drill or another, your answer lies there."

"Captain, how do you intend to fight the *Elita*? There must be a way to even the odds," said Hague.

"Well, first we have to find her but that will be a relatively simple matter so long as she continues to hunt merchantmen. As for battle... " Havelock paused, considering. "In a straight duel, she outguns us and probably has heavier guns that can out range ours. We cannot rely on superior manoeuvrability, though in those stakes I would tend to bet on the *Whirlwind*. We must also avoid any boarding action until the *Elita* has been pounded into submission, as she also has sheer weight of numbers on her side. No, we must endeavour to close range as quickly as possible, sailing straight into her guns if necessary, then keep her off balance until the job is done."

"I believe that is what Lord Nelson would do," said Corbin with a smile, causing everyone to raise their glass in salute of the famous admiral.

"I heard that Nelson said a brawl in the ocean is preferable to a straight line duel," said Rawlinson, drawing more than one incredulous gaze from the assembled officers.

Havelock smiled. "Well, there is a bit more to it than that, and far be it for me to criticise such a man as Admiral Nelson, but he does have a tendency to simplify things somewhat. If you have made your approach properly and caught your enemy off guard or without the wind, trained your crew to outshoot his, have officers and midshipmen who will keep the men steady, and have not tested Lady Luck too often in the past – then maybe, just maybe, drawing alongside the enemy and hammering constantly at him will carry the day."

"Is this not a job for two frigates, or even a small fleet?" Second Lieutenant Wynton asked, provoking Corbin to raise his eyebrows at the suggestion being raised out loud. Havelock was quick to counter the thought.

"The Admiralty clearly wants to keep as many ships at Spithead as possible, in preparation of the French invasion. Anyway," he grinned, "we have many counts in our favour. Remember, our crew are, by far, better trained. The *Elita* could have the biggest guns in the French fleet, but they will do them no good if they can only be fired once for every two salvoes we let fly. We will likely be in a position to dictate when and how the battle is fought – we will not even consider engaging unless we have the wind. The *Elita* will have been at sea for many months, while we are fresh. Finally, the *Elita* is worth a great deal of prize money if she can be captured so do not underestimate the effect of that on the efficiency of our crew!"

The last comment was met with laughter and not a little avarice, as everyone round the table stood to gain a great deal more than any of the crew. Hague raised his glass to Corbin "Well, that will do us all grand I think, and help some of us out a great deal, eh, Mr Corbin?" He said.

Corbin winced slightly and glanced at his Captain who deliberately avoided eye contact. He sighed. "It is true, Mr Hague, I am in need of funds. A small matter of accrued debts in the service of Lord Ashby and some very ill-advised investments to counter them."

"Gambling?" Wynton asked, suddenly sombre.

"Aye, I must confess Mr Wynton, gambling was the poor route I chose to reverse my fortunes."

"Has happened to many of us," said Wynton. "Unfortunately, gambling tends to work best when you do not have desperate need of money."

"Thems that have the money are those who can make the best stakes at cards," said Rawlinson.

"That's right lad," said Wynton. "And that's a lesson you should remember."

Hague, fuelled by a growing amount of wine, slapped Corbin on the back. "Never mind, Mr Corbin! We have our mission and the prize money is in sight! We have the best ship, the best crew and the best Captain for the job!"

"That much is true," said Wynton. He looked seriously at the other two lieutenants and the midshipmen. "Mark my words, all of you. We have a true seaman in our Captain, it is in his blood. You all heard of the Admiral Havelock?"

The lieutenants all nodded but Rawlinson and his fellow midshipman Buxton looked quizzically at Wynton, wanting to know more but hesitant to voice their ignorance. Wynton picked up on their expressions, and after pouring more wine for everyone, settled back in his seat, shifting to make himself comfortable against the hard wood.

"Well, the Captain's grandfather was also in the navy – made Admiral, he did. Led a squadron of three frigates against a French fleet off Guadeloupe. Now, he was outnumbered, to be sure, with four Froggie ships matched against his. But two of them were also ships of the line, huge great vessels that dwarfed his frigates."

The midshipmen looked incredulously at Havelock and then back to Wynton. "How could he have possibly fought against them?" Buxton asked.

"By all rights, he should have turned tail and ran, right?" said Wynton. "Well lad, that is what makes the difference between the likes of you and me, and a true hero. We might have scuttled off to find a squadron of third-raters and reported the position of the French, letting others do the fighting. But not Admiral Havelock. Oh, no. He approaches them, bold as brass, and they don't know what to make of him. He gets right up behind the two big warships and lets loose, sinking one and detonating the magazine of the other, with his first salvo, I heard. The two French frigates were shocked to inaction and quickly overwhelmed, then boarded. The whole thing took less than an hour and netted all crews a handsome prize."

Corbin smiled at hearing the story retold and he joined in with the applause of the others at its conclusion. He noted, however, that his Captain seemed distinctly uncomfortable listening to the story of his grandfather. Wynton had stood up, taking Corbin's attention as he proposed a toast.

"Gentlemen, I give you Admiral Havelock!"

"Admiral Havelock!" They chimed in, raising their glasses.

"For my money, a man every equal to Nelson himself!" Wynton said, who then noticed Hague's bemused smile. "I'm telling you, Nelson gets the glory these days – not that he does not deserve it – but there are others in His Majesty's Navy who are every bit as worthy."

Corbin grabbed the wine bottle and gestured for Wynton's glass. "Come, Mr Wynton," he said. "Let me refill you. Enough of Nelson, let us get back to the matter of the French quarry we will be chasing!"

Wynton sat down heavily in his seat and offered his glass. Corbin glanced at his Captain from the corner of his eye very briefly and was a little surprised, though gratified, to see Havelock give him an almost imperceptible nod of thanks for having changed the subject. He had not known what gave Havelock any discomfort with regards to his grandfather but Corbin had considered it his duty to ease the Captain's burden, whatever it might have been.

"What guns will the *Elita* be carrying?" Hague said, not catching the exchange between Corbin and his Captain. "How will they compare to our twelve-pounders?"

Havelock coughed, then answered. "Having two decks allows you to mount much heavier cannon behind the lower gun ports, as it balances your centre of gravity – you all remember the story of the *Mary Rose*, right? Classic case of a ship toppling over too far because of the weight of its armament. Still, we could be looking at guns as heavy as thirty-six pounders."

Wynton whistled. "I've only seen guns that large on a ship of the line."

"Well, that is the point, really," said Havelock. "That is why they are nicknamed super-frigates. I could tell you that she won't have many thirty-six pounders – but then I would have to admit that she will also mount twenty-four pounders. There may be a few guns, towards the stern or bow, that match ours but only on the upper gun deck. Make no mistake though, she is a powerful vessel."

"Forgive me, Captain," said Buxton. "But why does everybody here not think that we are beaten before we start? With guns like that, she can start firing long before we can and we should be hit before we even get into range."

Havelock opened his mouth to answer but was cut off by Hague. Corbin stifled a grin as Havelock smiled and waved Hague on, who was completely unaware that he had interrupted his Captain. "Lad, it is never as simple as that. First off, the French have got to shoot straight to hit you at range, which is never a given." Hague started counting off the points on his fingers. "Then, they have to reload, and the Froggie crews are not noted for their love of hard work. Our men will shoot straighter and quicker than them on any day of the week – it does not matter if you have the biggest cannon in the world, if your enemy is constantly pounding at you. Third, you have to point your guns towards the enemy in order to fire. And I'll lay good money that the Captain here will have a surprise or two for this Elita."

The evening continued and as the wine began to take its toll on the officers, the muffled singing of the crew elsewhere in the ship prompted them to join in with their own songs, Wynton leading the choruses with undisguised gusto. Finally, Havelock rapped his knuckles on the table to get their attention.

"My friends," he said. "We have a large task ahead of us, though it is one that I have no doubt we can complete, with the honour and dignity befitting one of His Majesty's Ships. We have escaped a long and drawn out wait here at Spithead, and in return, will demonstrate to the Admiralty just why the *Whirlwind* is one of the premier ships of the entire fleet!"

This raised a cheer from all the officers and Havelock had to raise a hand to continue, though he did so with a smile. "Get a good night's sleep, for we have a lot of work ahead of us tomorrow. Mr Corbin, would you be so good as to double-check the watches before you turn in. Whose is it now?"

"That would be Mr Buxton, Captain," said Corbin.

"Ah, that is why you were laying low on the wine, Mr

Buxton," said Havelock. "Good man. We enjoy our drink in the King's Navy, but duty must always come first. Very well, I bid you all goodnight!"

As one, the officers all stood and thanked their Captain before leaving. Corbin was the last to reach the door and he hesitated before leaving the great cabin.

"Something, Mr Corbin?" Havelock asked.

Corbin opened his mouth to answer then closed it again, thinking better. He paused and noticed his Captain's raised eyebrows. Closing the door, he turned back to Havelock. "Well, Sir," he said.

"You have doubts?"

"Yes, Sir. A few."

"Well, out with it man. I can spare you a few more minutes," Havelock said.

"Well... I understand that the Admiralty wants to keep as many ships here in readiness for anything the French do. But the *Whirlwind* is a fifth-rate ship. To put it up against one of these super-frigates, alone, seems folly. Do we really have a chance?"

"Oh, we have a chance, Mr Corbin," Havelock said quickly. "There is always a chance. However, I do understand and even, to a point, share your concern. The best ship to send against the *Elita* would be a sprightly third-rater, something that can keep up with her and yet still deliver a knockout blow. Mind you, that is exactly the sort of ship the Admiralty wants in British waters right now."

"I thought we might have been joined by another frigate, at least."

"Yes, that would have been preferable. But those are not the cards we have been dealt, Mr Corbin. We have our orders and must believe the Admiralty has its reasons for sending the *Whirlwind* and no other. It is entirely possible that those orders omitted some interesting piece of information that the Admiralty knows and we do not. Perhaps the *Elita* is ravaged by plague and has become short-crewed. Perhaps she has already been engaged by a British ship and has had trouble making repairs. Who knows?"

"Aye, you are right, Captain. If we were to second guess the Admiralty, we might all go mad."

"Oh, that is certain, Mr Corbin! What goes on in the Mad House, generally, could make anyone doubt their own senses. That said, we can normally trust our orders when it comes to engaging the French. Throughout the long years of war with France, the King's Navy has yet to suffer any truly significant losses." Havelock paused for a few seconds before continuing. "There is, however, something more pressing that concerns me."

When Havelock did not continue at once, Corbin prompted him. "Sir?"

"It is this list of ships that have been attacked, sunk or captured by the *Elita*," said Havelock. "Sixteen in three months? That is incredible good fortune for the French. Either the merchants are lining up to be taken or this Guillot is a very skilled captain. There is, however, one other possibility..."

It took Corbin just a second to see where his captain was heading. "There is more than one ship doing the raiding."

"Very good, Mr Corbin," Havelock said. "Yes, we could be sailing into a small French fleet. And if they are all fourth-raters like the *Elita*, we may be voyaging into a lot of trouble." He noticed Corbin's troubled face and then smiled slightly. "Take heart, Lieutenant. There are plenty of natural harbours along the African coast where the *Elita* may be re-supplying, allowing it to stay on station for an extended period while intercepting all merchants who must sail in the area. It may turn out that we are not even facing a skilled captain, just a lucky one. If that is the case, I think we can be luckier."

"I pray that is correct, Sir."

"You've served on a frigate before, Mr Corbin. You know it takes more than heavy guns and a fair wind to win battles with these ships."

"Yes, Sir. In that regard, I have few doubts. The *Whirlwind* is a good ship with a fine crew."

"And they'll be better by the time we reach our hunting grounds," said Havelock. "Even with the right winds, we will be voyaging for a good six weeks before we will have any chance of sighting the *Elita*. It is my intention to practice the men during that time. As well as sharpening them for the coming battle, it will also help keep their minds occupied during what will hopefully be an otherwise uneventful journey."

"As you say, Sir. Captain, there was one other thing... "

Havelock noticed his Lieutenant's hesitancy and cocked his head. "Yes, Mr Corbin?"

"You seemed a little perturbed when mention was made of your grandfather."

If anything, Corbin thought his Captain looked even more uncomfortable now. "A topic for another time, Mr Corbin," he said, a little briskly. "Check the watches, as ordered, then turn in. I want every man above deck at first light tomorrow. We'll announce our orders to them then, before setting sail. We can afford for the rumours to run wild until then."

"Yes, Captain. Goodnight, Captain," Corbin said, as respectfully as he could muster. Havelock nodded in acknowledgement, prompting Corbin to leave the great cabin and return to the main deck to monitor the changing watch.

CHAPTER THREE

As the crew of the *Whirlwind* gathered on the main deck, the air seemed to crackle with excitement and anticipation. By now every man had heard of the visiting marine sergeant and the letter that had been handed to the Captain, and few believed this could mean anything other than new orders with a good possibility of action against the enemy. Regardless of whether they would actually face the French in battle, every man was grateful that their stay at Spithead seemed to be over.

Few secrets could be kept long on board the cramped environment of a warship, but rumours and tall tales could easily subvert the truth when it was spoken. So, though there were men who had witnessed the purser make the final preparations for the long voyage, had even toiled to bring new provisions on board, their calculations or estimations on how long a voyage was expected carried less weight than another sailor who opined that hammering the French in the Mediterranean was their final goal, especially if he said it louder and with more conviction. Not every one was willing to accept what another said at face value, of course, and more than one of the crew bore the marks of a fist-fight as impassioned opinions had spun out of hand during the night.

Nearly three hundred souls made up the full complement of the *Whirlwind*, packed into two decks below the reach of sunlight. Now, they filled the main deck and hung from the main mast, standing shoulder-to-shoulder as they waited patiently for their Captain's address. With so many men gathered in one place, new opportunities for rumour mongering and storytelling abounded, and a quiet hubbub rolled with an irregular rhythm over the deck.

On the quarterdeck, Lieutenants Wynton and Hague stood at attention alongside the midshipmen, overseeing the crew as they too, waited. The Captain and Corbin stood behind them, near the prow of the ship, ostensibly discussing last minute changes and provisions, though it was entirely within Havelock's style to use the time to build up anticipation within his crew. As the muttering of the crew steadily grew in volume, it was clear that any wish to motivate them was working. When Havelock judged the moment right, he shook Corbin's hand and then walked purposefully across the quarterdeck to face his crew. Hands placed in a relaxed manner on the wooden railing before him, Havelock leaned forward slightly as he spoke.

"Men of the *Whirlwind*, your time idling here is over! We are about to set sail! Do you have it in your hearts to fight against the French?"

A loud and raucous cheer immediately met his words, persisting until he raised a hand. The crew fell silent almost immediately, as much out of curiosity for the mission as respect for their Captain.

"That is good! We have been ordered to the South Atlantic where we are to intercept the French frigate *Elita*. We have the permission of the Admiralty to sink her but it is my intention to take her as prize!"

Again, cheers erupted across the deck, this time fuelled by avarice and self-interest. Though most members of the crew would receive a tiny fraction of the prize money for a captured ship compared to any of the officers, it would still likely be far more wealth than they might earn in a year of hard toil anywhere else. This was the reason that even press ganged crew tended to stay on board, once they had become accustomed to a life at sea.

Holding a hand up once more, Havelock regained his

crew's attention, wanting to focus them on duty as much as the promise of riches.

"It seems the crew of this French ship believe they are the terror of the waves!" A few boos and jeers greeted this news as Havelock continued. "Thus far, the *Elita* has been responsible for the loss of more than a dozen English merchant vessels, all plundered or sunk. Right now, the crew of that French frigate are laughing at us, if you please!"

Havelock stood up straight, placing his hands behind his back as he mustered all the dignity he could.

"Shipmates, I say to you, that French crew has yet to meet a real English ship of war!" The massed cheer began once again at these words and Havelock smiled at his crew. "They think they prove their mettle by attacking merchant ships with but a couple of small guns! In a few short weeks, we will be in their hunting grounds and then we'll give them something to think about! We'll show them how His Majesty's *Whirlwind* fights, aye, and her crew too!"

The growing cries from the crew threatened to drown out Havelock's words; his eyes flickered across the deck, enjoying the moment, not willing to disrupt their enthusiasm as sailors congratulated one another and punched the air with excitement. Having one more thing to say, Havelock raised his hand and, again, received the rapt attention of his crew.

"Men of the *Whirlwind*, I ask for nothing less than your very best. We will soon be facing the enemy and I do not intend for us to be found wanting. Remember, you serve the greatest Navy the world has ever seen, on board one of its finest ships. Whatever hazards we meet, a Frenchman is but a Frenchman and we have always beaten him! Do your duty! God save King George!"

Havelock grinned openly as the crew responded to his speech with a roar that was almost terrifying in its volume. He turned to Corbin.

"Mr Corbin, would you be so good as to set us on our way?"

The Lieutenant's grin matched Havelock's, the man clearly as eager as his Captain at the prospect of action.

"Aye, Sir, with pleasure."

Havelock watched Lieutenants Hague and Wynton descend to the main deck with the midshipmen as they relayed Corbin's orders and the crew of the *Whirlwind* sprang from their perches to set the frigate in motion.

"Prepare to weigh anchor!"

"Stand by to loose the topsail!"

"Weigh anchor, jump to it!"

"Loose the staysail!"

"Loose the topsail! Put your backs into it!"

As wind began to fill the lowering sails of the *Whirlwind* and the frigate began to slowly pick up speed across the low waves, Havelock paced slowly to the stern of the ship, looking at the coast as it began, gradually, to recede from view. The cry of gulls milling above the masts mixed with the sound of the sea being split in two by the sharp prow of his ship and he breathed deeply, enjoying the familiar saltiness of the water anew as he looked forward to another voyage. He listened to the crew, feeling the natural rhythms of the ship as they went about their work in concert with shipmate, officer, sea and wind. Together, the entire vessel and its complement were like a single organism, one unit that, through him, would do the bidding of King and country. He paced back to the railings above the main deck but his eyes were focussed past the crew and sails, to the sea that lay beyond.

"On our way Captain, no problems reported," said

Corbin as he returned to the Captain's side, satisfied that everything on board the *Whirlwind* was proceeding as it should.

"Very good, Mr Corbin," said Havelock but he did not turn to the Lieutenant, simply keeping his gaze on the horizon. Corbin was about to ask a question but noticed the faraway look in other man's eyes. Picking up the lead, he stood quietly next to Havelock, both with hands behind their backs as they took in the wide panorama of the sea, conscious that the distance between them and land grew by the minute.

Presently, without changing the direction of his gaze, Havelock spoke, his voice almost soft. "You know, Mr Corbin, it is a funny thing."

"Sir?"

"I have faced stormy seas with waves crashing down onto the deck, I have met the French in battle and won, and I have dined with Admirals as they thanked me for a job well done. And yet... it is this moment, just as we set sail, that I have enjoyed every bit as much as the rest. It is funny, that so simple a thing could bring so much satisfaction."

Corbin smiled. "It is the sea, Sir. You have it in your blood. I think we all feel this way when first setting out on a new voyage."

"I pity those who are land bound, all those lords and army officers, no matter how privileged, who will never truly understand what it means to be on a ship like this, now, just as we set sail. It is more than a love for the sea, Mr Corbin. It is the discovery of what lies beyond the horizon, the parting of the veil, the knowledge that where we travel, few men have gone before us. Who knows what awaits us south? Victory? Disappointment? A sound thrashing?"

"Well, victory, I would wager, Sir."

"Aye, I think you may be right, Mr Corbin," said Havelock with a grin. "Gods, I would not be anywhere else!"

They stood together for a few minutes longer, watching the crew master the waves by sail and helm. Feeling he had luxuriated enough, Havelock turned to the Lieutenant. "As soon as we reach the Channel, let us have an hour's practice with the guns, Mr Corbin. We'll start as we mean to go on. By the time we meet the *Elita*, I want us to have the best practiced gun crews in the Navy."

"You'll have it, Sir," said Corbin before he faced the main deck to issue the orders. "Hands to quarters! Mr Hague, run out the guns!"

Once again, the crew of the *Whirlwind* sprang into action, this time to a very different rhythm.

Clinging to the wooden beams running across the ceiling for support, Bryant steadied himself against the swaying of the ship, taking care not to let the wet stairs send him crashing to the floor of the upper deck. Drenched through, he staggered past his cannon to join a group of men who were already feasting on a meal of beef stew and rum. Reaching behind his collar, he stripped his shirt off and wrung it in his hands, cold water pouring onto the wooden floor. The trickle ran under the feet of the sitting men as it made its way to drainage seams along the side of the deck.

"Rainin', is it?" asked Murphy, causing some of the other men to chuckle at Bryant's misfortune.

Bryant playfully shoved him, causing the smaller man to scramble in order to keep his food on its square tray. "Hey!" cried Murphy. "Just jokin'! An' anyway, look what

I saved for you 'ere. Complements of 'is Majesty."

Bryant's eyes lit up as Murphy threw aside a cloth, revealing a plate of stew he had kept by for the larger man. Sitting down, Bryant grabbed the plate with obvious relish.

"Ah, you're a good shipmate, Murphy."

A young man with a mop of ginger hair leaned forward into the circle of the gathered men. Brooks had been assigned to Bryant's and Murphy's gun crew soon after the *Whirlwind* had set sail and, upon revealing that this was his first time at sea, had been taken under their collective wing.

"So, Bryant, is it true that we're already in sight of the African coast?" he asked.

Bryant looked up from his meal with a puzzled look "We've barely been at sea for a week. What makes you think we have already made Africa?"

"I was listenin' to Jefferies and his mates talkin' back there," he said, indicating the stern of the ship.

"Heavens," said Bryant as he rolled his eyes. "What is it with you and Murphy? I keep telling the two of you, pay no attention to what Jefferies says. He may sound as though he knows what he is talking about but he knows as much about navigation as any of the ship's rats. He's barely been on more voyages than you, young Brooks."

Brooks actually looked a little crestfallen at this news. "So where are we then?"

"Somewhere off Southern Spain. I heard the Lieutenant mention something about the Cape of Trafalgar earlier this evening. Perhaps someone here has got a map we can look at?"

He was greeted by blank stares and a few heads shaking.

"Perhaps not," he said, sighing as he went back to his

food. Across the deck, casting eerie shadows from the few swaying lanterns placed at strategic positions in the rafters, another couple of gun crews had joined each other for food and some of them had begun singing, clearly enjoying their rum before starting their meals.

"So, Brooks, this really your first time at sea?" A weathered looking man seated to Bryant's left asked.

"Ah, yes, yes it is," said Brooks, vaguely wondering if he was being led down a path. As a new face, and one unfamiliar with the ways of a ship of war at that, he had already faced his fair share of ribbing, though most of it had been good-natured.

"You've been bearin' up well," the sailor remarked.

"Ah, Brooks is a natural born seaman!" Bryant declared. "Got his sea legs within hours!"

"That's good," said the sailor. "But it takes more than holdin' your guts steady to make a good seaman."

"Well give 'im a chance!" Murphy chipped in. "The lad's only been 'ere for a few days!"

"That's fair," conceded the sailor. "You pressed into this, boy?"

"Umm, no." Brooks said. "Volunteered. Always wanted to sail. And do my part, fightin' the French. Besides, if you live in Portsmouth, you're better off volunteerin' rather than waitin' for the gangs to come round."

Bryant reached forward and rustled Brooks' unkempt hair. "A real patriot, this one!" He turned to Murphy, who had started to lean backwards, an ear clearly cocked to a conversation among the group of men behind them. Bryant realised that the sporadic singing earlier had now stopped as the other gun crews talked in quieter tones, with some urgency, he thought.

"Murphy, wind your neck back in!" he said.

"Hush!" Murphy waved him back. "They're talkin' 'bout

the Cap'n!"

Bryant inwardly groaned but could not help but bend an ear himself. He quickly identified the hard voice of Jessop.

"Jefferies, yer a lyin' sod, an' we all know it!"

"Hey, listen to what I tell ya, or don't – all the same to me." Bryant had to strain to catch everything that Jefferies said. The man was quickly prompted by the others in his group to continue, despite Jessop's scepticism.

"Like I was sayin', there's a black cloud hangin' over 'Avelock. When I was servin' on the Dorchester an' 'Avelock was nothin' more than a lieutenant, we used to call it 'Avelock's Curse." Jefferies looked about his listeners with a certain satisfaction as he realised he had them hooked.

"What sort of curse is that, then?" asked one.

"Little things at first," said Jefferies. "A man slips an' falls to his death from the mainmast. Someone falls overboard an' no one notices for an hour. Sealed barrels o' pork go bad."

Jefferies took a swig from his metal cup as the others digested this information. "Then the weather turns against us, see, sails start shreddin', French ships start turnin' up when the sea should be clear."

"You survived though," pointed out Jessop.

"Well, yeah. 'Ad a good Cap'n back then."

One of the other men leaned forward, rubbing his chin. "There may be somethin' in this, you know," he said. "We've all 'eard about the Cap'n's grandfather, the great Adm'ral 'Avelock. Well, when I was last in Portsmouth, I over 'eard a bunch of old soldiers who had once served on ship with 'im."

"The Cap'n?" Jefferies asked.

"Nah, you fool, the Adm'ral. Anyway, they said 'is great

victory in the Caribbean was nothin' of the sort. 'E didn't go into battle against a full French fleet and 'e didn't win in less than hour, as they say now."

"So, what happened?" Jessop prompted.

"Well, an' this is just the soldiers talkin', mind. I 'eard that 'e sailed into a French port that was just launchin' a bunch of colony ships – you know, full of decent folk lookin' to make a life for themselves on one of the other islands. Caught the French nappin' and began sinkin' the colony ships until the French port surrendered. But that didn't 'appen until a lot of innocent women and children were sent to the bottom."

The men around him started shaking their heads. "Dirty business that."

"Dirtier that 'e got made Adm'ral for it."

"An' that the Cap'n can trade on the name – no guessin' that granddaddy's position 'elped 'im get a Cap'n's post," said Jessop. He glanced around the deck and noticed the interest his group had gained among Bryant's men. "Family ties like that matter more to the Lords runnin' the navy than bein' a good officer. You agree, don't you, Bryant?" he called.

Murphy scrambled back to his food, hunching over his plate. Bryant refused to meet Jessop's eye but said "That talk ain't wise, Jessop."

"Oh, really?" Jessop grinned as he stood and took two steps towards Bryant, bracing himself against the low ceiling to steady himself against the ship's motion. "Perhaps you would be likin' to do somethin' about it?"

Bryant turned to face Jessop, giving him a baleful look. "I'm eating. Besides, it won't be me that hangs you for mutinous talk."

A grin crept across Jessop's face as he stared hard at Bryant, who just shook his head and went back to his food, not wanting to play Jessop's game. He glanced up as a newcomer walked towards them. Dwarfed by most of the sailors on the main deck, yet distinctive in his simple dark blue uniform, Midshipman Rawlinson picked his way out of the shadows and walked up to the two antagonists.

"Jessop, good. Please come with me," he said.

"Why?" Jessop shifted his mass as he spoke, so that by bracing an arm against one of the rafters running above his head, he leaned over the midshipman in an attempt to intimidate the young man. Rawlinson blinked, not fully prepared for Jessop's insolence.

"Hobbs has reported some missing property, a matter of three shillings and a bone pipe. We are going to look into your belongings," he said formerly.

"I ain't stolen' nothin'," said Jessop turning his back on Rawlinson. "'Sides, I'm busy right now. Come back when I've finished eatin', boy."

"Sir!" The smirks of Jessop's friends were immediately cut short by the bark of Corbin's voice, as the Lieutenant stepped into the light from the stairs to the main deck. Though wet through with droplets of water streaming from his hat, his anger was unmistakable. He marched straight up to Jessop, completely unafraid of the larger man's muscles and demeanour.

"You will address Midshipman Rawlinson as Sir!" Corbin said, voice suddenly hardened from his usual manner. "Bosun!" he called.

It took just a few seconds for Kennedy to appear, no doubt already on his way once he had realised what was going on within this part of the gun deck. "Yes, Sir?" he reported, a little breathless.

"Escort Jessop to the brig. In the morning, he will answer to a charge of insubordination. You will then attend Mr

Rawlinson as he goes through Jessop's belongings and if the missing items are to be found there, a charge of theft will be added."

Jessop kept quiet but his face showed nothing but pure murderous intent as he glared at Corbin. The Lieutenant refused to back down and instead took one step closer to the man before he spoke.

"And if you carry on looking at me like that, man, I will see you swing from the yardarm!"

Expecting trouble, Kennedy grabbed Jessop's arm firmly but was surprised to find no resistance as he led the man down into the lower deck to the brig. Corbin nodded at the midshipman.

"Okay, Mr Rawlinson, about your business. The rest of you, get on with your food or I may decide the topsail needs replacing – and believe me, that is not going to be an easy job in this weather!"

The threat, however idle the crew may or may not have thought it, proved enough to force their attentions back to the food before them. Satisfied that order had been restored, Corbin walked the length of the upper deck to ensure no other trouble lurked and then returned to his post in the wind and rain above.

Having directly challenged a midshipman, Havelock had little choice but to condemn Jessop and force him to answer the charge made by Lieutenant Corbin. He was mollified somewhat by Rawlinson's discovery of the stolen pipe among the man's belongings, though no trace of the missing money had been found – not that anyone seriously expected it to turn up.

Once again, the entire crew of the *Whirlwind* lined the main deck but their mood was far more sombre than when they had last gathered in this way. They all knew they were to bear witness to the punishment of one of their own, and however unpopular Jessop may have proved with many of them, few liked to be reminded that it might only be the grace of God that spared them from a flogging. It was never a case of merely taking your licks, no matter how much a man thought he could face the pain – such men had never undergone the agony of a rope across the back. There was a humiliation to be borne too, the knowledge that the entire crew would be watching while the punishment was served.

Flanked by his officers, Havelock watched grimly as Jessop was brought up from below deck, escorted by the Bosun and two red-coated marines. He knew that, when in command of a ship of nearly three hundred souls, it was inevitable that more than a few bad apples would creep into the crew. Indeed, the press gangs were reported to be working overtime on shore and there was more than a little resentment building up on every ship in His Majesty's navy. Havelock had long ago determined that the iron rod was not the right approach to maintaining order on a ship of war, especially when one had a good Bosun to rely upon who could maintain a tight level of discipline. However, when a man turned his back on an officer, or even a midshipman, action had to be taken immediately. To defy Rawlinson was, when the matter was brought right down to its core, no different than Jessop casting two fingers up at one of the Captain's own commands. That way lay anarchy and chaos. As for the charge of thievery, he was probably doing Jessop a favour by publicly punishing him for it. Theft without comeuppance on any ship was likely to be met by a knife in the dark below deck, or a good shove while working at the top of one of the masts. Havelock had enough on his hands without having to contend with murder as well.

"All hands to witness punishment," called out Lieutenant Corbin, standing on the quarterdeck in full dress uniform, as were the other officers. His hand rested easily on the hilt of the sword at his belt.

Jessop steadfastly refused to look into the eyes of any of the crew as he was marched aft to face the Captain. When he stopped in front of the quarterdeck, he stood proud, staring at Havelock, who returned the look impassively.

"Jessop, you have been charged with insubordination to one of my officers and theft of property from one of your shipmates. What do you have to say?"

"Guilty as charged for insubordination, Cap'n," Jessop said. "And I would apologise to Mr Rawlinson for me manners. But I ain't no thief. That weren't me, Sir."

Havelock cast a look at the rest of the crew. "Does any man here have anything to say on Jessop's behalf?" He was answered by a deathly silence.

"If this man is found guilty of these crimes, the Articles of War allow for a maximum penalty of hanging..." said Havelock grimly. Still no one made a move to speak for Jessop which, given what he knew of the man's reputation, did not surprise Havelock in the least. Kennedy caught his eye and Havelock gave a nod to acknowledge him as the Bosun stood forward.

"Cap'n, I submit that Jessop isn't known as a thief by nature and that 'e has offered a full and frank apology to Mr Rawlinson. I would also like to bring to your attention that, when on duty, Jessop is a good sailor and a hard worker."

"Very well," said Havelock. He realised that Kennedy might be guilty himself of slightly overstating Jessop's case but it was the Bosun's task to defend the crew in any way he could. It was, in part, how he kept their respect and, thus, enabled him to keep discipline. After all, with so many witnesses, there was no way Jessop could have denied the charge of insubordination and an apology was a relatively painless way to avoid harsh punishment. Still, Havelock decided to take his Bosun's cue.

"Jessop, you have been found guilty of both charges. Seize him up," he said.

Those among the crew who were wearing hats took them off as the marines stood behind Jessop. The condemned man reached behind his back and took off his shirt before being led to the main hatch which had been opened for this purpose. The marines tied Jessop's outstretched arms to the hatch, forcing him to adopt a spread-eagled position as Kennedy removed his own hat and jacket and picked up his favoured flogging rope. Havelock nodded his thanks as Buxton handed him a thin red leather bound book. He took the Articles of War, which he opened and began reading from.

"Article Twenty One - If any officer, mariner, soldier or other person in the fleet, shall presume to quarrel with any of his superior officers, being in the execution of his office, or shall disobey any lawful command of any of his superior officers; every such person being convicted of any such offence, by the sentence of a court martial, shall suffer death, or such other punishment, as shall, according to the nature and degree of his offence, be inflicted upon him by the sentence of a court martial. Two dozen lashes."

He looked up briefly at Jessop, before continuing. "Article Twenty Nine - All robbery committed by any person in the fleet, shall be punished with death, or otherwise, as a court martial, upon consideration of the circumstances, shall find meet. Another dozen, Mr Kennedy."

The Bosun nodded as a marine on the quarterdeck began a quick drum roll, the sound carrying across the entire ship as it echoed off the unfurled sails. When the drum stopped, Kennedy reached back and then struck with his rope, the muffled crack causing most among the crew to wince in sympathy.

At first, Jessop just exhaled noisily with each stroke but after the fourth lash of the rope, blood started to streak his back and he began to grunt through gritted teeth with every blow. As the rope sailed down on his naked back time and again, the lines of blood began to cross one another and then flow freely, creating a crimson curtain that ran down the sides of his body. Finally, and to Jessop's gratefulness, the blows stopped.

"Three dozen, Sir," said Corbin.

"Very well," Havelock said. "Mr Kennedy, cut him down." As soon as the ropes were cut, Jessop sank to the floor, a slight strangled groan escaping his lips as he slumped heavily on the deck.

"Thank you, Mr Corbin," said Havelock. "Dismiss all hands."

"All hands, dismissed," called out Corbin. The crew began to disperse to carry on with their regular duties, though few spoke after witnessing Jessop's punishment. Havelock started walking the stairs to the main deck, musing that, for all his faults, the man had been brave enough not to cry out during the flogging. From experience, Havelock knew that such men could easily be a handful to discipline properly but were often a holy terror when facing a French boarding party. They certainly had their uses. Intending to retreat into his cabin for the rest of the morning to plot the next day's course, Havelock's eyes met with Jessop's as the man was being helped back onto his feet by the marines.

"I'm no thief, Sir," said Jessop, in obvious pain.

This simple statement caught Havelock by surprise and he found himself stopping to regard the man for a second before walking on.

"Sail to larboard!"

Havelock spun about from his inspection of the sail team on the forecastle and hurried across the main deck before vaulting up the stairs to the quarterdeck. Seeing Corbin already at the rails with an extended telescope, he hurried past Hague who called up to the lookout.

"Do you see a flag?"

"No, Sir," came the shouted reply. "Too far away!"

Sensing his Captain's approach, Corbin turned from the sea and passed his telescope. "A merchant, Sir. Can you make out its nationality?"

Havelock squinted through the telescope, taking a moment to bring the ship into focus. It was heading towards them at an oblique angle, though he could not see a flag flying – not that he expected to in these waters. Almost everywhere, the sea was nominally considered to be British but with war in the air, this was a disputed area. He tried to make out the arrangement of sails and pick out details from the hull in an effort to ascertain the ship's origin but while he guessed it might originally have had a French architect, the practice of taking prizes in battle meant that a ship could change hands a great many times in its life.

"Run up the colours, Mr Corbin," said Havelock. "We have nothing to fear from that vessel and we should be polite enough to announce our intentions."

"Aye, Captain. Run up the colours!" Corbin called to the crew and watched as the Ensign and Jack were hoisted into the air, fluttering in the stiff breeze flowing over the deck.

Keeping his eye trained on the approaching ship, Havelock finally smiled. "Ah, there you see. She answers – a Portuguese ship. Signal her, Mr Corbin. Have her run along side us a while. I wish to talk to her Master."

"Let's just hope they can understand British signals," Corbin said.

"Avoid code and she should get our meaning."

Gaining the attention of Midshipman Buxton, Corbin gave the order of signals required to bring the merchant alongside while Havelock remained glued to his telescope. The flags were run up on the *Whirlwind* and though Havelock knew they were in full sight of the incoming vessel, he guessed the Portuguese Master was cursing him at that moment. Merchants had schedules to keep and profits to earn, and were better off not dallying in the middle of the ocean.

It took nearly twenty minutes for the two ships to meet, the Portuguese ship lumbering in a long turn to match the *Whirlwind's* course. The crew of both ships lined the railings, trading greetings and well-wishes while Havelock stood on the quarterdeck, looking down at his civilian counterpart. Doffing his hat in a show of respect, Havelock shouted over the noise of the two crews.

"Hoy there! Greetings from His Majesty's Navy!"

"Hallo, English!" The reply came in a thick accent. He sounded faintly resigned. "*Stella Maris*, at your service."

The Portuguese crew continued to wave their greetings, some struggling to ask questions in pidgin English, interested in the *Whirlwind's* voyage and what weather lay ahead. The British crew on the main deck nearest Havelock fell silent, knowing they would learn far more from their Captain's exchange with the merchant's

Master.

"What news from the south?" Havelock shouted across to the Portuguese ship. "Have you sighted French shipping?"

"Three weeks past, chased by frigate!"

Havelock frowned impatiently at the ambiguous answer, irritated that he had to rephrase the question. "Was she French?"

There was a short pause before the Portuguese Master answered. "I believe so, yes. French, yes. We run and escape."

"Have you seen any other warships?" Havelock said and again had to wait while the Master translated the reply into English.

"Warships, no. No French, no English, no Espana."

"Have you sailed from the Cape?" Havelock guessed what the answer would be but wanted to be certain.

"The Cape, yes."

Making a few quick mental calculations, Havelock made some predictions of the Portuguese ship's recent course and back-tracked it three weeks. There was no way the Portuguese Master would have been able to identify the *Elita*. Indeed, if he had been that close, he would have been captured. It was within Havelock's authority to order the merchant to heave to in order for him to talk to the Master face-to-face so he could get accurate navigational information but, being three weeks old, it would have been of marginal benefit. It was enough to know, at this time, that a French frigate was still prowling southern waters.

"Thank you, *Stella Maris*. I wish you fair winds!"

Havelock watched the Portuguese master shrug and then bark orders to his crew to turn his ship away from the *Whirlwind* and back on to its original course. He was probably thanking his lucky stars that the English warship had not detained him longer.

Standing by his Captain to watch the Portuguese ship depart, Corbin asked "Useful information, Sir?"

"As much as it is," said Havelock. "*Elita* or not, we know there was a French presence in our hunting grounds three weeks ago – which means our voyage will likely not be wasted. The closer we get, the better our chances of intercepting her if she makes a break for French waters. However, I now believe the *Elita* is on an extended mission, which means she has her own harbour somewhere on the African coast. With a safe place to refit and re-supply, she could stay on station for months more, until her hold is full of stolen goods."

"Might the *Elita* be periodically unloading her cargo onto French merchants?" Corbin said.

"I considered that. Very risky. There is an excellent chance that such merchants would run into a British ship like us and then the cargo would simply come back into our hands. Still, if the aim was to disrupt supplies from the rest of the Empire rather than simply steal what she can, it might be a valid tactic. Especially if the *Elita* is trading stolen goods with natives for supplies on the coast. Yes, this bears some thought, Mr Corbin."

"Do you have new orders for us, Sir?"

"No, we continue south at our present speed. Depending on how large an area the *Elita* is patrolling we will be in her territory within two or three weeks."

Having completed his early morning watch, consumed mostly by the daily chore of cleaning the main deck with the large holystone, Bryant descended the stairs to the upper deck, looking forward to wrapping himself in his hammock for a few hours before being called onto duty again. The crew had long since become accustomed to the idea that they were back at sea once more, their days filled with the regular routines of maintaining the *Whirlwind* and keeping her on course. Now four weeks into their voyage, anticipation had been slowly growing again as the ship neared its destination. Gradually, talk among the sailors had turned away from promises of games of chance, or reminiscing of their home towns, to focus on war with France and her allies. They calculated the prize money the *Elita* and her cargo would bring them and divided it between the crew, taking into account losses borne during the fight (a subject which provoked some heated discussion in itself, as a few of the crew were happy to count off specific individuals as doomed). They then spent time surmising what could be bought with their own share.

The flogging of Jessop had long since passed from the minds of most crew but the man himself had seemed somewhat subdued afterwards, which came as something of a blessed relief to most. Bryant felt the whole atmosphere of the gun deck had changed since Jessop had kept to his own company more often, sparing weaker shipmates his own particular brand of cruelty and bullying. It was therefore of some surprise when Bryant climbed down in the upper deck and found Jessop in a recess beside a closed gun port, holding Murphy up among the rafters, the feet of the smaller man dangling freely as he gasped for air through Jessop's stranglehold.

"You li'l Irish rat," said Jessop. "I take a dozen for your stealin' and you're goin' to just stand there an' deny it?"

Murphy was clearly not standing at all and Jessop's grip had made him incapable of properly denying anything, though he made his best effort to shake his head. Sighing inwardly and preparing for the worst, Bryant marched over to the pair and laid a hand gently on Jessop's shoulder.

"Enough, Jessop! He doesn't know anything."

Jessop jerked his shoulder to remove Bryant's hand, though he did not relax his hold of Murphy. "Back away, this ain't none of your business! You ain't stickin' up for the rat this time!" he said, snarling.

Not wanting to provoke the already angry man but also keen to remove his friend from the ceiling, Bryant stood closer to Jessop, staring straight into his eyes. He spoke calmly and with conviction, wanting to diffuse the situation rather than get into another brawl that could easily be answered by the Bosun's rope.

"By my word, Murphy had nothing to do with the theft. He would not have been able to keep from telling me about it."

Face turning a murderous shade of red, Jessop swore and turned his attention to Bryant. "I'm tellin' you, I was fitted up!"

"I believe you," said Bryant quietly. That admission stopped Jessop in his tracks and he relaxed his grip on Murphy a little. Bryant took the opportunity to continue. "I really don't like you or what you do, Jessop. Take that as a gift. But I know you're no thief. You are too... direct for that."

Thoroughly confused, Jessop looked at Bryant, then at the suspended Murphy, then back at Bryant. Seeing no recourse beyond throwing a punch, a course of action that even Jessop realised would not portray him in a good light with the Bosun, he dropped Murphy heavily on the floor and spat. "Ain't worth my trouble anyway."

Murphy remained on the floor until he watched Jessop stomp away into the gloom. "Ah, me thanks, friend

Bryant!" he said, with some forced cheer. "I swear, 'e just came out of nowhere and 'oisted me up!"

"You certain he had no good cause?" Bryant asked.

"Hey, I'm tellin' you!" Murphy said in protest. "I ain't dumb enough to go rummagin' through Jessop's things!"

"Hmm." Bryant considered his friend and then decided that the matter was not worth pursuing at this time. "Come on, I'm tired enough to drop off right now."

Crossing the deck, they found a circle of men, the rest of their gun crew mixing with another, leaning on the cannon as they talked. As Bryant began unfurling his hammock and attaching it to hooks scattered among the rafters, Brooks piped up.

"Hey, Murphy, we were talking about what made us sign up with the *Whirlwind*. How about you?"

To his credit, Murphy actually began to look a little embarrassed. "Ah, well," he began. "You see, it was like this... umm..."

"He was pressed," said Bryant, smiling as he kicked off his thin leather shoes. "Too much to drink one night and then ran right into a gang. Woke up on board the next morning, with more water between him and land than he could ever hope to swim!"

"Aye, 'tis true," Murphy said. "Still, found it wasn't such a bad life. Some good people 'ere. An' the pay ain't bad – well, once you get signed up as a proper seaman an' get off the pittance they give the pressed men."

"What about you, Bryant?" Brooks asked.

"Oh, not much to tell," said Bryant, now beginning to become desperate for the peace of sleep. "Worked as a clerk for my father in his tannery until he made some very bad decisions and went bust. Tried gambling – wasn't so good at that either. Then played against a sailor one night and he told me that, up to a limit, a man joining the King's Navy was absolved of his debts. I was under the limit and, so, here I am. And here I go," he said as he climbed into his hammock. "I bid you keep it quiet, friends, I need sleep... "

"Yeah, me too," said Murphy, reaching for his own rolled hammock as he made a big show of yawning theatrically.

"So, what was goin' on 'cross the way, Murphy?" one of the men from the other gun crew asked. "Run into Jessop again? Thought 'e had calmed all that down."

"Tellin' me!" Murphy said. "I told 'im I 'ad nothin' to do with 'is theft but would 'e listen? Would 'e 'ell!"

"It wasn't you then?"

"I swear to God!" Murphy said "No! Bryant, tell 'im!"

"I'm sleeping," came the muffled reply.

"Well, I knew it weren't Murphy," said Brooks happily, keen to support his friend.

Bryant rolled over in his hammock and hooked open an eye, fixing it on Brooks. "And how, exactly, do you know that?"

Brooks suddenly felt very conscious as all eyes turned to him. "Well, it's obvious, yeah? Couldn't be Murphy."

Propping his head up, Bryant looked straight into Brooks' eyes. "I think you meant something more than that. What is it, Brooks?"

Putting his face in his hands, Brooks rubbed his eyes and sighed before looking back up. He was painfully aware that his over-eagerness was going to have consequences, though whether he would face them or if it would be someone else, he did not know. Still, he mustered the fortitude to continue down this path. "I saw someone going through Hobbs' things."

"Who?" Bryant persisted.

Brooks looked around the deck and leant forward as he answered in a quiet voice. "Jefferies."

"I might 'ave known it!" Murphy said.

"Keep your voice down," said Bryant in warning. "Brooks, are you sure about this?"

The boy just nodded, but Murphy had already been thinking along his own tangent.

"Eh, 'ang about," he said. "If you knew about Jefferies, why didn't you say anythin' before?"

Brooks shrugged. "It happened so fast. And Bryant, you always told me to keep my head down."

Closing his eyes from a weariness that came from more than a simple lack of sleep, Bryant muttered. "Guess I did at that."

The man from the opposite gun crew leaned back, considering this news. "Nah, doesn't make sense," he said. "Why go to all the trouble of stealin' a pipe, then givin' it to someone else?"

"No, it makes perfect sense," said Bryant, sighing. "Hobbs' pipe was not the only thing stolen. Think about it. You steal a few coins and a pipe. The pipe isn't worth that much and is easily recognisable, so you bury it in someone else's kit and watch them get the flogging as you walk away with the money."

"Oh, that's low," said Murphy.

"Indeed," said Bryant. "You then just make a few veiled accusations, the midshipman gets involved and before you know it, Jessop is having his own belongings searched. Up turns the pipe, then comes the flogging. No defence against that."

"An' no one questions it too deeply, as no one really likes Jessop," Murphy said.

Bryant nodded ruefully. "That's right."

"So what do we do?" Brooks asked, simultaneously a

little afraid of what might happen to him and yet thrilled to be part of a conspiracy of sorts.

"You don't do anything," said Bryant firmly as he swung himself out of the hammock. "Nor do the rest of you. I'm going to have a quiet word with the Bosun. What happens after that will be his business."

The *Whirlwind* had endured a short storm as it crossed into southern waters, but the sprightly frigate had ridden the waves in a manner that had warmed Havelock's heart, even as he stood on the quarterdeck, getting drenched from the unrelenting heavy rain and waves crashing against the hull of the ship, while watching his crew expertly handle the rigging and constantly changing conditions with deft hands. His officers, too, had acquitted themselves admirably, matching the endurance of the men under their command as they stood through each watch, ensuring the crew acted quickly but not so fast as to put their shipmates' lives in jeopardy.

The dispersing clouds and calming sea had marked the fourth day of the sixth week since the *Whirlwind* had departed Spithead, and driven on by the recent news imparted to them by the Portuguese merchant, the crew had steadily been building itself into a blind excitement. Many on the crew had learned how to handle the ship with steady hands, learning the ropes as it was called, but few were veterans of battle at sea. Havelock had made sure that his crew had constantly practiced with several gun drills every day since they left England and was now confident that any of his crews could keep to a constant rhythm of three shots every minute for as long as their ammunition lasted. In theory, that was enough to outshoot most French ships of war. However, gun drills were a far cry from having to do the same thing when there was an enemy vessel shooting back, cannon balls crashing through the decks, sending wood splinters flying with lethal force to maim your best friends as an officer stood behind you, shouting at you to reload once again and return fire.

There were a small number on board who had seen action before but many were new to the trade and their real test was to come. That was where the planting of discipline within the crew would bear fruit and Havelock was anxious to see the results of his hard work. For now, however, the crew were growing in eagerness to see a French ship in hostile waters and earn their chance for prize money. That, at the end of the day, was what made the wheels of the King's Navy continue to turn.

Even the loss of a shipmate, normally a source of ill omen and dire predictions, had been met without much negative reaction from the rest of the crew. Just two days previous, during the small hours of the mid-watch, a man known as Jefferies had plummeted from the mainmast into the sea. No one had noticed him missing until the end of the watch, by which time locating a man lost in the ocean might have proved impossible, even if Havelock was of a mind to turn the ship around.

In truth, Havelock suspected foul play, especially as no one seemed to mind the mysterious disappearance of the man who was known to be sure-footed on the masts. It happened, from time to time, an unpopular crewman would have an accident and no one would mourn his loss. Having quizzed the Bosun about the incident, Havelock had received the distinct impression that some kind of sailor's justice had been enacted for a crime that, had it come to his attention, would have merited the death penalty anyway. Certainly, Mr Kennedy had been evasive in his answers, taking each question in turn with a look that strongly suggested that Havelock did not really want to become involved. Having sailed with Kennedy for several years in one capacity or another, Havelock had come to trust and rely upon his Bosun, and this seemed to be borne out by the quiet acceptance of the crew over the death of Jefferies. Maybe Havelock would hear the full story when they returned to port. But probably not.

Though the sea had calmed over the past day, the wind remained strong, filling the *Whirlwind's* sails as it sailed down past the African coast which lay out of sight some distance over the eastern horizon. With his ship skimming through the sea at a fair rate of knots, Havelock enjoyed every small twist and turn transmitted through the hull to his feet on the quarterdeck, feeling the *Whirlwind* literally cut through the water, parting it to leave a long wake behind. He smiled. Calm seas, a stiff wind, an enemy nearby and a double watch of lookouts constantly scanning the horizon for sails. This, more than anything, was what it meant to be the captain of a frigate in His Majesty's Navy. The frigate was, after all, a hunter, able to roam the ocean in search of prey that would leave heavier and more powerful ships of war far behind.

Havelock's musings were wrenched back to the here and now by a cry from the top of the mainmast.

"Sail to starboard!"

Looking up at the men on the mast, Havelock followed the line to where they were pointing, roughly thirty degrees off from the starboard bow. Raising his telescope, he scanned the horizon until he found a familiar arrangement of sails.

"What do we have, Captain?" Corbin voice came from behind him.

"Frigate, a big one. Two-decker, if my eyes are not

mistaken," said Havelock. "Unmistakably French. Sailing across our path."

"She is in our lee, Sir. The advantage is ours."

"Indeed, Mr Corbin. I believe we have found our quarry. Pass the word – beat to quarters. Ready the larboard guns."

Corbin turned back to the main deck and shouted triumphantly to the crew. "Beat to quarters! Jump to it! Run out the guns, to larboard!"

He was answered with a cheer as crewmen leapt to their stations. Those on deck had heard the lookout report a sail on the horizon and the news flashed into the lower decks like wildfire. Along the length of the *Whirlwind's* hull, gun ports were opened and cannon loaded before being rolled out, ready to fire. Marines, under the command of their sergeant, lined up on the main deck, ready for the Captain's order to scale the masts for sniping positions or to otherwise line the forecastle.

"Run up the colours!" cried Havelock over his shoulder, and the dual flags of British nationality were soon flying proudly, announcing the *Whirlwind's* intention to do battle with the French ship as she closed inexorably on its position.

Lowering his telescope, Havelock gazed at the horizon, where the enemy ship was just beginning to materialise out of the haze. Smiling grimly, he spoke quietly to himself.

"We have her."

CHAPTER FOUR

Havelock's attention was riveted on the French ship, as were any crewman who had the luxury of standing idle as he awaited orders that would throw him into action. Though the French crew must have spotted the *Whirlwind* long ago, she made no effort to change course and the two ships sailed ever closer to one another for nearly an hour.

During that time, the British crew had plenty of opportunities to think about the coming battle. For many, their previous anticipation gave way slowly to a creeping fear. Memories of crippled sailors leaving battered ships at port percolated in their thoughts, along with stories from the older and wiser hands on board that they had listened to just a few days past. The tales of hardship, of blood flowing across the deck and masts falling to crush sailors beneath did not seem so frivolous now as the *Whirlwind* inched towards its enemy. For many of the crew, the thought of their own mortality was only now just beginning to cross their minds. There was an inevitability about their fate that seemed irresistible.

Not everyone on board had such dark thoughts, of course. On every ship of war there would be those who simply did not believe they could ever die while so young, while others took the idea of the invincibility of the King's Navy and their own national superiority to heart.

For his part, Havelock was enjoying a moment of supreme calmness, as he often did before battle. He knew the French vessel enjoyed certain advantages over his ship but he was also aware of the odds in his own favour. The *Elita* would have heavier guns that could out range his own, but this would be countered by their fast closing speed. He guessed the French would have, at best, the opportunity to fire two salvoes at range before he could respond and he did not intend to present an easy target when they opened up on the *Whirlwind*. It was true, too, that the French had many more guns than he possessed, lined up on two decks. However, Havelock had yet to meet a French crew that could fire as efficiently as well disciplined British sailors and the biggest cannon in the world would do them no good at all if his men could fire two or even three times while they struggled to reload.

He was painfully aware that the *Elita's* crew greatly outnumbered his by perhaps as much as three to one but Havelock trusted in his own ability not to be caught off guard by a sudden manoeuvre that would send the French frigate crashing into his own before her crew swept over the railings. A dozen different scenarios played through his mind during the long wait as the *Whirlwind* closed the distance with the *Elita*, imagining stroke and counterstroke as he tried to place himself in the French captain's position and predict just what might be his first move.

The French frigate began to loom high before him and Havelock raised his telescope once more, this time sighting individual crew running about the deck of the *Elita*, following their captain's orders. On the quarterdeck of the ship, he saw the unmistakable uniform of a French captain, also looking at his enemy through a telescope. Havelock resisted the temptation for a cheerful salute and instead contented himself with the thought that while the French crew stirred on their ship, his were standing at attention, calm and collected. What a sight it must have been to that French captain!

Of course, it was equally possible that the French

captain was arrogant enough to think the coming battle was a foregone conclusion, given that he had the larger ship. That was something Havelock intended to disabuse him of very quickly.

"Sergeant!" Havelock called, and the red-coated commander of the *Whirlwind's* marines stepped up behind him.

"Sir!"

"Get your men up into the masts," said Havelock. "As high as you can go without falling off. Their own marines are likely to have a height advantage over you, so make sure your men shoot well."

"Yes, Sir! We'll send them Frogs packin'!" The sergeant stomped off, bellowing orders at the two lines of marines who had stood at attention on the quarterdeck with their muskets held steady in front of their chests since the *Elita* had first been sighted. Jumping to obey, they split into three groups, each heading to one of the tall masts of the *Whirlwind*. Slinging their weapons across their backs and climbing up the rigging, they began to take positions high above the deck, where they would be able to snipe choice targets on the deck of the French ship.

"He has still made no change in course, Sir," said Corbin who, after having performed one last tour of the ship to see all was in order, had returned to his captain's side.

"He will, Mr Corbin, you can be sure of that," said Havelock. "On our present course, we'll sail right behind him and unload a salvo into his stern. He won't chance us crippling him like that. No, he'll make a move, just watch out for it."

The two officers, satisfied that their crew and ship was ready to fight, kept their eyes glued on the *Elita*, straining to see the first hint of a move by the French captain. They did not have to wait for long.

"Sir, movement among the sails," said Corbin.

"I see it – she's coming about!" Havelock said. He called down to the crew on the main deck below him. "Steady, men, she'll get a hurried shot or two at us – and then she'll be ours!"

He almost did not notice the cheer a few of his men gave as he watched the *Elita* begin a steady turn towards his ship. The two light coloured bandings that ran the length of the ship's hull were obvious to his eyes now, each line marking the position of one gun deck. The ship had its larboard side to them but he quickly noticed its gun ports were closed.

"She is going to cut across us!" Havelock said. "Helm, steady as she goes. Aim straight for her until I give the word, then hard to starboard!"

"You see their plan, Sir?" Corbin asked.

"Aye, I do. They are going to try steal the wind advantage from us by reversing their course and coming past us. A fine gambit but easily countered."

As the *Elita* continued its turn, prow pointing briefly at the *Whirlwind* before continuing to move on, its starboard side was revealed. Everyone on deck could see the two layers of gun ports being thrown open before cannon were rolled out. For the next few seconds, time seemed to slow down for Havelock as he watched the guns of the *Elita* slowly line up on the prow of his ship. Then the French ship disappeared in a roiling cloud of thick white smoke.

Havelock heard a couple of popping sounds as cannonballs penetrated the sails above his head but the rest of the shot went speeding past the *Whirlwind* to raise large spouts of water in its wake. This was enough to cause Midshipman Rawlinson to duck. Corbin turned round instinctively to admonish him.

"On your feet, Mr Rawlinson! Where do you think you are?"

Extending his telescope, Havelock made a quick calculation as he watched the French canon being rolled back into their gun ports for reloading.

"We are going too fast, they won't get another chance to fire – Helm, hard to starboard, now! Bring us in line with that ship!"

With a deft twist, the *Whirlwind* responded instantly to the wheel, the crew on the main deck automatically adjusting the spread of the sails to match the command. With less than a hundred yards separating the two ships, they sailed in parallel, each racing the other in an attempt to steal a lead and either take or retain the advantage of being on the windward side of the duel.

"Mr Corbin, if you would be so good as to teach these Frenchmen how an Englishman shoots..." said Havelock.

"Aye, Sir. Gun crews, fire!" shouted Corbin, whose order was immediately relayed by Wynton to the gun deck. The entire ship shook and rolled as the eleven larboard guns fired simultaneously, instantly obscuring the *Elita* with a thick bank of smoke. Havelock caught a glimpse of bright light flashing from the French ship before it disappeared but before he could shout an order to his crew to hold them steady, the Whirlwind shuddered as it was impacted by the *Elita's* broadside.

The cry of men was pierced by flying splinters as heavy shot smacked into the side of the ship. Overhead sails ripped and Havelock saw one man fall from the mainmast into the sea. He sensed immediately that the damage was light, the French crew having aimed high by waiting until their ship had rolled to one side, as was typical for their captains when trying to de-mast an enemy.

"We'll win the race to reload, Mr Corbin," he shouted.

"Doubleshot the guns. Let's see if we can counter some of their heavier firepower!"

"Aye, Sir. Doubleshot the guns!"

Sailing onwards, the two ships sped forward from their shroud of gun smoke and Havelock was gratified to see his regular gun drills had paid off in terms of accuracy. The entire starboard side of the *Elita* was blackened and pitted, and three large, ragged holes in the hull marked the areas where cannon had been blasted by incoming fire, rendering them useless. Even so, Havelock could not help but marvel at the size of the French frigate, its quarterdeck towering over his own position and the two gun decks appearing even more intimidating at this range. All the more so as, while the two ships raced side by side, it was painfully obvious that she was every bit as fast as the *Whirlwind*.

"Fire at your discretion, Mr Corbin," Havelock said, preferring to leave the cycling of the guns to his lieutenants while he watched, hawk-like, for the slightest twitch from the *Elita* that would reveal its captain's intentions. He did not have to wait for more than a few seconds before the guns of the *Whirlwind* roared again, blanketing the area with smoke. Still, Havelock's ears were becoming re-accustomed to the noise of battle and he heard the distinctive crack and splintering of shot smashing into a wooden hull, even as he heard the cries below deck to reload. He smiled as he saw the damage revealed by the clearing smoke. More French cannons had been put out of commission, and several jagged holes very low on the *Elita's* hull would see it taking on water in hard turns.

Watching the French crew work to recycle their own guns, Havelock saw them roll out their cannon even as the order to do so was relayed on his own ship. He realised then that the French crew, while no match for his in a straight race, were certainly more competent than others he had faced in the past. Wincing in preparation of the assault, Havelock realised that the *Whirlwind* was to receive the full weight of the French two deck broadside an instant before his own guns could respond. He heard the cry to fire from the *Elita* before it once again disappeared in smoke and he was knocked to the deck by a jarring impact that left him breathless.

Arms covering his head, Brooks tried to crawl for cover next to his gun carriage before he was hoisted to one side by Bryant. The gun deck was flooded with a dim light from open gun ports and gaping holes in the hull, dispersed by the smoke that hung still in the air. The smell of spent powder mixed with the almost overpowering stench of blood and sweat while everywhere men shouted orders or howled in pain as they clutched splinter wounds or stumps of limbs.

The sights and sounds of battle terrified Brooks and he wanted to do nothing more than curl into a ball. Squeezing his eyes shut tightly, he moved his hands to his ears but nothing seemed to shut out the terrible noise of explosions and men shouting as they fought.

"Return fire, you British dogs!" Hague shouted through the din, straining to be heard.

Hearing the voice of an officer, Brooks reacted automatically and tried to stand. Wide-eyed, he put a hand out to steady himself against the nearest rafter but then slipped, falling hard on the wooden deck. He was shocked to discover he was soon wet through then realised it was from the tide of blood that was slowly spreading across the floor. He became aware that Bryant had shoved a rope in his hands and was yelling at him to pull.

"Come on, run out the gun lads!"

By reflex alone, born from countless drills, Brooks braced himself against the side of the hull and pulled, sensing the heavy gun carriage rumble past before an immense crack thundered from the weapon, bathing him in smoke once more. Whimpering, he stayed motionless until Bryant hooked an arm under his and lifted him up once more.

"Snap to it, lad," Bryant said. "Not long to go now, we have them on the run." He turned away from Brooks briefly to shout for powder and sighed with relief as a young boy, no more than nine years old or so, came scampering through the death and chaos to deliver a metal box of cloth-bound charges.

"Reload," roared Hague. "Doubleshot!"

Murphy scampered to Bryant to take the charges, instinctively keeping his head low, before springing back to the front of their cannon, beginning the process of swabbing it out to receive a new round. Bryant turned Brooks round to face him and, looking straight into the young man's eyes, sought to penetrate his fear.

"Brooks, you hear me?" he shouted, trying to maintain an element of calmness in his voice. "There's no point trying to hide, lad – there's nowhere they can't get you. All we can do is make sure we fire faster than they do. You with me, lad?"

With a slowness that seemed agonising to Bryant, Brooks blinked and looked back at him.

"Stick by me, I'll see you right," said Bryant. "Now, grab the shot and help Murphy!"

Casting a look around his feet, Brooks quickly found the stack of cannon balls in their brass stay and, lifting one out, carried it round to the front of the cannon, taking great care not to look at the massive French warship that loomed close outside their open gun port.

Behind them, Hague wiped his brow, his silk handkerchief now ruined by sweat and powder. Seeing the gun crews remained more or less firm, he quickly trotted to the rear of the gun deck, taking care not to hamper the reloading of any of the cannon. Seeing Wynton at the top of the stairs on the main deck, he called for the older lieutenant's attention.

"Four guns out of action!"

He watched Wynton nod in understanding as the man turned back to relay this to Corbin. He then turned back to the gun deck and, on seeing the crews were completing their reloading cycle, looked out of the nearest gun port to check the position of the *Elita*. Seeing that it still sailed directly at their broadside and that the roll of the *Whirlwind* was just right, he barked the command.

"Fire!"

Hague had to brace himself against a rafter as the whole ship rolled to starboard from the recoil. Through the dirty smoke, he could see many of the crew on this deck were scared, but was gratified that towards the prow of the ship Jessop's team, at least, was alternating between whooping in triumph and cursing the ancestry of their French counterparts. Their attitude was beginning to become infectious and the neighbouring cannon crew had started to join in.

"Reload!" He shouted. "Steady men, remember, that is only a French ship out there and any one of you is worth ten of them!"

From the far end of the gun deck, Jessop's team responded with more promises of what they would do to the French and even some members of the other crews began to smile in a grim fashion.

Brooks had slipped into automatic in concert with Murphy and Bryant as they cleaned their cannon, loaded it with charge and shot, rolled the carriage out and then fired, before pulling it back to start the process again. He glanced up once to see Bryant staring out of the gun port towards the enemy vessel.

"How are we doing?" Brooks asked.

Bryant hesitated before answering. "Looks pretty even at the moment. Keep firing, lad, that's the key. Those Frogs will soon give up if we can fire more often than they can."

His overly confident words caused Murphy to flicker a questioning look at him. Bryant could only shrug. He knew that the *Whirlwind* had been hit hard but he also realised that while the *Elita* had suffered more crew and gun losses, she could weather the damage far better than they. Even though both ships had suffered in these exchanges, the *Elita* had started with more cannon and crew to service them and she still enjoyed that numerical superiority.

Stunned for a few brief seconds, Havelock did not realise that he was being helped to his feet by Lieutenant Corbin. As soon as he saw he was being aided, he put a hand out, forcing the man to back away. It would not do for his crew to think he had been wounded.

Comforted by the thunderous sound and rocking motion that signified the *Whirlwind's* guns had been fired once again, Havelock cast a look at both the *Elita* and his own ship. The French ship sported several holes in her hull from which cannon had been blasted from their carriages. Breaches lower down the hull had grown in number but, on the ship's present course, rode high enough out of the water not to cause any significant problems to her captain.

Casting an eye to the *Whirlwind*, Havelock saw men lying on the deck and smoke rising up from open hatches. More critically, the top third of the foremast had been shot away, leaving the sail to hang down uselessly. That would cost him some speed and agility. He looked at Corbin.

"Damage report?"

"Complements of Mr Hague, we are down to seven guns against the French," said Corbin. "We are also beginning to take on water in the hold."

"Get a crew down there to begin pumping it out," said Havelock. He thought for a second. "If we stay as we are, that ship will just overwhelm us by weight of guns. We need to break them, and quickly."

"What are your orders?"

"Get the gun crews to load the starboard cannon but tell them to keep the gun ports larboard open. I don't want the French getting a whiff of this until they actually see what we are doing."

Corbin left Havelock's side briefly to relay the instructions down to Wynton and then returned, a question on his lips. "You are going to cut across behind them, Sir?"

"It is worth the gamble. We trade the chance for a knock-out blow against the possibility of handing them the wind advantage." Havelock said. By making this manoeuvre, he would be placing his ship on the leeward side of the *Elita*, which he was well aware, might be a decision he regretted later.

Looking back at Wynton, Corbin received a nod and reported to Havelock that the starboard guns were ready for firing. Watching the *Elita* intently, Havelock began timing their reloading cycle.

"Let's see if we can catch them off balance," he said, as much to himself as Corbin. As the first French gun was rolled out, Havelock shouted his order.

"Helm, hard to larboard! Bring us behind him!"

Havelock instantly noticed that the *Whirlwind* was a little sluggish to respond, indeed, it felt as if the ship was lumbering as it made the turn. However, it was quick enough to put the crew of the *Elita* on the back foot, as they watched the *Whirlwind* make its harsh turn to sail behind them. Their gun crews were still running out cannon from the open ports on their starboard side, only to find the British ship had disappeared from their view.

As the *Whirlwind* held its course, perpendicular to the *Elita's*, the range between the two ships dropped dramatically and, for the first time, the marines high among the masts found themselves able to target the crew on the deck of the French vessel. The crack of musket fire rang out time and again from above their heads, small puffs of smoke from the guns instantly dispersing in the wind. On the *Elita*, half a dozen men dropped to the deck, either dead or clutching at wounds, while others scampered for cover. To his credit, Havelock noticed, the French captain did not flinch, even though his quarterdeck was the main target area for the marines.

Returning to a straight line course, the *Whirlwind* began to pick up speed again and her crew watched as they sailed within a stone's throw of the *Elita's* stern, her gold-etched name plate clearly visible to all. Havelock almost snarled his next order.

"Mr Corbin, run out the guns. Crew to fire at will."

He barely listened as his order was relayed to the gun deck but watched intently as the *Whirlwind* sailed past the French frigate. From prow to stern, his guns fired one by one as they lined up on the rear of the *Elita*, where she was most vulnerable. Havelock momentarily rued the thought that if he possessed heavier guns, his shots would be capable of passing right through the ship, smashing every deck as the shot travelled the full length of the vessel. However, he quickly put this idea aside as, over the course of twenty seconds, he watched his crew put the full weight of the *Whirlwind's* guns into the stern of the *Elita*. The deck below the elegant great cabin was wrecked almost instantly and everyone on board the British frigate heard the cries of the dying and wounded inside the French ship, even above the thunderous rumble of cannon fire. Havelock was particularly gratified to see the French captain dive for cover on his main deck when he realised just what the *Whirlwind* intended to do.

Propelled forward a few steps by Bryant's heavy slap on his back, Brooks nevertheless managed to raise a smile as he looked out of the open gun port.

"You see, lad?" Bryant said enthusiastically. "You can always rely on the Captain! Caught the Frogs completely off guard with that one!"

For his part, Brooks was just as happy to now be working on the other side of the gun deck, where the devastation of smashed wood and broken bodies was far less apparent than his last station. However, Murphy was also jumping with excitement and the good humour of the pair was infectious.

One of the last guns to fire in the volley that had wrecked the *Elita's* stern, Bryant had grinned as he closed the firing catch of his cannon. By the time the frigate had floated into view of his gun port, its rear quarter was already a mess, a tangle of wood planks and struts that veiled the destruction within. Knowing that the wreckage could provide little hindrance to his shot, Bryant was left to imagine just how much damage he had dealt to the internal structure of the ship.

"Reload!" The inevitable order came from Hague, the triumph in his voice unmistakable. "We have them on the run now, men!"

Rolling their gun carriage back, Murphy looked out of the gun port as they continued to sail past the *Elita*. When he saw the larboard side of the French ship, he smiled.

"They still 'aven't rolled out their guns!" he cried happily. "We're goin' to mash 'em!"

"They ain't turnin', either!" Brooks shouted back.

"They ain't dead yet," said Bryant calmly. "But we are still better shots and we can still reload quicker than they can. Hop to it, lads, let's get ready to give them another taste of British metal!"

Together, they worked in perfect synchronisation as they readied their cannon once more, even sparing a laugh for the news filtering from forward that Jessop's team had boasted they could reload quicker and shoot straighter than the rest of the gun crews put together.

Having finished loading their cannon, the three of them ran the carriage out of the port and Murphy scrambled past the other two in order to poke his head out of the hatch. He stared at the French ship as it first sailed away from them and then began to turn.

"Oh, she's comin' back for more!" he said.

"Hold your fire!" shouted Hague behind them. "On the Captain's word and not before!"

"She's in a bad way, Sir," said Corbin as they both

watched the *Elita* begin to make its turn back towards them.

"We are both in a bad way, Mr Corbin," Havelock reminded his lieutenant. "We are taking on water, have a damaged foremast and many guns on our larboard side out of action. We may have fresh guns on this side but then, so does she. I wonder... Oh! Did you see that?"

Havelock's sharp eyes and experience at sea caught the odd motion of the *Elita* a fraction of a second before Corbin did. Coming about to match the *Whirlwind's* new course, the frigate heeled hard to starboard, the weight of its masts listing it heavily as the rudder steered it through the rolling water. It began the turn as smoothly as Havelock had come to expect but, suddenly, the ship seemed to catch something in the water and he saw some of the crew on board lurch forward as their vessel decelerated suddenly.

"What was that?" Corbin asked. "Surely they could not have struck anything?"

"They might as well have," said Havelock with a growing smile as the reason for the *Elita's* strange movement dawned on him. "We holed her on the starboard side, remember? While the wounds were above the waterline, as soon as she turned and rolled onto her side, they would have been underwater." He sighed. "Her captain won't make that mistake again."

"Can we not use it to our advantage?"

"She might be as slow as us now and will favour starboard turns. Still..." He thought for a second. "Mr Corbin, instruct the gun crews to check their fire. They are to wait for my command."

Corbin was puzzled but obeyed without comment. "Aye, Sir."

He looked quizzically at his Captain until Havelock

noticed his attention. Havelock gestured to the *Elita*.

"She has yet to run out her guns on this side."

"Did we hit her harder than we thought?" Corbin asked.

"I don't think so. Our guns are not that powerful, though I fancy her rearward cannon may not be firing any time soon. No. Watch what she does next."

They both stared intently at the *Elita* as the frigate continued making its ponderous turn, swinging round until its prow faced them. Once the turn was complete, the ship righted itself and began to pick up speed, closing the distance between them rapidly.

"She's going to ram us?" Corbin asked incredulously.

"No, I fancy her captain intends to board us. I believe I can put a stop to that though!" Havelock said and raced to the stairs leading to the main deck, climbing down them two at a time. Maintaining his pace, he carried on downwards into the gun deck, where he acknowledged Lieutenant Hague with a nod.

"Listen to me, men!" Havelock shouted to gain the attention of the gun crews. "That French ship means to board us! We have scared her crew with our fine shooting so much, they no longer wish to play!"

He smiled openly as the gun crews cheered, some of them reaching through their open gun ports to shake a fist at the approaching frigate.

"However," he shouted, regaining their attention. "We have better things to do than dally with French sword play! Stand to your guns and prepare to fire! On my word and not a second before!"

The crew leapt to their feet, the gunners standing with a hand on the firing catch of their cannon, all eyes on their Captain. Walking smartly towards the nearest gun crew, Havelock stared out of the gun port, watching the

Elita as she sailed closer, timing the motion of both the French ship and his own. He noticed the cannon's crew looking at him expectantly.

"You've done well today, men," he said, congratulating them. "What is your name?" he asked the nearest.

"Err, Brooks, Sir, err, Captain."

"Well, stand easy, Brooks," said Havelock, keeping his voice even. "We are going to try a little trick the French often like to play here."

The motion of the waves constantly rolled the *Whirlwind* slightly as it sped across the ocean and it was this movement that Havelock began to time. Satisfied that he had the measure of it, Havelock stood back.

"Ready men, on my word and not a second before..." he said. "Ready... Fire!"

His view instantly disappeared in a wave of smoke but soon cheers from the forward gun deck told him that the hit had been solid. A few seconds later, the stern of the *Whirlwind* had passed out of the cloud and he leaned forward across the cannon again to judge the results. He liked what he saw.

The *Elita* had been hit hard but Havelock's timing had sent the full weight of fire into the frigate's masts and sails. Striking from the front, the combined shot had snapped the *Elita's* foremast like a twig, sending it crashing into the mainmast which now leaned precariously. With sails now tangled and out of trim, the French ship slowed noticeably, leaving the *Whirlwind* to skip ahead freely across the waves.

Havelock put a hand on Brooks' shoulder. "That," he said, "is how we halt a French frigate! Well done indeed, lad!"

The raucous cheers of the collected gun crews followed Havelock as he first shook Hague's hand and then returned to the quarterdeck. He found Corbin waiting for him there, a broad smile on the man's face.

"A fine shot, Captain!"

Casting a look back at the floundering French ship, Havelock had to agree.

"Aye. It was. Thank you, Mr Corbin."

Walking behind the mizzenmast, the two officers stood, arms folded, as they watched the *Elita* recede into the distance. By now its captain was not even trying to keep pace as the *Whirlwind* skittered away, instead taking the time to begin repairs to his masts and sails.

"He'll be stranded for some time, trying to make good the damage you caused," said Corbin.

"True, but we have our own wounds to heal before we can think about going into battle again. One or two good salvoes from that ship and we would have been in serious trouble. Gods, but she can hit hard!"

"We are rigging the foremast now, Captain, and should have near full mobility within the hour," said Corbin.

"Good. She won't be her normal sprightly self until that is fully repaired though. What else do we have to contend with? Has Wynton given you the full list?"

"Minor breach on the starboard side below the waterline. The pumps are keeping pace at the moment but we'll have to stop to patch it. Four cannon knocked off their carriages, Kennedy thinks they are all serviceable. A lot of damage to the gun ports and fittings larboard but it can all be repaired, given time."

"We gave better than we took then. Casualties?" Havelock asked.

"Considering what might have been, light. I'm told seventeen dead or dying, nearly half as many again injured and unable to report for service." Corbin tried to look on the good side. "Still, I think we dealt far worse."

"Yes, but then they can afford to take worse. Another race is about to start, Mr Corbin, the one for repair. If we can patch this old girl up and locate the *Elita* again before she can make good the damage we handed her, she'll be ours. If she beats us..." He trailed off, not wanting to think about facing the larger ship while the *Whirlwind* was still battered.

"What are your orders, Captain?"

"Set course due east. We'll find a natural harbour on the African coast and make repairs. I think we can also take the opportunity to send out teams for water and fresh food – the crew certainly deserve it." Havelock thought for a moment. "Speaking of which, give them an extra ration of rum tonight. They fought well and are worthy of the recognition."

In spite of the wind streaming in from gaping holes in the side of the hull the atmosphere on board the *Whirlwind* was jubilant. Already exhilarated to have survived a clash with a French frigate, Captain Havelock's granting of an extra ration of rum for all men had been received extremely well. In the flickering light of the gun deck, someone had produced a fiddle and many sailors were dancing wherever there was room, their shipmates clapping and joining in with familiar songs.

Having toured the entire length of the gun deck, linking arms with any man he found dancing before spinning off to the next group of happy souls, Murphy was getting fairly exhausted. Though he had consumed his own rum some time earlier, he was on the look out for anyone who did not feel the need to drink in order to have fun. As usual he was disappointed. In the end, he trotted and skipped his way sternwards, where he found his own gun crew in happy debate with their neighbouring teams. Crashing down on a bench next to Bryant, he grinned at everyone present.

"To the *Whirlwind*!" he said, holding up a fist in place of a full mug of rum. The others joined in with his toast with a more meaningful handful.

"No arguments 'ere," said one of the revellers. "An' 'ere's to the Cap'n!" he added, invoking another round of raised mugs. Murphy sniffed around hopefully to see if anyone was going too steady with their drinking but a shake of the head from Bryant dashed his hopes.

"So what happens now, then?" Brooks asked.

"No doubt the Captain's sailing us somewhere to make repairs," said Bryant. "And then it will be back to find that ship."

"Won't the Frogs be making repairs too?" Brooks said.

"Aye," said Bryant. "But I think it is fair to say we got the best of the last battle." The group responded with another heartfelt cheer. "You did well today, lad," he added, looking meaningfully at Brooks.

"I,,, I went to pieces at the start."

"Many men older than you do likewise, in their first battle," said Bryant. "Battle on board one of his King's ships is a scary thing. All you can see is the murderous enemy out of your gun port, and that is exactly where the damn cannon balls are going to be coming from. Takes a lot to stand and do your job in the face of that. You never know where the next hit is going to come in."

"True 'nough," said Murphy. "But I was watchin' you, lad. Once you saw what needed to be done, you got your 'ead down an' stuck at it."

Bryant slapped Brooks on the shoulder. "Can't ask for more than that in a gun crew," he said.

"How did you all fair?" Murphy asked of the other guns

crews.

"Carriage rolled over Tailor's leg. 'E's with the surgeon."

"Buckley took a hit. Been cleanin' 'im up from the deck. Ain't a pretty sight."

"We lost Stefans too. Hull buckled in front of us, 'e lost his arm. Bled to death 'fore we could get 'im down below."

The group fell silent for a few seconds as they considered the loss of their shipmates, the pain endured by others and their own fate. The spell was broken by Bryant raising his mug again. "Hey, we're still here, lads."

He was greeted by murmurs of thanks and appreciation. Battle at sea was never routine, no matter how many times a man lived through it and they were all grateful to be alive.

"I say it was down to the Cap'n that we did so well," said Murphy with some conviction.

"Aye, masterful," said one of the other crew members. "Kept 'is 'ead as we closed range, didn't allow the Frogs to put 'im off. Then a quick turn and we're racin' 'em, tradin' fire as we go!"

"Then that lovely turn," said Bryant. "Took them completely off guard, just as they were about to fire. And we went sailing past their stern, with all the time in the world to take our shot!"

"Never thought I would see a French ship up that close," chipped in Brooks. "Not while there were fightin' Frogs on board!"

"You remember that moment, lad," said another sailor. "That 'ain't somethin' you see often!"

"And that's the God's honest truth," said Bryant, in full agreement. "For my money though, the masterstroke of the Captain was that aimed shot at their masts. Stopped them near dead in the water!"

"Couldn't believe it when the Cap'n came down 'ere – and walked straight to our gun!" said Brooks, excitedly.

"Well, 'e did more than that, Brooks," said Murphy. "Looks through the gun port, asks your name, and then congratulates you – personally!"

Brooks looked somewhat embarrassed. "I think that was for all of us," he said quietly.

"Don't you knock it back, lad," said Bryant. "He'll remember that incident as well as you do. From now on, the Captain knows who you are!"

"If we could all be so lucky!" Murphy said, raising a few chuckles from the gathered men.

Trying to shake the complement off with a laugh, Brooks suddenly turned serious as he considered something. "One thing I didn't get, though. We had been poundin' away at the side of the French ship all the way through the battle. And then, just one shot, boom, the masts go. How did the Capt'n know how to do that?"

"Was wondering when you would ask that," said Bryant with a satisfied smile. "The gun carriages we carry here give the cannon very little elevation – just enough to lob a shot over a good distance. Now, you can change the elevation of your guns... you remember how, from your drills?"

"Err, yes. Use blocks and wedges to lift the barrel up."

"Aye, that's right. But it takes time to do that. You have to lift the entire gun up, get just the right amount of elevation the Captain asks for, settle the gun back down – and that is not just us doing that but every cannon on this side of the ship."

Bryant threw his head back to drain his mug, settling it down on the bench next to him. Out of the corner of his eye, he saw Murphy peer hopefully into the dark recesses of the mug in a vain hope of free drink and smiled to himself as he saw the small man's nose wrinkle in disappointment.

"There is a quicker way of shooting to a ship's masts," he said, seeing that Brooks was fully engaged in his explanation. "In fact, it is something the French do damn near all the time."

Cocking his head with a puzzled expression, Brooks said "Yeah, the Cap'n said somethin' about a French trick."

"Well, not really a trick," said Bryant. He raised his forearm across his face, palm flat. "As you will be well aware by now, a ship does not lie flat in the water. It will move depending on what the sea is doing, how the sails are rigged, where the rudder is and so on. It will pitch up and down," he said, raising his hand up and down. "It will also roll," this time rocking his hand from side to side.

Brooks nodded but it was clear from his face that he still did not fully comprehend.

"Well, we British are told to fire when the side we are shoving the guns out of is at its lowest point of that roll." Bryant demonstrated by tilting his hand. "That side of the ship will just be rising, and so our shot goes in a more or less straight line, straight into the side of the enemy's hull. We do it to cause as much damage as we can, knocking out his guns early on in the battle. Obviously, if a ship cannot shoot back at you, he cannot fight."

"And the French fire at the high point of the roll?" Brooks guessed.

"That's right," Bryant said. "Their shot tends to go up into the masts and sails. They aim to cripple a ship early on in the battle, taking away its ability to move effectively. If they can do that quickly, you have no choice but to surrender or watch them move to a place where your guns can't reach and have them pound you into the sea."

"And so that's what the Cap'n did," said Brooks.

"Exactly. He saw what the Frogs were going to do and decided to stop them quickly. We were lucky and it worked."

"Lucky?"

Bryant smiled. "We in the King's Navy are known to be good gunners but our aim is not like that of a sharpshooter. Our reputation comes from being able to fire together and to reload quickly – that is really all there is to it. The shot from these cannon can go all over the place – that's why ships have to move so close together in order to fight. It is possible for the guns to fire much, much further but you would be lucky to hit the coast at those ranges. And remember, you haven't got to worry about one gun reaching its target but eleven of them in the *Whirlwind*. One little cannon ball is not going to do a lot of damage. But a whole storm of them will."

Brooks stared hard at the floor for a few seconds, then looked up with a smile. "I think I've got it," he said.

"Oh, you 'ave more to learn yet," said Murphy. "Like takin' the wind out of another ship's sails. That's a good one. You see..."

"Whoa there, Murphy," said Bryant. "No need to over burden the lad. He doesn't need to learn everything tonight!"

Brooks seemed about to protest but Bryant shook his head firmly. "Just concentrate on what you are doing at the moment, young Brooks. Learn to handle the guns and rig the sails. Everything else is easy, so master those and you'll be well on your way to being a valued shipmate. You'll pick up the rest as you go on."

Brooks nodded, a little disappointed but then perked up. "So, there are lots of tricks like that, then?"

"More than any one man has a right to know," said another sailor in answer. "But I would bet my ration of rum for the next month that the Captain 'as 'em all pegged."

"And what are you reckonin' will 'appen when we next meet them Frogs?" Murphy asked.

"The Cap'n will pull somethin' out the bag," said the sailor confidently.

"Aye, but we have some hard work ahead of us," said Bryant, causing the sailor to nod in agreement.

"What do you mean?" asked Brooks.

"Well, we have plenty of damage that needs fixing, as you can see," Bryant said, sweeping an arm to take in the shattered hull larboard. "But the Frogs have their own repairs to make too. If we can fix the *Whirlwind*, make her battle worthy again and find that frigate before they can do anything meaningful, she'll be ours. They'll probably surrender after the first shot!"

"And if they fixed their ship too?" Murphy asked, a little mischievously.

Bryant sighed. "Well, then, we'll have to start all over again." Seeing Brooks' face fall a little at this, he smiled. "Don't worry, lad. Trust to the Captain. He'll see us right."

"Aye," said Murphy. "I certainly 'aven't 'eard Jessop and 'is mates goin' on about 'Avelock's Curse since the battle."

"Like us, they're all too full of rum tonight," said Bryant, ignoring Murphy's waspish comment about chance being a fine thing. "They'll start off again soon enough. So long as we ignore them, they can't do any harm."

The gathered sailors murmured their agreement. The

conversation meandered after that, as they discussed the possibility of re-supply during the voyage and the fresh food it might bring, before Brooks leapt in with an excited comment from the battle and the whole fight was recounted yet again. It would not be the last time that night.

With the setting sun at his back, Havelock luxuriated in the warm evening wind that swept across the deck of the *Whirlwind*. He had already noted the presence of sea birds high in the sky but was nevertheless gratified to hear the lookout announce the presence of land dead ahead.

"We made good time," he said to Corbin.

"Aye, she is a fast ship, even with a few scratches."

"Call all hands on deck, Mr Corbin," Havelock said. "It is time we told them of our intentions. It will also do them good to see land."

Corbin dutifully relayed the order and the other lieutenants and midshipmen descended below deck to stir the crew. They arose in groups and gaggles and Havelock was pleased to see that some were alert enough to see land. Word of this rippled through the assembling crowd and more than one sailor had a smile on his face as he looked up expectantly at his Captain.

Waiting until he received a nod from Corbin that all hands were present, Havelock strode confidently up to the front of the quarterdeck and, in his customary manner, spread his hands on the wooden railing. Satisfied that he had the attention of every man on board the *Whirlwind*, he began his address.

"Today, you have fought in a manner that befits a crew in his King's Navy. I am proud to have each and every man jack of you with us on this voyage! It is no exaggeration to say that we gave the French a damn good thrashing!"

Though they might have expected praise from their Captain, this did nothing to dampen the enthusiasm and excitement of the crew. They responded to his words with an impassioned cheer that Havelock let run long and loud. When they finally subsided, he continued.

"We have proved that no matter what ship the French bring to battle, a good British frigate with a hard-working and disciplined crew will win the day every time!"

Another cheer erupted but, sensing that it might partly be fuelled by rum, Havelock held a hand up to still them.

"We still have work to do," he said. "As you no doubt have already seen, we approach land. We will find a safe harbour and put ashore for repairs. And though there is much to be done, spare a thought for the poor Frenchmen, at sea with no means of making landfall!" The crew gave the appropriate cruel laugh at this. "Through your excellent gunnery, they are far worse off than we! We will see to the *Whirlwind's* slight wounds and then head back west to find our prey. And this time, we shall see her surrender, striking her colours as we approach!"

The volume of the crew's jubilant cries made Havelock both wince and smile. For any faults individuals may have, he knew that, collectively, there was a good crew on board this ship. He gave a nod to Corbin.

"All hands dismissed!"

Before the crew could return to their duties or sleep, depending on which watch they had been placed on, a new voice rang out from the crowd. Havelock quickly realised that it was the Bosun who had called aloud.

"Three cheers for Captain Havelock," Kennedy shouted

out. "Hip, hip..." As one, the crew raised their voices in a genuine salute of their commanding officer's skill.

Taken aback, Havelock opened his mouth to say something but found he did not have the words. Instead, he just smiled again and nodded at his crew in gratitude. He turned to walk to the rear of the quarterdeck as his men finally dispersed.

He was surprised to find that tears had started to well up, unbidden, in his eyes.

CHAPTER FIVE

The sea threw itself against the shore, breakers rearing up as they smashed into the pristine white sand and smooth rocks. The coast looked as if it had never been disturbed by the intrusion of civilised humans. Struggling to climb out of the jolly boat with a modicum of dignity intact, Hague readjusted the long sword at his belt and hopped into the sea, another incoming wave immediately soaking him up to the chest. As he staggered to the shore, he kept an eye on the rest of the crew dragging the jolly boat in, alert for any mishaps that might drag them under but they seemed quite accustomed to the conditions. Hague had occasionally seen sea rise up like this on the tip of Cornwall and had to remind himself that nothing separated him from the raw strength of the Atlantic Ocean on the beaches of this land.

Two other boats had already been dragged up onto the shore and he saw Lieutenant Corbin organise various parties, mixing marines in among sailors where he thought prudent, but giving enough latitude to those he felt worthy of trust. He was surprised to see him assign one man to a party of sailors who were going inland alone, a sailor he thought Corbin had been partly responsible for disciplining earlier on this voyage. Perhaps the Lieutenant thought the others would be a stabilising influence or perhaps he just did not much care for what happened to the man while they spent time here. The last sentiment might not have been one worthy of an officer in the King's Navy, but it was one that Hague could readily identify with. Some men were beyond reach, shrugging off the harshest discipline like water from a duck's back.

As Hague stomped up the beach, leading his rowing

party, he listened to the tail end of Corbin's orders as the Lieutenant pointed at his men and then directed them into their groups.

"Do not stray too far and always make sure you are within five minutes' run of the shore," said Corbin. "The wildlife round here may not be used to men and many creatures will bite before asking questions. If you see any interesting insects or snakes, believe me, you are better off leaving them alone. If you see any large predators, back away from them carefully. If you meet any natives you *will* show them all respect. Remember, this is their land and they know it better than you do. Party leaders, you have instructions and you know which direction I want you to head in. Mr Hague, you are with me – I believe you have some experience in dealing with the natives of Africa?"

Hague was caught a little off guard. "Eh? Ah, yes, Mr Corbin," he said, recovering quickly. "But that was some time ago and nowhere near this place." In truth, he had spent part of his childhood in South Africa while his father had run a merchant's agency there and while he had picked up some of the native tongue, he was well aware that the speech varied from tribe to tribe.

"You are the best we have, Mr Hague, and if we encounter any natives we may save a great deal of time if we trade with them."

"Right you are, Sir."

Corbin stared hard at the assembled parties. "Remember what I said about the natives. They may prove to be of great benefit to us. However, keep in mind the only experience they may have had with white men could be with the slave ships of the Americas. So, mind your manners as they may appear less than receptive. Only respond in kind if they prove outwardly hostile. Any questions?"

A few sailors shook their heads, which Corbin took to mean that at least a few of his warnings had hit home. He was on a strict timetable from Captain Havelock, who had remained on the *Whirlwind* to oversee the repairs. Having been given a list of requirements – ranging from a good stock of wood, replenishing that used for repairing the hull, to necessities such as fresh water, food and appropriate wood to be used for brushes – Corbin had split the men on the beach into three separate parties, tasking each with searching for just one of these goods. He was to lead a fourth group with Hague, in the hope of encountering natives and trading with them. With any luck, a little diplomacy would reap more rewards than the entire crew scouring for supplies.

"Very well, then. Off you go and good luck!"

Striking off in four different directions, the landing crew of the *Whirlwind* entered the tree line running along the shore and disappeared from sight.

Leading the way for his party of six, including two marines, Bryant hacked at all plant life within reach of his broad knife as he struggled to get past a particularly thick knot of branches. He had only been leading his group for little more than twenty minutes and already he felt exhausted. Wiping his brow with the back of his arm, he glanced around.

Though they had seen no wildlife, strange calls that may have come from birds or something else best not imagined, constantly rang out. The shrubs and trees were nothing like he had seen before and he noticed their leaves tended to be thick and rubbery to the touch, though here and there a very exotically coloured flower poked its elaborate petals out of the verdant mass as it strained for just a portion of the sunlight trickling through the canopy. The very air lent an ominous feel to the area, especially for men used to serving on board a ship that, while retaining its own specific odours, at lest felt the breeze once in a while. Here, it felt as if the wind never penetrated the trees, and as a result, the air was thick, cloying and very damp.

"This ain't no work for a sailor," said Murphy, and though he wished the small man would stop griping, Bryant could not help but agree. He had never imagined anything like this when he had signed up.

"Be just our bleedin' luck to run into damn natives," said Jessop. "Bad move from the Cap'n, not issuin' us with guns. What are we goin' to beat an attack off with? Sticks?" he asked, twirling a particularly heavy branch that Bryant had cut down earlier.

"I doubt he was wild about the idea of giving you a firearm, Jessop," replied Bryant, without breaking his stride.

"You'll be glad of a decent gun if we get ambushed," said Jessop, his eyes beginning to scout out the surrounding shrubs.

"You're beginnin' to worry me now," said Murphy nervously and his eyes too began to dart from left to right as he watched the vegetation. "Anyway, them marines 'ave got guns. If they see any... I saw somethin' move!" he suddenly exclaimed.

As one, they froze, casting anxious looks about them. Bryant was the first to stir from the spell and shook his head. "You're just jumpy, Murphy, calm down. There's nothing here but us."

"Probably just a pig or something, Murphy," said Brooks, not entirely convinced by his own words.

"Pig?" Jessop asked, his attention caught by the prospect of fresh meat.

"There ain't no pigs in Africa," said Bryant wearily. "Only where civilised folk settle. They have other animals here – buffalo, I think."

"What's a buffalo?" Brooks asked.

"Like a cow. But bigger. I think Hague would know."

"Yeah, an' of course, Corbin takes the one man who knows somethin' about the area for 'imself," said Jessop.

"Officer's privilege." If Bryant had the time or strength to shrug, he would have. He stopped and turned round to face his party. "Look, we ain't going to get attacked, there are no natives here and no pigs. Let's just find clean water, as we were told by the nice Lieutenant, and then we can be out of here. Agreed?"

Even Jessop nodded at the wisdom of this. By now they were all wet through, hot and feeling miserable, each longing for the familiar comforts of the *Whirlwind*.

"Right," said Bryant with some finality. "We'll go a little further and then you'll have to take over here, Jessop."

"Why me?" an irritated Jessop said.

"Because I am getting tired, and for all your faults, you are as strong as anyone else here."

Jessop grunted, perhaps unsure of whether he should carry on complaining or accept Bryant's words as a complement. As one, they started walking again but stopped almost immediately when a low, base growl echoed among the nearby trees. Murphy began to ask what the sound was but Bryant urgently waved him to keep quiet. None of them moved as they began to look around once more. It was Brooks that spotted it first.

"Up there," he said in a whisper, pointing to a spot among the branches of a tree just a few yards ahead of them. Bryant cocked his head and squinted as he tried to peer through the leaves and saw a flash of dull yellow. Moving very slowly, he shifted a nearby branch aside and looked into a pair of blinking golden eyes, narrowing as they considered the new arrivals. Stretched languidly along a thick branch just a few yards off the ground was a lithe-looking cat, its fur dappled with dozens of dark coloured spots. They watched its powerful hind muscles tense as it bared two inch long fangs and spat at them. It was clearly at least as large as a sizeable dog and seemed a lot more powerful.

"Gods, it's a lion!" Murphy said, beginning to shake in fear.

"Ain't a lion," said Bryant. "They live on plains."

"So what is it?" Brooks asked. "Is it dangerous?"

Bryant was at something of a loss. "Some kind of cat. Probably wont attack if we just go round it."

"I can eat cat," said Jessop with confidence as he strode past Bryant, brandishing his stick. Ignoring the warnings of the other members of the party, he jabbed upwards at the animal, trying to dislodge it from its perch.

At first, the cat simply tried to swat his stick away but it began to hiss violently when Jessop connected hard with its flank. It sprang to its feet and leered down at him, teeth bared just a yard away from his head. Thinking that perhaps there might not have been as much meat on the cat as he had first thought, Jessop turned and skipped back to the safety in numbers of the rest of the party.

Tensing for a split second, the cat launched itself with amazing speed at the man's back. Acting purely out of instinct, Bryant lashed out with his knife but only drew a thin line of blood down the cat's ribs.

Moving with a surprising agility for his size, Jessop had already retreated behind the marines, who now found themselves staring into the piercing eyes of the large cat as it crouched, tensing itself for a leap. The nearest marine struggled to unlimber his musket, fiddling at his belt for the ammunition pouch. With a ripple of honed muscles, the cat threw itself forwards, claws digging into the man's shoulders as fangs sunk into the side of his face and neck. The man screamed at an unbelievably high pitch and fell backwards, pinned under the weight of the animal. Screams turned to a gargle as the cat tightened its grip on his neck and rear claws started raking at his stomach, tearing apart the red uniform to stain it with a darker flow of blood.

The second marine, hesitating only a second as he watched the demise of his squad-mate, dismissed any thought of firing his musket and instead reversed it, swinging the butt of the weapon against the shoulder of the cat. It was a weak and hurried blow, which skittered off the creature's hide with no appreciable effect.

By this time, Bryant had recovered enough to step forward and slash with his knife across the cat's haunches, leaving a deep, bleeding cut. The cat released the dead marine and spun around, spitting as it bared its fangs once again. Bryant locked eyes with the animal and saw that it was gauging him carefully, looking for an opening through which to spring and take him down. Shuddering, Bryant crouched, ready to try beating the cat's reflexes by rolling to one side when it leapt.

He was spared the attack by the marine who, yelling with a primal fury he had managed to find deep within, set about the cat with the butt of his musket. The cat shrunk downwards, trying to escape the blows as he swung and jabbed with the weapon. Seeing the animal otherwise distracted, Jessop jumped back into the fight, hammering away with his heavy stick about the cat's head, knocking it insensible almost immediately. As soon as the animal began to move sluggishly under the repeated attacks, Bryant built up the nerve to approach it once more, burying his knife into the cat's neck. He was rewarded with a brief spray of blood, then the cat fell limply across the legs of the dead marine.

Brooks and Murphy crept back from where they had retreated, staring curiously at the animal, its fur now matted with both its own blood and that of the marine. Bryant, Jessop and the remaining marine looked at one another in some relief, the latter two at first beginning to smile and then laughing nervously.

For his part, Bryant was just angry. "You satisfied now, Jessop?" he demanded. "Is the filling of your belly worth the life of a man?"

Jessop started to shrug but then turned to face the last marine. "Hey, sorry 'bout your mate an' all."

The marine cast a glance at his fallen squad mate. "He knew the risks. Anyway, I won't miss 'im."

Glancing back at Bryant, Jessop had something of a look of triumph. "You see?" he said. "Could 'ave 'appened to any of us. An' now we 'ave what we came for – fresh meat!"

Opening his mouth to argue further, Bryant thought better of it, realising that there was no way to get through to the man. He sighed.

"Have it your way. Let's get this animal strung up to a branch. Jessop, you'll help Brooks carry it back."

Frowning, Jessop looked as if he were about to argue the point but the look in Bryant's eyes made him think that here, alone with Bryant's friends, might not be the safest place to complain. Shrugging dismissively, he began looking for a suitable branch from which the cat could be hung and carried.

Even though four marines and twice as many sailors surrounded him, Corbin still felt distinctly uncomfortable as he watched the dark-skinned natives gather in the clearing. It soon became clear they outnumbered his party by at least four to one and though he might have the advantage of swords and firearms on his side, Corbin did not fancy taking chances with this many armed natives who were, literally, just a spear's throw away.

Whereas the other parties had been sent at oblique angles from the beach into the tree line, Corbin had led his party directly through it and they had chanced upon a trail within minutes. Deciding that it was created by natives rather than animals, Corbin had given orders for them to follow the path. It had not been long before they realised that they were not alone among the thick vegetation as they saw shadows flitting from tree to tree beyond the trail, and, having arrived at the clearing, Hague suggested they wait where they were for the arrival of their hidden escort.

The arrival of the first black face at the edge of the clearing had set all their pulses racing but a slow feeling of dread began to spread throughout the party as more and more dark figures stepped out of the trees. Each brandished a primitive looking spear and was clothed only in a short loincloth with a variety of bones and beads hanging from their necks or woven into their black hair. Corbin was left in no doubt that these people would prove to be utterly lethal if provoked and he could not decide if their expressions were a reflection of mere curiosity or... hunger?

Later on, Corbin would reflect on how well Hague had handled himself during the encounter. Showing no outward sign of fear, the Lieutenant had stepped forward and raised his arms in greeting. He began speaking in a strange tongue that seemed impossibly fast to Corbin.

One by one, the natives overcame any hesitation they had, though they did not relax their grip on their weapons. Three started talking to Hague and the conversation became increasingly animated. After a short time, Hague stopped talking, apparently considering what to say next. After he felt the silence had persisted just a little too long, Corbin slowly stepped up to Hague's side.

"Well, you certainly seem to have mastered the tongue, Mr Hague," he said.

"Ah, yes Sir. Unfortunately, we are talking two different languages," he admitted. "Let me try again."

Turning back to the natives he restarted his negotiations, though Corbin could not help but notice that far fewer words were being used, replaced instead by a lot of gesturing and finger pointing. After a while, it seemed as though some progress had been made, especially when the hand movements pointed to various items the party was carrying and Hague had made motions that indicated eating and drinking. The three natives directly opposite them suddenly seemed to get quite excited and kept gesturing towards the marines that accompanied the sailors. It took Hague a few seconds to work out what it was they were after. Reluctantly, he turned back to Corbin.

"Ah, it seems they want guns."

"Guns? They know what guns are?" Corbin was a little confused. "They know how to use them?"

"These people may have a simpler way of life, Mr Corbin, but they have seen the white man before and are well aware of what guns can do. What do I say?"

Corbin thought for a moment. "Well, what do we get in return?" he asked.

Looking a little apologetic, Hague grimaced slightly. "I

am not entirely sure, Sir. I've tried explaining what we need and where we want the goods brought. I think we'll get what we are after and it will be brought to the beach. Frankly, I would rather start haggling within sight of the ship than in this clearing."

"That is a very fair point," Corbin conceded. He sighed. "Well, we can spare the guns, and if they get us what we need, I can't say that we will make landfall here again. Might even give those damned slavers something to think twice about."

"My thoughts exactly, Sir," said Hague, smiling with some satisfaction.

"Very well. Make the arrangements, Mr Hague, then we can leave this place."

Becoming anxious to leave the clearing, and the natives, far behind, Corbin watched Hague conclude his business with some impatience. A small commotion from the men behind him made Corbin turn around to see what the disturbance was, keen not to have anything alarm the natives now they were closing a deal. He saw a marine, not part of his detail and clearly out of breath, being interrogated by a few of the sailors.

Taking care not to make any sudden movements that could over-excite their hosts, Corbin nodded to the natives and walked back through his own men to see what the commotion was about. One of his sailors, sensing the presence of an officer, turned round and raised a curled finger to his forehead in salute.

"Beggin' your pardon, Sir," he said. "This marine's just come from the brush party. Says they found somethin' you really need to see. Won't say what."

Corbin looked expectantly at the marine who had begun to recover his breath, though not his composure. "Well?" he asked.

"Complements of Mr Kennedy, Sir," said the marine. "He told me to find you and to not mention what he had seen." The man did not seem apologetic at all in his evasiveness and he cast a meaningful glance at the sailors in Corbin's party. The Lieutenant quickly picked up on his meaning but was puzzled.

"Okay, stand easy man." Corbin said. "We'll make sure Lieutenant Hague has finished here and is making his way back to the beach. Then I will join Mr Kennedy."

The stench filled the air around the trail, a powerful, sickly smell that overpowered that of the vegetation or the sweat of the men present. On the rough soil lay five bloody patches, ripped clothing and raw flesh scattered around them, the odd bone poking up to gleam white among the sodden mess. A discarded musket and tattered red uniform identified one of the patches as having once belonged to one of the ship's marines.

Kennedy rubbed his short beard as he took in the scene. "Bad business, this."

"Who else has seen this?" Corbin asked.

"As soon as my men came across it, I told 'em to get back to the beach. I then sent the marine to find you."

Corbin found himself at something of a loss. "What happened here?" he said, finally.

"Never seen anythin' like it, Sir," said Kennedy. "It's like they 'ave just been ripped apart. Some kind of animal, it must be." He shook his head, unable to imagine what kind of beast could do this. "I have 'eard of attacks by creatures in Africa before, Sir, but nothin' like this. Nothin'."

"Can you arrange for them to be buried?" Corbin asked.

Kennedy replied at first with a bitter laugh. "Well, I can cover what's left, Sir. Not much to be done beyond that."

"Okay, Mr Kennedy. Do your best."

A sharp crack marked the arrival of something large passing through the vegetation, causing them all to spin round. His nerves on edge, the single marine cocked his musket and brought it to bear down the trail.

"Whoa," said Murphy, holding up a hand and smiling. "We're friendly!" His eyes then tracked down to the bloody patches and stinking flesh on the trail in front of him, opening wide as he began to realise what they probably were. Corbin noticed four other men behind him, carrying heavy loads. He hurried to stand in front of them but was too late, for they were soon all gawking at their dead shipmates.

"Did we set up a signal fire?" Corbin asked as he flashed a grimace back to Kennedy. He had hoped to keep this scene quiet. Now, it was unavoidable that rumours would sweep through the ship.

"Sorry, Sir," said Murphy. "We was on our way back to the beach when we 'eard voices."

Bryant stepped forward, trying to avoid staring at the blood and gore as he adjusted the weight of his dead party member across his shoulder. "Lost a marine, Lieutenant," he reported to Corbin. "To that," indicating the dead cat now suspended from a pole.

Corbin shook his head. The death toll of this little expedition was beginning to rise beyond all reason. "We'll talk about it later," he said. "Get back to the beach."

Seeming as if he wanted to say something else, Bryant instead took one more look at the raw flesh before them and then instructed the rest of the party to follow him as they left the trail.

After watching them trudge away to disappear into the trees and shrubbery, Kennedy spoke up. "You think this was caused by one of them beasts, Sir?"

Corbin eyed the dead sailors out of the corner of his eye before facing the Bosun. "I don't see how, Mr Kennedy. Seems too small and it did nothing like this to the dead marine that group was carrying. Do what you can here and then make sure everyone gets back to the beach. We should leave as quickly as possible."

"No arguments from me, Sir."

The midday sun beat down hard on the *Whirlwind*, blinding any man foolish enough to look upwards for more than a few seconds. However, the constant breeze coming from the sea was a blessed relief to everyone working above deck or on the side of the hull. Within the bowels of the ship, anyone unlucky enough to be working just cursed and sweated.

Appearing to be everywhere at once, Havelock moved form prow to stern, monitoring all aspects of the repairs, occasionally making a suggestion to the work teams and, once, rolling up his sleeves to help move a large wooden splint to the foremast before it was hauled up into the sky.

Lieutenant Hague had briefly appeared back on board, asking permission to trade firearms with a native tribe he had managed to locate, though he had also been vague about what they were receiving in return. In the end, Havelock had reluctantly agreed to the exchange, though it went against his grain to trade advanced weaponry with primitives. On balance, however, he had much preferred to win his race to repair the *Whirlwind* and locate the *Elita* once more before the French frigate could make good its own damage. This did not stop him from keeping an eye trained on the beach when the natives emerged with their offerings. He did not have much experience in dealing with such people and had heard of many trades turning rotten in the closing moments. He was glad to have Hague on his crew, who seemed to have at least some affinity with the tribe.

Once the beached jolly boats had been filled with supplies from the natives, as well as wood, food and water from the parties that had been dispatched, they were turned around into the sea by their crews and then oars were plunged into the churning waves as they struggled to fight the initial current and head back to the *Whirlwind*. Havelock waited on the quarterdeck for Corbin to climb up the side of the ship and make his report, though he had already seen through the telescope that less men were coming back than had been originally dispatched.

Corbin was only faintly apologetic in his tone but he gave a full and frank account of the landing as he had seen it, which Havelock appreciated. He regretted the loss of life but paid close attention to Corbin's report of the supplies that had been gained.

"We have some fresh water, as I said, Captain," he stated. "But far more milk, from the natives. Seems that is what they usually drink, not sure what it is from though."

"Best not to ask, I imagine," Havelock said.

"Aye, Sir. The natives were also able to supply us with some kind of cloth and wood, though it will need working by the carpenter," Corbin said. "And they gave us all the nuts, roots and fruit we could carry – that should keep the men happy for a few days. Some fresh meat was brought in by our parties, though I doubt it is enough to go round."

"Officers and crew from the landing parties first," said Havelock. "Anything left can be dished out by the Bosun as reward for hard work."

"As you say, Sir."

"You have no idea what caused the deaths on shore?"

"None, Sir," Corbin said. "I don't know what could have done that. One party lost a marine to some kind of wild cat. We buried him on the beach while waiting for the natives."

"Good. I'll mark the other deaths in the log as victims of an animal attack as well."

"Sir, with respect, I am not sure... " Corbin started.

"Yes?"

"Nothing, Sir. How go the repairs?"

"Well enough, though she'll never be truly right until we can pull into a proper dock," Havelock said, a little wistfully. "The foremast is being supported by a tight splint and we daren't risk a topsail on it."

"That will only drop our speed and mobility a little, Sir," said Corbin.

"I would have preferred not to lose anything when in a fight with a ship like the Elita. The odds are close enough as it is. Still, we must play the cards we are dealt. The repairs to the hull and gun ports, at least, have proceeded apace. We have even started on the fittings, fixing the non-essential things. It all goes towards... "

"Sail to starboard!" The lookout cried far above them, breaking Havelock's train of thought.

"Damn!" He muttered and drew up his telescope with lightening reflexes as he stared out to sea, slightly northwards.

"What is it, Sir?" Corbin asked.

"She's back again," said Havelock quietly to himself, before handing the telescope to Corbin and pointing to where he should look.

"This is the third time," Havelock said. "She keeps appearing, in the same place every time. Stays a few minutes and then appears to retreat. Never gets close enough for identification. The best I can do is tell she is a three-master. Can you see anything else?"

Corbin squinted hard but a combination of distance and haze foiled his efforts. "Sorry, Sir, no. Could it be the *Elita*?"

"I don't see how. Repair her masts and sails, then get here so soon? Then again, if it were a British ship, why would she not approach? It's damned peculiar."

"Could it be a companion ship to the *Elita*? Maybe a replacement?" Corbin said.

"That might explain a few things," Havelock said. "I think we have to assume she is indeed hostile, until we know better. I have a bad feeling in my bones about that ship and I am damned if I know why."

"What are your orders, Captain?"

Havelock took the telescope from Corbin and raised it to view the distant sails once again.

"She is already retreating back north," he said. Then, to himself, he muttered. "What is it you want?"

Dropping the telescope, Havelock made a decision. "I don't like this. Prepare to set sail, Mr Corbin, set our course due west until I give the word. The crew can carry on with the repairs as we travel. We'll try to sweep round and approach from behind. If she turns out to be friendly, we'll discover soon enough why they have been playing silly beggars. If she is a French ship, we'll have the windward advantage once again."

"Right you are, Sir," said Corbin as he turned to the main deck to begin relaying orders. "All hands ready! Prepare to weigh anchor!"

They did not see the mysterious ship again after they set sail, though Havelock posted a double watch among the lookouts and constantly scanned the horizon himself through the telescope. He had ordered the *Whirlwind* to sail due west with all speed until late afternoon, then changed course to sail north for nearly three hours before sweeping back east and then south to run past the coast. Hoping that he had plotted the manoeuvre accurately, Havelock moved to the prow of the ship where his telescope was never far from hand. If he had done this properly, they would now be behind the ship, assuming it had not spotted them at some point and simply fled the area. As the sun began to dip ever lower in the west, with shadows lengthening on deck, he began to fear that this was exactly what had happened.

From time to time, he shouted up at the lookouts among the masts, as much to see if they remained awake and alert as hoping a query from him might suddenly cause the ship to materialise in front of them. Still no vessel showed itself and Havelock's hopes began to fall. Corbin made regular reports as the crew continued to work on repairing the *Whirlwind* but Havelock knew the ship was already fit for battle. What remained was of a superficial nature only.

Twilight was descending when one of the lookouts gave the cry Havelock had been waiting for.

"Sail to starboard!"

Grabbing his telescope and quickly extending it, Havelock glanced up at the lookout to see where the man was pointing and then followed suit himself. Focussing the glasses, he soon picked out a three-masted ship, sailing west away from them, into the setting sun. He could not have asked for a better position.

"Mr Corbin!" he called, summoning the Lieutenant from the main deck. "Change course to follow her! And order the men to beat to quarters!"

Corbin complied as Havelock returned to his place on the quarterdeck. Around him, the crew of the *Whirlwind* rushed to their positions, manning sail, rope and gun as they prepared to go into battle once again. Orders relayed, Corbin climbed the stairs to the quarterdeck and announced that all crew were ready for action.

"This is perfect, Mr Corbin," said Havelock excitedly. "You might find yourself in a position like this just once in your career!"

"Sir?"

"We are cloaked by the night sky, Mr Corbin," Havelock said in explanation. "While she is silhouetted against the fading sun. Thus, we can approach unseen while maintaining an eye on her at all times. Her captain will never know we are here until it is too late."

"A credit to your navigation, Captain," said Corbin, not without a hint of reverence as he realised the position of superiority in which Havelock had managed to place them.

"Now we can see just who she is," said Havelock. "Lieutenant, run up the colours but order the crew not to light any lanterns. We must not give our position away. Let them chat among themselves for the next hour as we make our approach but when we get close, I don't want to hear a single sound from this ship."

For two hours, the *Whirlwind* closed the distance with the other ship, gratifying Havelock that his was still the faster vessel, even with a damaged foremast. Night was now completely wrapped around the frigate, causing crew moving across the main deck to take a great deal more care when traversing ropes and fittings. Though the western sky was quickly darkening, it was still pale enough for everyone on deck to see the ship before them, growing steadily larger. The entire crew, having at first been disquieted with the news from shore of a few deaths, now held their breath in excited anticipation. Having had the order to beat to quarters, there were not many who did not automatically presume they chased an enemy. The veterans among them knew the position of advantage they had been placed in and appreciated the seamanship of the Captain, their words of praise serving to steady the nerves of younger sailors who still remembered their first battle with the *Elita*.

Havelock and Corbin were once again at the prow, this time seeking to penetrate the growing darkness in an effort to identify the ship they chased. Corbin had already remarked on its large size.

"Aye," said Havelock. "That is a ship of the line, and no mistake. Third-rater at the very least. Perhaps seventy guns. Maybe more. This does indeed explain a great deal."

"The list of missing merchant ships?"

"Indeed. I always wondered whether the *Elita* was operating alone and now, it seems, we have our answer. This is as much part of our mission as capturing that damned oversized frigate."

"Are we wise to pursue such a ship thus, Captain?"

"We are in no danger at this moment, Mr Corbin," Havelock reminded him. "If she did see us, we are fast enough to sail away before she could make a decent move. That's if she proves hostile. If that is a British ship, we may have found a valuable ally in our mission. If not, it is our duty to do what we can to disable or sink her."

"A daring idea, Sir," Corbin said diplomatically.

"We have complete surprise, and are approaching unseen from the stern. Few of their crew will be alert and we should get several volleys in before any reprisal is possible. We will then make the decision to fight or run, depending on how badly damaged she appears."

"A frigate conquering a ship of the line always makes for a fine tale, Sir!"

Havelock handed his telescope to Corbin. "Now you are thinking like an officer of the King's Navy! Here, see if you can make out any markings. There is a flag flying at the stern but I can't make it out. Can younger eyes do better?"

"I'll try, Sir," said Corbin, holding the telescope aloft and squinting as he tried to focus on the tiny fluttering cloth trailing the ship. He spent over a minute trying to gain a steady glimpse. When he did, he dropped the telescope straight down to his side, clearly excited. "It's French, Sir!"

He looked back at Havelock who now wore a wolfish smile. "Time to make some history, Mr Corbin," said the Captain. "We'll retire to the quarterdeck – but do so down the larboard side of the ship, reminding each man that he must keep deathly quiet for the next few minutes. I'll do the same starboard."

Pacing carefully down the main deck, Havelock stopped every few feet to remind one sailor then another to keep his spirits up but also to keep his mouth shut. Everything depended on silence now, as one errant noise could spark the interest of a lookout on the French warship. While the *Whirlwind* would be difficult to see, its huge white sails made sure that it was not impossible.

With both ships travelling in the same direction, it took nearly twenty minutes for the *Whirlwind* to close range, and still Havelock wanted to get even closer, intending to sail within point blank range of its stern and then heave hard to larboard, sending a volley of cannon fire directly into the rear of the ship, just as he had done with the *Elita*. While his small guns would have a limited effect on the huge ship of war, they would be at their most effective at this point.

During this interminable wait, the crew sweated with apprehension and excitement. They knew the advantage was theirs but, being forced to silence lest they be discovered too soon, each man was locked in his own private thoughts of what might happen in the next few minutes.

Guiding the *Whirlwind* slightly off the French ship's beam in order to avoid his sails cutting the wind from its own masts, Havelock forced himself to relax, not wanting to appear too eager in front of his crew. Quietly, he gave Corbin the order to fly the colours, run out the starboard guns and wait his signal to open fire, imagining the enemy captain to perhaps be sitting down to a fine meal in his cabin, maybe with his officers. They would soon be rudely interrupted as the full weight of metal from the *Whirlwind's* guns came crashing through the huge glass windows.

Yard by yard, the distance between the two vessels shrank, the French ship of the line now beginning to tower somewhat over the British frigate, its three layers of gun decks making the *Whirlwind* seem almost puny by comparison. Yard by yard, Havelock counted down the seconds until he judged the time to be right. He waved to get his Lieutenant's attention.

"Now, Mr Corbin," he said, in barely more than a whisper. "Make the turn, hard to larboard."

CHAPTER SIX

Leaning far over with the force of the turn, the *Whirlwind* pulled hard to larboard, sweeping behind the massive French ship of war. Havelock could not help but marvel at the size of the enemy vessel as he ran to the railings of the quarterdeck to get a better view. Looking to his left the windows of the great cabin buried within its stern were level with his position on the *Whirlwind*, though he was a little disappointed that no lights were flooding out of them. The possibility remained, however, that the captain of this other ship had retired early and was about to be roused from bed by a very painful alarm.

He hissed over his shoulder. "Mr Corbin, open fire!"

The order was quietly relayed back until Lieutenant Hague, on the gun deck, received it. He shouted to ensure the order was not misunderstood by any of the cannon crew. They, in turn, had already been primed to fire when they saw the stern of the enemy lying in full view of their gun port. However, the stern of this ship of the line was so vast that they were still able to fire almost simultaneously, with the forward guns blasting away just a few seconds before those at the rear of the *Whirlwind*.

Thunderous explosions and bright light, temporarily blinding those who had become accustomed to the night sky, tore the darkness apart and the familiar smell of spent powder filled the air. Already, Havelock could hear Hague's order to reload float up from the gun deck and then the *Whirlwind's* speed had carried it past the smoke cloud of its guns and he looked eagerly at the enemy ship to see the results of his surprise attack.

The windows of the great cabin had been shattered by

the assault and large sections of the stern had buckled under the weight of the frigate's metal. Havelock was somewhat irritated that no cries from the wounded could be heard, nor had any fires started. He passed a few course corrections to the helmsman, sailing the *Whirlwind* on a tight line that kept the French ship in line with his guns, then focussed his attention back on the enemy.

Havelock was somewhat nonplussed to see a lot of figures on the deck of the warship and not a little alarmed when he realised that the huge vessel was already changing its course to match his own. His lieutenant noticed this as well and ran up to his side.

"Were they expecting us, Sir? Is this a trap?" Corbin asked.

Mystified, Havelock shrugged. "Makes no sense. To just stand and take the damage we inflicted if you know what the enemy is up to. And yet, Gods, they reacted quickly! Their lookout must have spotted us right at the last moment – you see they are not yet running out their guns?"

The *Whirlwind's* second volley drowned out Corbin's reply, the bright flashes lighting up both ships. When the smoke cleared, both Havelock and Corbin peered through the darkness to gauge the results of the attack. The side of the French vessel was pitted with holes and powder burns, large chunks of the hull planking beginning to splinter and peel away from their mountings.

"A fine shot!" Corbin said.

Havelock was a little less jubilant and instead wore a puzzled frown. "Have you seen their sails?" he asked, disquieted.

"Sir?" Corbin peered into the dark once more and, gradually, began to realise what his Captain had seen. The sails of the French ship were billowing out as if capturing all the wind for miles around and yet they were ragged, with huge holes and tears stretching across their entire span. The mainsail was split in two, straight down the middle and yet, impossibly, both sides were bent forward as if taking the wind. They should have been fluttering like flags, threatening to tear their neighbours apart.

"Damnedest thing I ever saw," said Corbin. "How is that thing sailing?"

"It shouldn't," said Havelock flatly. "That is impossible. Just what the Hell is going on here?" He thought furiously for a few moments. "It doesn't matter right now. Let us throw another volley at them, then extend and come round their prow – we'll send a shot down their length from the other direction, see if they like that!"

Below in the gun deck, they could hear Hague ordering the running out of the cannon as they prepared to fire once more. The *Whirlwind* raced alongside the larger ship, the frigate's speed beginning to tell as its prow started to push past that of its enemy. Havelock watched as, one by one, gun ports started to open on the side of the French vessel and smiled grimly. There was no way they were going to get every port open for a broadside before he fired again and, hopefully, the *Whirlwind* would have moved past many of the enemy guns before they were given the order to shoot.

It was therefore with some surprise that they watched a single cannon on the warship fire, its loud crack and puff of smoke instantly dispersing into the night. Feeling a slight tremor through the quarterdeck, Havelock realised the shot had impacted the *Whirlwind* on its hull, somewhere amidships. About to make a comment regarding poor French discipline, Havelock was amazed to see another cannon fire independently, then another. Soon, the whole side of the warship was clothed in individual smoke clouds as other guns fired, on their own or, at best, in pairs. A continuous staccato blast filled the air, like the low rumbling of thunder. The effect on the crew of the *Whirlwind* was quite unnerving as they endured not a single massive blast but a continuous salvo that lasted for nearly half a minute, until their frigate was able to make headway past the ship of the line. The incoming attack seemed almost light enough to be ignored and then, without warning, a nearby shipmate would lose an arm, leg or even head as a random cannon ball came crashing past.

Pulling ahead, the *Whirlwind's* crew did their best to ignore the losses and continue the business of sailing or reloading their cannon, enjoying a brief respite from the battle as the frigate prepared itself for a new line of attack. On the quarterdeck, Corbin and Havelock exchanged worried looks.

"Who fights like that?" Corbin asked. "It goes against everything we have been taught."

Havelock shook his head, clearly confused. "I don't know who we are fighting here. Pirates, maybe, who have managed to capture a ship of the line and did not bother to remove the French flag? Somehow it does not seem likely."

"Are we to break off the attack?" Corbin said.

"No. We have hurt them more than they have hurt us. We are still in good fighting form and if they are as ill-disciplined as they appear, we have the advantage." He tried hard not to think about the unnatural way the sails of that ship were moving.

"Is it your intention to swing round the prow and attack them from the other side?"

"No, Mr Corbin. To do so would force us to launch an attack on their undamaged side, starting us afresh, as it were. No, we'll cap the T across their prow, fire, and then turn hard about larboard to come down this side again. We'll present our undamaged guns to their damaged hull."

"Very good, Sir. With your permission?" Corbin asked, indicating that he should leave to relay the orders. Havelock nodded him away and looked back at the French ship again, trying to understand what it was he was fighting.

Once the *Whirlwind* had cleared the enemy vessel's prow by sixty yards, Havelock raised his hand to Corbin, who bellowed orders to turn to starboard, bringing the frigate's guns to bear on the warship's prow. Havelock suddenly coughed, nearly retching, as he struggled to find a handkerchief to shield his mouth and nose. Now they had moved downwind of the French ship, he noticed the vile stench that seemed to pour off its deck. It was like nothing he had experienced before, the odour almost overpowering, a mixture of rotting meat, decay, and the pungent aroma of seawater kept in a bucket for too long. He noticed that the other crew on deck were also suffering from its effects, some running to the far railings to heave the contents of their stomachs into the ocean.

"Gods, what is causing that?" Havelock muttered. He knew the French navy did not value hygiene in the same way as British crews but for them to serve on a ship like that stretched the realms of his imagination. The thought of taking the ship of the line as a great prize seemed somehow less appealing and he knew lots would have to be drawn in order to send a skeleton crew over to man it.

Rocking as it fired, the *Whirlwind* launched another salvo at the French ship as they sailed across its path. Several balls bounced off the curved prow, the thick wood serving as effective armour as it deflected the attacks. Others managed to punch through and the elegant figurehead, a painted sea nymph, was shattered in an instant by a single blast.

"Hard to larboard, Mr Corbin," said Havelock. "Bring us about and ready the starboard guns!"

He heard the gun crews pound across their deck as they ran from one side of the ship to the other, urgently loading the starboard guns before opening the gun-ports to run them out. As the Whirlwind continued its long, sweeping turn that would send it sailing past the enemy vessel from the opposite direction, Havelock crossed the quarterdeck to see if the opposing captain, pirate or not, would accept another exchange of fire or whether he would try to follow the *Whirlwind* in its turn. Instead, he was alarmed to see the sails of the French ship billow out as if filled with the wind from a hurricane.

The giant ship of the line surged forward with unbelievable speed, its prow splitting the sea in two as it travelled, creating a huge wake behind it. For vital seconds, Havelock was speechless as his mind turned – surely no ship had any right to move that fast?

Dimly, he began to realise what the enemy captain intended and he shouted for Corbin urgently.

"Prepare to be boarded! All hands on deck! Now, Mr Corbin!" He had to fight to keep his voice even lest he risk frightening the crew.

Below the main deck, the gun crews had been spared much of the strangeness that had perturbed their Captain and, indeed, morale had remained high as they realised they were getting far more shots into the enemy than she was throwing back. Casualties had been light and they had yet to lose a single cannon.

"All hands on deck," shouted Lieutenant Hague, his voice carrying above the sound of men in battle. "Prepare to receive boarders!"

"Here we go," said Murphy, clearly unhappy about the prospect of hand-to-hand fighting.

Brooks looked up worriedly at Bryant who smiled back reassuringly. "Don't worry," he said to both of them, as he drew a cutlass he had stashed next to their gun carriage. "You two stick by me, I'll watch over you."

They raced onto the main deck where they were directed by Corbin to form up behind a line of marines who were already loading their muskets. Beyond the red uniformed soldiers, they could see the French warship closing rapidly, like a leviathan of legend surging from the darkness. Bryant cast an eye about the railings behind him and pulled a heavy wooden peg from its hole, about two feet long.

"Here," he said, handing it to Brooks.

"Belaying pins?" asked Brooks, confused.

"Feel the weight of it," Bryant said. "Almost as good as a sword, trust me."

Murphy chipped in as he drew a small knife from his belt. "If a Frog comes up to you, bash 'im over the 'ead with that. 'E won't get up again, I promise you."

Brooks looked from the belaying pin, to Murphy and then back to Bryant. "I'm not sure I can do this," he said, fear beginning to creep into his voice.

"Course you can lad. If you can fire a cannon while we take fire, you can do this. Both of you, stay behind me at all times. I'll look after you."

All around them, sailors held a variety of weapons, either belaying pins taken from the ship or an assortment of knives, cutlasses and axes they had filched or bought for themselves. The marines, their uniforms and weapons a strong contrast to the sailors behind them, obeyed the orders of their sergeant step-by-step, and now stood ready, muskets braced and ready to open fire on the first Frenchman that dared to climb over the railings of the *Whirlwind*.

"Stand ready, men," called Captain Havelock from the quarterdeck. "Remember, you are fighting Frenchmen and every one of you are worth at least ten of them!"

This served to begin steadying the nerves of sailors who had yet to face a boarding action and the veterans among them smiled viciously at the words. Looking at their faces, Brooks realised that there were many on the ship who actually relished the chance to get to grips with the enemy face-to-face. Oddly, he found that strangely comforting.

"What, in the name of God, is that?" A voice said from somewhere within the gaggle of sailors. A second later, they were all gasping as a powerful stench of rotting decay and seaweed rolled over the deck of the *Whirlwind*. Even the normally well-disciplined marines visibly staggered, their muskets dipping for a brief instant before they responded to the sergeant who bawled at them for dropping their guard.

Bryant looked over his shoulder to see how his shipmates were reacting. Murphy was making caustic comments about not wanting to be the one who was tasked with cleaning the French ship when they captured it. Brooks just looked green as he clasped his hand over his face.

"Brace yourselves!" Corbin cried as the French ship sailed the last few yards. Veering hard to their left, the warship's prow thundered into the side of the *Whirlwind*, forcing everyone on board to take a step back to steady themselves. With a grinding of wood upon wood it slid down the hull of the *Whirlwind*, snapping rails and buckling planking as it went. The side of the French ship rose at least four yards higher than that of the frigate's and everyone on deck looked upwards, steeling themselves for the Captain's order.

As they watched, a dozen lines with heavy metal hooks were thrown over, falling to ensnare themselves among the rigging, masts and hatches, effectively binding the two ships together. Then, a score of faces appeared at the side of the warship and men began to either clamber down the lines or simply drop to the deck of the *Whirlwind*.

The marines opened fire immediately, dropping several boarders to the deck of the frigate. Their sergeant bellowed an order for them to fix bayonets as a huge planked board suddenly became visible high up on the deck of the French ship. Standing vertical for a few seconds, it was then allowed to drop, smashing into the main deck of the *Whirlwind* with a dull thud that was felt by every man on board. More boarders appeared at the top of the plank and they poured down it unsteadily, using it as a ramp to gain access to the frigate.

"At them, men!" shouted Havelock who, they saw, was already advancing, sword in hand, towards two French sailors who had dropped onto the quarterdeck. "Throw them off our ship!"

With a cheer, the sailors on the main deck advanced, eager to smash in the brains of the nearest boarder. Bryant waved Murphy and Brooks forward, brandishing his cutlass.

Together, they pushed past the marines, who were only just completing their orders to fix bayonets. Bryant deliberately steered them away from the ramp, where he knew the fighting would be fiercest. Instead, he positioned his team to defend the ship against any boarders who still chose the risky route of using the lines or jumping onto the deck. One of the early jumpers stirred before them, obviously just winded from his fall. Bryant smiled confidentially at Brooks and Murphy.

"I'll show you how it's done!"

Stepping forward as the man rose Bryant swung downwards with all his strength, burying his cutlass deep into the man's shoulder. His nose wrinkled as he realised the foul stench that covered the deck of the *Whirlwind* seemed to be emanating from the French crew themselves and he was surprised to feel as if the blade had not passed through flesh and bone at all but something a little less substantial. Any puzzlement was soon forgotten as the wounded man rose to his feet, cutlass still lodged in his shoulder. Swinging an arm in a wide arc, the man caught Bryant in the chest with a terrible strength, sending the sailor sprawling into Brooks.

Bryant looked up in horror and disgust at the Frenchman's face. Crooked teeth leered at him from a lipless mouth, and the man's skin was stretched and sallow, greying as it rotted. Just a few wisps of mangy hair graced the top of his skull but their attention was drawn to his eye sockets. One was empty, a dark pit of blackness that nevertheless seemed very aware of their presence. The remaining eye dangled by a single cord, bouncing on his sunken cheek as he moved.

"Gods!" Struggling to his feet, Bryant eyed his cutlass, still stuck in the man's shoulder. Steeling himself he leapt forward a step and grasped the hilt of the weapon. He was rewarded by a sudden spear of pain as the man swept an arm at him, this time using nails that had grown into steel-hard claws. Four lines of blood began to stain the shirt around Bryant's stomach but he ignored the injury and heaved at the sword. Begrudgingly, it gave way and he pulled the cutlass free, slowly becoming aware that no spray of blood followed it.

The man swung at him again but Bryant jumped out of the way and brought the cutlass hard over his head, into the forearm that flailed at him. It was severed cleanly and fell to the deck. The man did not even grunt in pain as he lumbered forward to take another swipe with his other arm. Eyes growing wide with horror, Bryant yelled inarticulately, a mixture of anger and horror at what he was fighting. He thrust the cutlass forward, driving it into the decomposing chest of the man, holding his enemy back at arm's length as his opponent tried to claw at him with the remaining hand.

Knowing that he was about to do something he would likely regret, Murphy edged forward, circling the man who remained pinned on Bryant's cutlass. Raising his knife, he charged the man from behind stabbing down with the blade again and again into his neck and base of the skull. The man seemed to lose strength under this assault and sagged, falling to his knees.

Bryant put his foot on the chest of the man and withdrew his cutlass, then kicked out, sending him sprawling. He followed up and, like a madman, chopped away, cutting into the man's head and chest. After a dozen strokes, he realised Murphy's hand was on his arm, bidding him to stop. Bryant looked down at the cut and rotting carcass that lay before them.

Rooted to the spot, Brooks was petrified. Murphy had some choice words to say: "I told you! Didn't I tell you?" he said, almost triumphantly. "Them French are startin' to use the dead in their armies and now they are 'ere on the sea!"

Down by the ramp, their shipmates had begun to realise the nature of the enemy they faced and the line of *Whirlwind's* sailors began to buckle as men retreated. Their officers called out to hold steady but the sailors ignored them, some running across to the far side of the frigate at full stretch before realising they were trapped on a ship in the middle of the ocean. The fighting dead continued to pour down the ramp in ever increasing numbers, fanning out on the deck of the *Whirlwind* as they sought to engage their living enemy.

"Back, back!" Bryant shouted, hustling Brooks and Murphy back among the crowd of other sailors.

"What do we do?" Murphy kept asking. "What do we do?"

"You fight, sailor!" Lieutenant Wynton roared, as he hacked at an approaching corpse.

"Them's zombies!" Murphy squealed, and his hysteria began to spread to the crew nearest him.

"Fight them or join them!" Wynton cried as he deflected a blow from the plank with his sword and then twisted the blade, sweeping it in an arc to sever the head of the creature, causing it to stumble away and crash to the deck, unmoving.

The wave of walking dead crashed into the living across the deck of the *Whirlwind*, gouging, biting and hacking with claws, teeth and an assortment of unclean weapons. Several British sailors fell under this onslaught, paralysed into inaction by their fear. Their screams served to galvanise the others who began to fight with the desperation of men who realise they have nothing left to lose. All along the line, men fell to the deck, disembowelled by wicked claws or gasping their last breath as a pair of pallid hands choked them to death. Elsewhere, animated corpses were pinned down while their skulls were crushed, thrown over board or simply torn apart by frenzied sailors driven far beyond fear.

Taking his place in the centre of the line, Bryant fought like a demon as he swung and hacked at anything moving that did not have a beating heart. He had quickly learnt that a solid blow to the skull could at least slow a zombie down and a decapitation would stop it moving altogether. Failing that, severing limbs at least made them less effective.

Brooks and Murphy cowered behind him, occasionally lashing out with a weapon when one of the infernal creatures came too close. Murphy guessed his small blade was going to be of limited benefit in this battle and turned to gather a belaying pin in his other hand. Taking care to keep Bryant between himself and any zombie, he batted away any claws or weapons that threatened to hurt his friend while another corpse took his attention. Brooks held his weapon close to his chest, standing rigid as his eyes constantly darted left and right, expecting to see a zombie come stumbling through the line to claim his life at any moment.

Aiming a hard kick into a zombie's knee with his heel, Bryant forced it to the ground, feeling a bone break under his blow. The creature flailed at him with a rusty cleaver but he knocked it to one side and swung his cutlass down hard into the centre of its skull, splitting it apart in a shower of grey putrefying ooze. He glanced at the ship of the line, still locked in an embrace with the *Whirlwind* and saw that another score of zombies were shambling down the ramp. They kept together as a group and stumbled directly towards his part of the line.

"Watch out, here come more!"

Though approaching at no more than a slow trot by human standards, the zombies formed a dense wedge that crashed into the line of sailors, buckling it by their weight alone. Men scattered as the zombies struck out at anything within reach that lived, slashing faces with claws and sinking battered swords into chests, seeming to relish the spurt of warm blood that washed over their cold, dead features.

Bryant fought hard to keep his position but even his efforts had to give way to the inevitability of the zombies' assault. He found himself confronted by a pair of the foul creatures, each armed with old-fashioned short swords, and was immediately forced onto a defensive posture, parrying each blade as it tried to sneak in to gut him. Timing his riposte, he waited until one of the zombies stabbed at him again and then swung wildly, knocking the sword to one side. He stepped up to the same creature and slammed it with the full weight of his body, throwing it off balance even as its companion turned to face him. Ducking under its swing, he drove his cutlass upwards, piercing the centre of its face with the tip of his weapon. It sunk in several inches without much effort, the zombie twitching its limbs several times before going limp.

As he withdrew his cutlass, he was suddenly aware of a heavy weight bearing down upon him, before a splitting pain in his shoulder announced the return of the first zombie, sinking its sword into his flesh. He cried out and rolled away, carrying the creature with him. Twisting his body, Bryant continued his roll until he sat astride the zombie, gagging at being in such close proximity of its foulness. Holding his cutlass across his chest with his off hand on the back of the blade, he drove it down across the zombie's neck, severing its head instantly.

Rubbing the creature's gore and flaking skin off his arms and clothes as he stood up, Bryant began looking anxiously for his friends. He panicked as he realised they were no longer with him.

The rush of the zombie wedge into their line had taken

Murphy completely by surprise and he had retreated ahead of them until his flight was halted by the railings at the side of the Whirlwind. He glanced longingly at the open ocean and, for a brief second, considered leaping into the dark sea, believing it better to drown than be torn apart by these infernal creatures.

Heavy footsteps caused Murphy to spin round, instinctively raising the belaying pin. The reflex saved him as a knife sailed into the wood. He yelped and took a step away until he felt the railings dig into his back. Three zombies advanced, reaching for his throat. Crazed by fear, he struck out wildly, hitting nothing but slipping on something on the deck – whether it was blood or water, he did not have the presence of mind to question. Falling heavily, Murphy covered his head for protection, his vision filled with the sight of three dead men bending down to tear him apart.

An angry cry, unmistakably human, caused him to peer up with a single eye. The head of one of the zombies flew above him and into the sea as an axe bit through its neck. The weapon was reversed in mid-swing to land a blow straight into the chest of the second as Jessop, consumed with fury and covered in blood trickling from a dozen minor wounds, dove into the fight. The third zombie turned from Murphy to grab at the burly man but he head-butted it in return, sending it stumbling backwards as he heaved upwards with his axe. Carrying the impaled zombie with it, Jessop strained as he lifted the creature off its feet, above his head and over the railings. Having cast his enemy into the sea he spun round to catch the last zombie in the side of its skull, dropping it instantly.

Bending down to Murphy, Jessop heaved the small man to his feet and snarled into his face. "On your feet and fight, you li'l Irish maggot!"

Murphy had seen the man angered before but the pure hatred and deadly intent he saw now were beyond anything he had witnessed in a human being. In spite of his fear, he was very glad that Jessop was on his side and he regained his footing, brandishing his weapons to show the man he was back in the fight. Satisfied, Jessop turned back to the fray, twirling his axe as he sought a new enemy to smash apart.

Murphy heard a familiar voice cry out in desperation and he looked around to see a mop of ginger hair near the mainmast. Pushing through the press of sailors and side-stepping a leering zombie, he raced towards his friend as Brooks confronted another of the decomposing boarders.

Backing away and swinging wildly with his belaying pin, Brooks was petrified as he faced the cutlass wielding zombie, constantly giving ground before its attacks. Nearly tripping on a loose rope, Brooks cried out as he sank to one knee and raised his weapon up in reflex. The zombie hacked sideways, slicing into the belaying pin and leaving only a stump in Brooks' hand. Shouting out desperately for help, Brooks managed to regain his balance and started to back away again, only to find himself pinned against the mast. He closed his eyes, raising the remains of his weapon as he waited for death.

Seeing what was about to happen, Murphy let loose an inarticulate war cry as he jumped forward past a stumbling zombie and then crouched, tensing his muscles and dropping his near useless knife. Leaping upwards, he caught hold of a rope that had broken free from somewhere high on the mainmast, and swinging across the few remaining yards, he let the full weight of his momentum carry forward into the blow he made with his belaying pin. Landing the weapon squarely on the back of the zombie's skull, he shattered it completely and, landing lithely on his feet, he stepped over the corpse as it crashed to the wooden deck.

"Brooks, lad!"

Slowly, Brooks opened his eyes "Murphy? Where did you come from?"

Sporting a long, ragged cut on his left cheek Havelock had been fighting for his life since the French ship had crashed into them. Two boarders had jumped from the side of the larger ship, falling straight to the frigate's quarterdeck. Havelock at first thought they had both broken their necks from the drop, but had been horrified to see them rise, their milky eyes staring at him from deep, sunken sockets as they reached for him with wickedly sharp claws. The flash of bloated, rotting flesh had stalled him for only a brief second before he realised, whatever the nature of the enemy, it posed a very real threat to his ship.

Precise strokes of his sword had at first disabled the zombies, depriving them of their arms, then dispatched them as he learned, like so many of his sailors after the initial clash on the main deck, how to fight these unnatural foes. He had backed away as more creatures started dropping onto his deck like sacks of wheat, before stirring from their fall and advancing. Quickly joined by Corbin and a handful of marines, Havelock had led the defence of the quarterdeck against ever-rising odds.

Now coated with sweat under his ripped jacket, his hat lost long ago and sword wreathed in a sickly grey ichor, Havelock fought side by side with his Lieutenant as another pair of zombies advanced towards them. Only the Marine Sergeant now survived on the quarterdeck and he flanked Havelock on his left side, using his sword as skilfully as either of the naval officers.

Working together, their swords flickered out as one and the two zombies dropped to the deck, their heads rolling for several yards before coming to rest. Already, more zombies were clambering over the side of the ship that towered above them, preparing to drop downwards. Havelock spared a glance to the main deck, trying to gauge the ebb and flow of battle. He immediately saw that, while his crew had taken horrific casualties, they had steadied from the fear of confronting the fighting dead for the first time, and now formed a credible line that held firm against the tide of zombies. Away from this scattered skirmishes took place all over the ship. He took a single glance at the number of unmoving rotting corpses lying on the deck and quickly decided that far more zombies lay within the French ship and that his crew would, inevitably, be overwhelmed sooner or later.

"Mr Corbin!" he called, arresting his Lieutenants attention. "We cannot go on like this."

"Captain, what are we facing?" Corbin said breathlessly, a hint of hysteria beginning to rise in the man's voice.

"We haven't got time to ponder that now! We have to get away from here, Corbin, do you hear me?"

Havelock grabbed Corbin by the arm and shook him, forcing the man's attention on him. Corbin seemed to waver for a brief second, then locked eyes with his Captain.

"What are your orders?" he asked, to Havelock's relief.

"Gather as many men you can. Then sever those lines holding us to that ship. Once they are cut, we sail."

He saw Corbin's eyes dart with foreboding to the roiling battle on the main deck. He gave the man's arm another firm shake, forcing Corbin to look at him again.

"Lieutenant, this is very important. If we cannot get away from that ship, we are doomed."

Corbin took a shaky breath. "I understand, Sir. You can count on me."

"Good man. Now, go. The sergeant and I will hold them here. Their swordplay is no match for ours!"

Taking just a second to gather his courage, Corbin ran to the stairs leading to the quarterdeck and ran down them, two at a time. A zombie had started to climb them to flank the Captain's position but Corbin, bracing himself against the banister, kicked out with his boot, pitching the creature overboard. He spotted half a dozen sailors battling a trio of zombies just ahead and he leapt into the combat, slashing with his sword as he aided them in braining or decapitating the decomposing French.

"You men!" He called "With me! We must cut the lines!"

He could sense the sailors' relief as they realised that, at last, they had some real direction. Some of them even grinned as they gathered their weapons and followed their Lieutenant to the other side of the ship where they set about cutting the lines that bound the ships together, while two of their number stood guard with belaying pins, ready to attack any zombie that strayed too close.

After the nearest lines had been cut, the ships began to float apart and the team moved forward, eager to cut the remaining tethers. Corbin looked up and spied another group of zombies setting foot on the ramp, another wave designed to slowly wear down the defenders and whittle them away to eventual defeat. He shouted to gain the attention of the two men standing guard over the line-cutters.

"The board! Pitch it over the side before they come down!" he said, pointing up at the advancing zombies.

The sailors at first seemed dubious about intentionally getting so close to the dead but a further word from Corbin sent them sprinting.

Getting a purchase on the wood, they strained, raising it a few inches from the deck but the weight of more zombies walking on the board threatened to tear their grip loose. Seeing the danger, Corbin ran over and, skidding to a halt, dropped his sword and grabbed the board to add his own strength to their efforts. Straining together they slowly raised the board and, moving to one side, spun it around so it broke free of its mountings on the larger ship. Board and zombie alike fell into the gap between the two ships and were instantly swallowed up by the sea.

Looking towards the prow of the *Whirlwind*, Corbin saw that almost all the lines had been cut. He began shouting orders that would set them underway but the frigate was already shuddering as it began to scrape past the French ship, as if it were aware that to tally longer would mean its own desecration and eventual corruption.

"Set the mainsail," shouted Corbin and his line-cutters began scuttling up the rigging to obey. On the other side of the deck, men still battled with the dead but they had all sensed the *Whirlwind* begin to move and there was an instant change in their demeanour. Morale improved instantly and those still fighting redoubled their efforts while those who had defeated their immediate foes either scrambled up the rigging or grabbed lines to bring the sails into line, or else prowled the decks, quickly dispatching any zombie that leapt from its ship to the frigate's deck.

In less than a minute, the *Whirlwind* had cleared the hull of the French ship and the last zombie had either been cast overboard or cut into inanimate pieces. Corbin ran back up to the quarterdeck to greet his Captain. He found Havelock stooped over the marine sergeant, hands pressed to the man's chest which was stained with a spreading shade of dark crimson. The sergeant's face was deathly pale, matching that of the zombie that had finally claimed his life with a wicked strike to his heart.

Without turning his head to face Corbin, Havelock asked "Are we all set, Mr Corbin?"

"Aye, Sir. We are on our way."

Regarding the sergeant for just a moment longer, Havelock laid the man's head gently on the deck and then stood up. "But for a few more moments and he would have lived through this. He was a good fighter, Mr Corbin."

"That he was, Sir."

Walking slowly to the stern of the *Whirlwind*, Havelock looked into the darkness, watching the French hulk lie still and motionless on the ocean.

"We are not pursued," he remarked.

"I don't understand, Sir. I saw how fast that ship closed with us – it was like lightning! Why do they not chase us?"

Havelock stared at the zombie ship until it finally disappeared into the darkness.

"I don't know. I just don't know."

CHAPTER SEVEN

Throughout the small hours until the breaking of the dawning sun above the eastern sky, the crew of the *Whirlwind* often resembled the walking dead they had fought earlier that night. Going about their duties automatically, many were dull-eyed and uncommunicative. The constant banter among sailors was noticeable by its absence and orders from officers were obeyed without comment or argument. Stunned by their supernatural encounter, each member of the crew tried to assimilate, in his own mind, just what had happened, even as he mourned lost shipmates.

Having been ordered by their Captain to make good repairs and return the frigate to fighting fitness, the crew of the *Whirlwind* found their ship to have suffered only superficial damage. The sporadic firing of the French vessel had failed to do much more than smash the rigging of the mizzenmast and dislodge a couple of guns from their carriages. The damage to the crew themselves was more substantial and morale plummeted as men were ordered to clean the deck. Whereas this usually meant hours of back-breaking labour with the holystone, today it saw sailors prepare the bodies of their shipmates for burial at sea, sealing them in sailing canvas, while throwing the corpses and severed limbs of unmoving zombies over the hull. Even then, they had to strain to remove the countless pools of blood from the wooden deck, each a reminder of just how hard they had had to fight in order to survive.

While most of the *Whirlwind's* crew who had been killed in the attack were easily identified, a few were not. In areas of the deck where the walking dead had swept forward quickly, trapping sailors behind their line, there remained only a few gruesome scraps of bloody flesh and clothing, mere puddles were men had once stood. Corbin noted the similarity of these finds to the remains of the crew that had been killed on the African coast, and he mentioned his theories to the Captain. Evidently, the ship of the dead had known where the *Whirlwind* was for quite some time and was not averse to deploying its crew on land.

It was not until this gruesome task had been completed that Havelock allowed his crew to resume their normal watch patterns, permitting those off-duty to find whatever rest they could below decks. There was a brief period of excitement as a call rang out that another zombie had been found on the gun deck, having apparently clambered up the hull from where it had been tossed into the sea, to enter the ship through an open gun port. It had lurked in the darkness of the lower decks until a sailor had strayed too close to its hiding place. Stumbling out of the darkness, the creature had terrified the man, who ran up into the daylight, screaming. A small party of sailors eventually steeled themselves to descend onto the gun deck, where they had dispatched the zombie. A thorough search of the ship turned up no more enemies but it had rattled the nerves of everyone on board even further.

All across the gun deck, sailors who were not assigned to the current watch set their hammocks swinging from the rafters but few actually crawled into them. Most gathered in small groups, speaking in huddled whispers as they tried to come to terms with what they had seen, keeping an envious eye on those who did sleep.

Bryant, Brooks and Murphy sat quietly at a table hastily placed across the centre of the gun deck, the crew of two other cannon opposite them. Conversation was sporadic, each man preferring to keep his own council as they hunched over under the light of a single swinging lantern above them. It was Murphy who broke the silence.

"So what 'ave the Frogs turned upon us?" he asked.

No one answered for a few seconds, then Bryant sighed. "I don't know, my friend, truly I don't."

"I told you they was usin' the walkin' dead – zombies – as sailors!"

One of the other cannon crew stirred at this. "It don't seem credible."

"Trust your own eyes," Murphy said. "What do you think we was fightin' last night?"

"It was the dead," Brooks piped up softly. "Face's rotting – and they didn't go down when you hit them!"

"Not without a solid blow to the head," said the sailor. "I saw one comin' at one of me mates, both arms 'acked off. Still it came forward, trying to bite 'im. In the end, we stuck an axe in its chest and 'eaved it overboard. Not 'fore it got Buxton though. Poor lad."

"And that smell!" Brooks said. "I lived near the factories of Portsmouth and never smelled anything so bad."

"T'was the smell of death," said Murphy.

"It was the stink of something that had lain at the bottom of the ocean for years," said Bryant. "I don't know, Murphy, your idea of the Frogs using the dead to fight this war – there's something wrong there. That ship, I swear, had been dragged from its resting place on the sea floor. It was like, I don't know, a ghost ship or something."

They paused there, mulling over this new idea but were interrupted by heavy footsteps and a curse as somebody walked into a gun carriage. Jessop headed their way but his feet were unsteady. They quickly realised that, somehow, the man had managed to get his hands on a rather large quantity of rum. Given the circumstances, they could not blame him but still grew alarmed when they realised he was heading in their direction. No doubt his own gun crew had retired or else become tired of his banter and he was searching for more company.

Tripping over his own feet, he staggered across to their table, bracing himself on Bryant's shoulder before collapsing on the deck. He grinned as he looked into their upturned faces.

"We showed them Frogs, eh? Dead or alive, British is best when it comes to the sea!" He raised his mug in salute, showering Bryant with the strong smelling drink. Jessop reached forward to ruffle Murphy's hair, though the action nearly unbalanced him. "I even saw you start to fight towards the end, ya li'l Irish maggot!"

"Ah, yeah," said Murphy. He turned back to his friends. "Jessop 'ere, 'elped me out in the fight."

"Just 'elped you out?" Jessop roared with laughter, the volume seeming entirely inappropriate for the subdued deck. Many of those in the hammocks turned to complain but held their tongues when they saw who was talking. He leaned over, placing his face right next to Bryant's. "I'm tellin' ya! Your little friend 'ere was in a bad way. Three of them dead men – three, I tell ya – had 'im pinned. 'E was all curled up, ready to die."

Murphy grinned nervously. "Can't say anythin' against that. Jessop, 'e just comes out of nowhere, swingin' 'is axe. Took care of all three!"

"An' ya got balls after that," Jessop said to him. "Out the corner of me eye, I saw ya save Brooks! Worthy of a drink, methinks!" Jessop swigged from his mug then handed it to Murphy.

Brooks smiled his thanks but Murphy was consumed

with Jessop's rum until the mug was snatched away. He smacked his lips but Bryant was less impressed.

"You seem in a good mood, Jessop," he said.

"Well, why not?" The burly man asked. "We won!"

"And, presumably, you do not think it strange, the enemy we fought?"

Jessop seemed ready to answer with more bravado but, instead, he seemed to consider Bryant's words. Pushing in between Brooks and Bryant, he sat heavily at the table.

"The other men don't like to talk about it," he said.

"I imagine, like us, they are just grateful to be alive."

"You all think it is some Froggie plot?" Jessop asked.

Murphy nodded but Bryant answered for them all. "I don't think so. Not unless the French have found a way to drag a ship up from the seabed, crew and all."

"It might help if we knew which ship it was," said Brooks.

"No, I thought about that," said Bryant. "The French have dozens of ships of the line, probably hundreds throughout the years – and we don't know how old that ship was. We might have seen her nameplate if we had approached her differently, but it would have been smashed by our first salvo."

"I saw it," said Jessop, with a sly wink. The other sailors around the table looked at him dubiously, prompting him to continue. "True as I'm sittin' 'ere, I saw it. We was the first gun crew to fire – it was untouched before we let rip. I saw the nameplate. Even in the dark, it was as bold as brass."

He seemed to saviour the attention until Bryant nudged him. "Well?"

"It was the *Deja*. Never 'eard of it though."

The sailors all tried to recollect the names of French ships of the line they had run across or head heard tales of but all shook their heads as they drew blanks. Still, as Murphy pointed out, the British and French captured and re-captured each other's ships so often, it was almost impossible to keep an accurate track of names. Jessop, though, had been doing his own thinking.

"Now, 'ang on, Bryant," he said. "You said the Frogs can't raise a ship from the bottom of the sea. An' that makes sense. So 'ow come it was there at all?"

Bryant's look was a little incredulous. "Well, I think that is why they call it a mystery, Jessop. Some kind of ghost ship, you hear stories like this."

"Yeah, but I've been thinkin'," said Jessop. "An' I've never 'eard of a ghost ship firin' at someone. An' I sure as 'ell 'ave not 'eard of a ship bein' boarded by the livin' dead."

Knowing that he would be better off not hearing any more, Bryant nevertheless sighed and asked "So?"

"That Jefferies, thievin' scum that 'e was, talked a lot of nonsense. But I remember 'im talkin' about 'Avelock's Curse. An' it seems to me there is some sense in that."

"It fits with what Jefferies said," Murphy interjected before Bryant could speak. "The men die in droves but nothin' bad 'appens to old 'Avelock. 'E survived just fine. Barely a scratch and, remember, the sergeant of the marines died just a few feet from 'im. Must 'ave taken a blow meant for the Cap'n!"

"Don't you start that," Bryant warned Murphy, before he was interrupted by Jessop.

"Think about it," Jessop said insistently. "We're 'ere, in the middle of the ocean. An' we just 'appen to come across a hulk of a Frog ship, crewed by nothin' but the dead. It leads us on, lurin' the Cap'n far from land and then turns on us." He sat up straight, draining his mug before turning back to look at them all, deadly serious.

"You know what one cursed man can do to a ship..."

"And you can stop that talk too, Jessop," Bryant said, his voice quiet but stern. Again, he was ignored as one of the other sailors chipped in.

"What're sayin', Jessop?" he said. "You talkin' about the Cap'n 'ere, not some green pressed man or midshipman you can just 'eave overboard when no one is lookin.'"

For the first time, Jessop seemed a little uncomfortable, as if the weight of what he was saying was only just becoming apparent to him. He shifted uneasily in his seat and swilled his mug, hoping to find more rum within. "There are ways," was all he said.

"Blow that for a game of soldiers," said the sailor. "I ain't bein' any part of this." He stood up from the table, retreating into the darkness of the gun deck to find his hammock.

"And that's good advice for all of us," said Bryant, standing up himself. He was arrested by Jessop's hand grabbing his arm.

"Think about it," Jessop hissed. "If it comes down to him or us... I say we make a move if that damned ship turns up again."

"What's going on here?" The soft voice of Midshipman Rawlinson surprised them all, his small form stepping into the light of their lantern.

Jessop started but quickly recovered, standing up straight, if a little shakily, and hooking a finger to his forehead. "Nothin' goin' on 'ere, Sir," he said. "We was just talkin'."

Regarding them all, Rawlinson seemed to be considering what to do and Bryant wondered how much the Midshipman had heard. He had no idea how long the young man had been on the gun deck, nor whether he had been paying attention to their conversation.

Finally, Rawlinson seemed to make his mind up. "You should be sleeping. You all have your regular watches ahead of you." He regarded Jessop. "I am not going to ask you about illicit rum or smell your breath, Jessop, given what we have all been through. But I suggest you return to your hammock now."

Relieved, Jessop bowed his head and crooked his finger to his forehead again. "Right you are, Sir."

The Midshipman watched them all rise from the table to find their sleeping places, then turned to leave, mounting the stairs to the gun deck. Next to their gun carriage, Bryant helped Brooks tie up one end of his hammock as the new seaman dealt with the other. Murphy, with typical speed, had already climbed into his own but he rolled over to regard his two friends.

"So, if it ain't a ghost ship, what was it?" he asked.

"I really don't know what you call a hulk like that," said Bryant, beginning to feel weary now that he saw his hammock in front of him.

"A ship of death," Murphy mused.

"A death hulk," said Brooks softly, causing the other two to look at him curiously. The name was to stick.

"Very good, Mr Rawlinson. Inform Mr Kennedy and tell him to keep an eye out," Corbin instructed the Midshipman. The news of talk among the crew verging on the mutinous was not welcome but he could not find it in his heart to blame the men. The pitched battle of the night before, that had seen dead men boarding the *Whirlwind*, had rocked him to his core, and it had taken a great deal of effort to portray the image of a calm, disciplined and unruffled officer of His Majesty's navy. Inside, Corbin wanted nothing more than to return to

England with all speed.

Captain Havelock had spent the night personally overseeing repairs and passing an encouraging word where he could which at least some of the crew had seemed to appreciate. He had then spent several hours in his cabin, plotting their next course of action, but Corbin now spied him on the quarterdeck, enjoying the morning air as it swept over the frigate. Vaulting the stairs Corbin joined his Captain, needing to inform him about the state of the crew's morale but also eager to hear of their next destination.

"Lieutenant," Havelock greeted Corbin as he approached. "Are we fighting fit?"

"Aye, Sir. She's battered and scarred but as ready to join battle as she ever was."

"The *Whirlwind* will see us through," said Havelock, gazing at his ship with not a little fondness. "And then she'll carry us back home."

"Complements of Mr Rawlinson," Corbin said to change the subject. "Many of the crew are uneasy about last night. Some are taking matters a little too far."

"Talk of mutiny?"

"Not outright, I believe. But Mr Rawlinson was present during a conversation below decks that made him feel uneasy. I had him instruct Mr Kennedy to keep a reign on things, without letting it boil over."

"Very good," Havelock said. "We must give the men a little latitude today – a flogging would work against us in the end."

"What are your intentions today, Sir?"

"Why, we have two enemies, Mr Corbin, both of whom we have hurt a great deal, I believe," said Havelock with a grin. "It is my intention to locate one or both, and finish them off!"

"Yes, Sir. I believe I know which one I would rather face," Corbin said.

Havelock winced briefly but quickly recovered. "Last night, the enemy had the advantage of us not knowing what we faced. Now we do and I am confident we can compensate for that."

"Your pardon, Sir, but what do you have in mind? She had a distinct turn of speed about her. We saw that as she came into board us."

"True. But I saw nothing to indicate she was particularly manoeuvrable. So, we use that. Keep to her stern, avoid her prow. It even seems that we have little to fear from her broadsides – their return fire was lacklustre at best. As for the *Elita*, I would be surprised to see her even halfway to fighting readiness. We really gave her a bloody nose."

"That we did," Corbin said, heartened to see his Captain had a firm plan.

"I'll address the crew once they have had some rest. Still I would like to know just who it was we faced last night," Havelock said.

"Ah, yes. More news, courtesy of Mr Rawlinson. He overheard one of the gun crews talking about our first salvo. Apparently they saw the nameplate of the ship before we attacked."

"And?"

"He said it was called the *Deja*. Mean anything to you, Sir?"

Corbin was taken aback when he saw his Captain blink dully at him, cast a look to the main deck, and then back, this time with a more urgent look in his eyes. He leaned forward, talking quietly.

"The *Deja*? Are you sure, man?"

"As reported by Mr Rawlinson, Sir. You have heard of it?"

Havelock's expression was one of utter confusion. "That's impossible," he mumbled, as he pushed past Corbin, not seeming to notice the Lieutenant, walking down the stairs to the main deck before disappearing below and retreating into his cabin. Corbin heard the door shut with a dull thud, leaving him totally perplexed.

Believing that his Captain simply required a little time to digest the news, whatever it might ultimately mean, Corbin patrolled the ship, talking to Kennedy, Rawlinson and Hague, ensuring their duties were being attended to and no other problems were arising. All three reported that the crew, as a whole, were beginning to become surly and while no one had transgressed the Articles of War directly, it could only be a matter of time. As he moved from deck to deck, Corbin became aware of a tension settling on the entire ship. It was nothing he could really put his finger on – just a slight delay in a salute, perhaps, or a sideways look of contempt as a sailor worked on the rigging. He could not help but contrast the attitude of the crew to Havelock's earlier buoyant mood when talking about defeating the two French ships. It was if everyone knew something he did not.

The ship's bell rang twice before Corbin realised that Havelock had still not emerged from his cabin, signifying the Captain had secluded himself, without word, for over an hour. Concerned, he finally steeled himself to approach the great cabin and, once outside the oak door, rapped on the wood.

No answer came and he knocked again with still no response. Hesitantly, beginning to fear for his Captain's health, Corbin pushed the door ajar and peered inside.

Havelock did not acknowledge Corbin as the Lieutenant entered. He was sat at his table, back to the long lead-lined window, turning an old-fashioned sword over and over in his hands as he inspected its blade.

"Sir?" Corbin asked, with some hesitation.

It took a while for Havelock to respond and when he did so, his eyes did not take their intent gaze off the sword.

"What is it, Mr Corbin?" he said quietly.

"Sir, Mr Kennedy and I have some concerns over the crew. Morale, you understand."

Again, it took Havelock some moments to reply and when he did so, it seemed as if he were far away. "Ah, yes, morale. The key to a good ship, Mr Corbin. We must do something about that."

Feeling unsure of himself, Corbin took the liberty of sitting himself down at the table, opposite Havelock. He had never seen the expression on the man's face before. He would have described it as... haunted. He was about to venture another question when Havelock spoke once more.

"My grandfather's sword," he said by way of explanation. "Given to him by the First Sea Lord. Now I keep it in here, a memento to past glories of the old man."

"He was a true hero, Sir," Corbin said carefully.

"Oh, yes. The scourge of the French. Certainly helped my career along, I can tell you. There was no doubt about my finding a ship, even if peace should suddenly break out. Ever since I was a midshipman, having the name Havelock was always useful."

"Sir? Is there something awry?"

With care and a little reverence, Havelock set the sword down on the table. Finally, he met Corbin's gaze and his eyes seemed to clear slightly.

"What do you know of my grandfather's great victory? The one that earned him his admiralty?"

"Very little," Corbin admitted. "But I have heard plenty

of stories. How he engaged a fleet of two ships of the line and two frigates off the coast of Africa, sinking one after the other, constantly keeping them off balance. I have also heard people say it actually took place at Guadeloupe and that the port there was sacked as a result."

"People like to gossip. They rarely get it right," Havelock said.

"That is true, Sir," Corbin said. After a brief hesitation, he then asked "Would you care to tell me what really happened?"

Havelock took a deep breath. "This is not something I have ever done, Mr Corbin. As is the way of things, a glory in a family's past rarely holds up to close inspection. However, I believe you have been pulled into something terrible and, as such, you certainly deserve to know the truth. Though I would be much appreciative if this were kept between ourselves, assuming we make it back to port."

"You can rely on my discretion, Captain."

"Only a few in my family and certain members of the Admiralty and Imperial Administration know what I am about to tell you. They would not be pleased to learn that you also know the truth. I accept your word of silence as an officer of the King's Navy, Mr Corbin, but I want you to understand the repercussions possible if you should break that word, for any reason. It would mean the end of your career."

"I understand."

Placing a hand on the hilt of his grandfather's sword, Havelock began to speak. "You were right about my grandfather's victory taking place off the coast of Africa – not far from our current position, if I am not mistaken. Nowhere near the Caribbean. I have no idea how that rumour started. Anyway, my grandfather had not been sent down to this wretched part of the world as we have, with orders to hunt down a commerce raider. No, he *was* the commerce raider. Specifically, he had been tasked with destroying a French convoy en route to the east."

"So there was no great battle?"

"Oh, a battle there was," said Havelock candidly. "You see, that convoy was filled to the brim with colonists. Just men and women searching for a new life overseas, no great silver train or other valuable cargo. However, not even the French are callous enough to risk sending so many people so far without some form of protection. Present with the convoy was a ship of the line, a real bruiser of a vessel, I have been told."

"Just the one?"

Havelock smirked. "Sorry, Mr Corbin, yes, there was just one ship of the line. No other warships were in that convoy. Still, it must be said, the defeat of any ship of the line by a single frigate is an action worthy of recognition and could well aid a promising captain on his way to becoming an admiral."

"Indeed."

"However, the actual details of the battle were kept secret, hence the rumours that grew."

Corbin looked puzzled. "But why? If it was a great victory, why not publicise it?"

"Because hunting down ships packed with colonists is something the British people like to think the French do, not His Majesty's Navy. And also because of the manner by which the ship of the line was sunk. You see, my grandfather's frigate could keep the single warship off balance alright, he had the wind and benefit of speed. So, he could pick off the colonists' ships as he pleased while the larger vessel lumbered after him. Towards the end of the engagement, the French ship deliberately placed itself between my grandfather and the rest of the convoy, leeward and at a terrible disadvantage. This move enabled the remaining colonists to escape but the warship paid for it heavily. Unable to defend itself properly, my grandfather was able to sink it with relative ease – though I understand it did take a bit of time." Havelock mused for a second and then added: "That French captain was the true hero that day but no-one ever got to hear about his selfless courage."

"Ah." It was an unworthy response to the tale, Corbin knew but he had been left confused and not a little deflated at this admission. They sat in silence until a thought crossed Corbin's mind. "Sir, what business has the Admiralty in ordering the destruction of colonists anyway?"

"Happens more often than you may think," said Havelock. "After all, a newly discovered land is just a rock in the middle of the sea until you put people on it. With people come towns, forts, garrisons and trade. On the other hand, hunt colonists and you not only keep land bereft of civilisation. You also delay the spread of French imperial interests. And you can understand how that very much concerns the Admiralty, not to mention Parliament and the Royal Court."

"I can, Sir, yes," said Corbin. With Britain's trade and Empire dependant on her ships being able to range freely on the ocean, the spread of a rival power across the globe could only mean a curtailing of their domination – and profits. While pondering this, Corbin suddenly realised that the Captain had deliberately left something out. This was confirmed when he looked up at Havelock and saw the man's eyebrows lift in question.

"I appreciate the confidence you place by telling me all of this, Sir," Corbin said. "But why are you telling me now?"

"The name of the French ship of the line sunk by my grandfather was the *Deja*," said Havelock simply.

"No!" Corbin exclaimed, amazed by the coincidence. He then slowly began to realise that Havelock did not think it a coincidence at all.

"You know, it's funny," said Havelock, almost conversationally. "I have been aware of sailors under my command talking about the Havelock Curse for some years now. But I never gave it an ounce of credence until today, when I discovered the name of that bedevilled ship."

"You believe that the *Deja* your grandfather sunk and the ship last night are one and the same? That is... impossible!"

"I believe it shows a wonderful symmetry. A man commits callous murder in the past and is never made to pay for his crime. The victims, searching for recompense, finally receive the chance to make his descendants answer for those actions."

"This is madness!" Corbin said.

"Really? You saw the nature of the enemy we fought last night. How else do you explain it? Think of it – how many years might they have roamed the ocean, not able to rest until they found my grandfather, not even knowing he was dead? Discovering no resolution, they eventually happen upon his grandson. If you were they, what might you do?"

Corbin shook his head, not wanting to follow where his Captain was taking him. "So you think, what, they disappear into a watery grave every day and rise as the walking dead at night, ship and all?"

"I know not how this works, Mr Corbin," said Havelock flatly. "I am no expert in such matters. Perhaps they never return to the sea floor. Perhaps they have only just risen, sensing my presence. All I know is that I have been called to account for the sins of my grandfather."

"So... what do you intend to do?"

Havelock paused, thinking. "A mark must be set for justice," he said finally.

"Sir?" a confused Corbin asked.

"Come, Lieutenant," said Havelock, standing up from the table and straightening his jacket. "The crew must not be allowed to mutiny. Call all hands to deck. It is time I addressed them."

Looking into the eyes of the sailors who stood on deck, hung from the rigging and slouched against railings, Havelock could see a variety of emotions, all of them negative. Bitterness towards him for losing so many crew last night, resentment at being so far from home, fear from facing a nearly unstoppable enemy. There was anger, too, aimed at both himself and the walking dead. That was good. Wherever it was directed, he could use anger, shaping and moulding the crew's fury into a credible weapon.

As a whole, the crew had been notably lax in responding to the order to assemble on deck and now they stood, sullen, a low grumbling forming an undercurrent to the sound of the *Whirlwind's* prow cutting through the waves. Havelock had faced sailors disgruntled with their lot many times in the past but this was the closest he had been to a complete breakdown of discipline and he realised that a single rousing speech would not solve the problem. He had to give the crew something tangible and it had to come soon.

"Men of the *Whirlwind*," he said. Thankfully, enough

respect seemed to remain among the crew that the sound of their Captain's voice was still enough to silence them. "We have fought a bitter and dreadful enemy, the likes of which have never been faced by a crew of His Majesty's ships. But we survived! We took their full measure and have lived to tell a tale that will mark our place in history!"

Casting a quick glance around, Havelock noticed that his words had an effect on his officers, but that he was failing to reach many of the crew. He decided to change tack and pursue another course. "But we still have a duty to perform," he continued. "We have discovered the reason our merchantmen have been suffering so badly off the African coast and it is up to us to bring victory to King and Empire. The French have debased themselves by allying with an unholy force, one capable of raising a ship long since sunk. But think of this; that ship has been sunk once and it will be sunk again! We withstood a boarding action from a ship of the line, against an enemy already dead and we beat them! Why? Because we are a British ship of war, and we have no equal on the ocean!"

No cheers greeted him this time but Havelock could see a few wry smiles begin to spread throughout the crew. Whatever their background, there were few sailors in the navy who did not believe in the inherent superiority of the British at sea and a call to duty never went amiss. Now to complete the turning of the tide. The only thing stronger than a sailor's patriotism was his avarice.

"We all have our orders. The frigate *Elita* is still at large in these waters, and a fine prize she will make for all of us! I assure you, she is still hurting after our first encounter and the next match will see us pounding her into submission before swinging over the railings and defeating her French crew. We then sail for home – to riches, fame and glory! My friends, you will all be heroes and many a tavern will fall silent as you recall your time on the *Whirlwind* as you faced the very worst the enemy could muster and yet remained victorious!"

Still no outright cheers but smiles had turned to a few chuckles as the crew began to consider what life would be like back in England with the notoriety a mission like this brought, as well as the lifestyle that could be had for a frigate's prize money. Havelock smiled broadly at his crew, encouraging those who were beginning to leave their fear behind.

"And if that ship of the dead comes for us again," he said, catching their attention. "Well, we will simply send it back to the hell from which it came!"

The crew, he thought, were more resigned to their mission than elated by the possibilities but that suited him. Anything to stave off a potential mutiny served his purposes for now. He was about to instruct Corbin to dismiss the crew when a single voice rang out across the main deck.

"And when will your curse be visited on the rest of us, eh, Cap'n?" The challenge came from a sailor leaning with his back against the mainmast. It was not so much the man's words that angered Havelock as his lazy and uncaring demeanour.

"Mr Kennedy," Havelock roared. "Discipline that man!"

Pushing his way through the crew, the Bosun confronted the sailor, who just smirked at him. Kennedy reached forward and grabbed the man roughly by the shoulder, propelling him forward in front of the Captain.

"A dozen lashes, Mr Kennedy," Havelock said.

Corbin, at his side, leaned forward and whispered

quietly, so no one else would hear. "Sir, do you not wish to read the charges and remind the crew of the Articles of War?"

"No need for that, Mr Corbin," Havelock said. "He knows what he has done wrong." He then raised his voice so the whole deck could hear his words. "Proceed, Mr Kennedy."

The crew kept their eyes fixed solidly on the deck as the Bosun's rope rose and fell against the condemned sailor's back, a loud crack ringing out a dozen times. His punishment complete, the man was led below decks, though he appeared strong enough to still walk by himself. Waiting until Corbin gave the order to be dismissed, the crew slowly dispersed, refusing to jump to their posts with any speed. To a man, they all steadfastly refused to look up at any of the officers.

"Damn that man," Havelock hissed to Corbin. "I very nearly had them until he brought on that flogging. Now we have to produce some results and quickly."

"Might it have been wise to spare the flogging, Sir? You said earlier... " Corbin asked.

"Absolutely not!" Havelock turned to face his Lieutenant, a look of shock on his face. "It matters little where we find ourselves. Complete discipline must be maintained at all times, utterly. I cannot have anyone challenging my authority, openly or otherwise. Inform Mr Kennedy; any talk that can be considered mutinous is to be dealt with in the severest manner."

Corbin appeared to hesitate for a brief second but then left the quarterdeck to find the Bosun. Havelock remained behind to consider his next course of action and wonder what fate would next bring for his ship.

CHAPTER EIGHT

Having set course southwards to take advantage of the prevailing wind, Havelock observed the activities of his crew as they scurried about the main deck. Under their Captain's eye, none seemed willing to speak out but he could only guess what they might be saying below decks, and he chafed at having to rely on his Bosun and junior officers to maintain discipline. They were good men, he knew, but the situation was balanced too finely on the knife edge for him to relax his grip. Crews had mutinied for far less than his crew had faced. If the *Whirlwind* finally returned home, fully intact and with victory, it would be a miracle of some proportion.

The frigate, for all the trials it had been matched to, was performing admirably – he had that at least. Slicing through the waves, the ship seemed to almost enjoy a sense of freedom as it was carried by the wind at speed. Havelock wished he could permit himself to enjoy this moment for this was when the *Whirlwind* felt truly alive but his mind constantly churned over the possibilities of his next encounter at sea.

That he now faced two potential enemies did nothing to raise his spirits and he was caught between suppositions. On the one hand, if he was right about the *Deja*, he was fighting an enemy that had a much more powerful vessel, could not be truly destroyed and was determined to find and sink his own ship. Then again, what if it was part of some French plot and the name of the ship was a mere coincidence? What ramifications might that have on the war at large and the Empire in general? For his part, both the *Deja* and the *Elita* now knew of his presence in these waters and if they were allied, might they not seek to join battle with the *Whirlwind* simultaneously? That was a battle Havelock was certain he could not win.

He had spoken with some bravado to Corbin earlier when they had discussed how to fight the *Deja*. Certainly, he believed he could navigate the *Whirlwind* to stay out of the warship's arc of fire and away from its prow, thus stalling any further attempts at boarding, especially if he had the wind's favour. That alone could not win a battle though and he had to find some way of sinking the ship – but how to sink a ship that had already been raised from the bottom of the ocean at least once?

Though they scoured the ocean for prey now, Havelock had little doubt that he need not search for the *Deja*, as he firmly believed the ship would find him. It should have been his grandfather in this place and this time, of course, but he had benefited from the actions of the past as much as grandfather had, perhaps more so, given his command history. While other captains languished in port on half pay, Havelock had never lacked for a frigate. He could not help but feel that a final confrontation between the death hulk and himself would somehow complete a chapter of history, allowing someone, somewhere to turn the page.

He was far more comfortable fighting the *Elita*. Though it was, in theory at least, a superior ship, he would stand by the shooting and seamanship of his own crew on any day. If the *Whirlwind* could be coaxed into soaking up a broadside or two from the French ship, he believed he could pound her crew into surrender in return. That victory would be all he needed to bring his crew back into line, as defeating a so-called super frigate would raise morale to the sky and get his men believing they could fight anything afloat, and win.

When it came down to final considerations, the nature

of the enemy they faced mattered less than the opinions of a newly press-ganged sailor. He was the captain of a British ship of war and the French could be damned, dead or alive!

Rubbing his chin as he contemplated these matters, Havelock drew his hand across stubble and cursed himself for having been so inattentive. While he might have excused one of his sailors for poor hygiene after the last battle, it could never be accepted from an officer, much less the Captain. At the same time, he was somewhat grateful to have a more earthly concern to deal with. He began to make his way to his cabin when a cry from the lookout arrested his attention.

"Wreckage, to larboard!"

He looked up to see where the lookout pointed and drew his telescope to match the direction indicated, just slightly off line from the ship's course. It took him nearly a minute to spot the debris, just a few shattered pieces of wood thrown about by the gentle waves, and he turned to the helmsman behind to give instructions that would bring the *Whirlwind* closer.

"Two points to larboard, if you please."

As the ship approached the scattered wreckage, sailors began to line the railings, eager to get a glimpse. When on a long voyage, sailors quickly learned to give any new development their full attention. Elevated on the quarterdeck, Havelock had a better view than most and he quickly ascertained that the wreckage was strewn over a wide area, though it represented only a few hull planks and hatches. Presumably the rest of the stricken ship was already at the bottom of the ocean, though he had already caught sight of several bodies floating in the sea. A commotion from the main deck caused him to turn and he saw Corbin order the Bosun to fish something out of the water.

Kennedy hoisted a long hooked pole over the side of the ship and lowered it downwards into the water, his skill and strong arms belying the unwieldy nature of the tool. With a deft motion, the man snared something and quickly drew the pole upwards, hand over hand. Reaching over the railings, he grabbed the coloured cloth snagged on the hook and wrung it dry before passing it to Corbin. Before the Lieutenant had started unfurling the ragged flag as he walked to the quarterdeck, Havelock had already identified the red, white and blue colours as belonging to a Union Jack.

"One of ours, Sir," said Corbin as he mounted the steps up to Havelock.

"It is good news of a form, Mr Corbin," Havelock said. "The work of the *Elita*, no doubt. It means we are on the right course."

"Not the... other French ship?"

"No," Havelock said flatly. "That ship is only interested in one target on these seas. It would not stop for anyone else."

"So who do you think this belonged to?"

"Some poor merchant or trader, probably. I know of no other British warships in the area."

Corbin looked thoughtfully at the flag. "Does this mean the *Elita* is now fully repaired?"

"It need not be completely seaworthy to engage a merchant but, in truth, that is something I have been giving some thought to."

"Sir?"

"We are relatively far from the coast now, especially for a ship that was dismasted in its last engagement," said Havelock. "To make it to some safe harbour after our battle, make repairs, then sail here and sink a merchant vessel in this time? Doesn't seem credible to me."

"You have consulted the charts for possible island harbours?"

"I have but nothing is obvious. However, the charts do not list every small lump of rock in the oceans. We must be cautious about presuming the plans and capabilities of our enemy until we have more information. I am guessing the *Elita* is still hurting from our last encounter but I have no wish to sail into a trap and be sunk."

Brooks sighed gratefully as he dropped his wooden burden to the deck and held his back as he stood up straight. He had at first welcomed news that Bryant's crew had been tasked with aiding the ship's carpenter in making repairs to the decking on the forecastle. Working at the prow, Brooks had expected to benefit from a constant soothing breeze unsullied by the odours of shipboard life but he had not foreseen the backbreaking labour as the carpenter constantly called for new materials and tools.

He nudged Murphy as he cast a look back down the length of the ship, watching the Captain and First Lieutenant examine the flag that had been hoisted from the wreckage.

"What do you think they are talkin' about?"

Murphy followed his glance and sniffed. "Officer talk. Probably discussin' tactics and the like."

"Which ship do you think they are plannin' to fight?"

"If they 'ave any sense, the Frog frigate."

Bryant joined them, straining to drop his own load of wooden planks as lightly as he could on the deck. "If I know the Captain," he said, "he'll be planning to face the *Elita* but preparing to fight the death ship."

"Death hulk," corrected Brooks.

"Hmm? Ah, yes. Of course."

"So, what are you two plannin' to do if we face them zombies again?" Murphy said, immediately causing his two friends to furrow their brows. Neither wanted to reflect on the events of the last battle but the question served to concentrate their minds.

"The Captain won't let us be caught off guard again," said Bryant. "He's too canny for that."

"Yeah, but we 'ad the advantage last time – can't get a better set-up than we 'ad."

"True, but we didn't know what we faced then. You mark my words, the Captain won't make the same mistake again."

"And if it is the Frogs – the living Frogs – we end up fighting, we'll win, right?" said Brooks with a confident smile.

"It will still be a hard battle, make no bones about that," said Bryant. "She'll pound us with cannon and you best keep your head down, lad. And then, even if we win the duel, the French may not surrender immediately. That will mean we have to board the ship, and there are far more of them than there are of us."

"Ah, Bryant, still grumblin', eh?" Jessop's familiar growl caused more than one of Bryant's crew to roll their eyes.

"I thought you were managing the supplies today Jessop," said Bryant, immediately feeling a little weary.

Jessop shrugged. "The ship still ain't quite right, know what I mean? Not everyone is being watched all the time, an' the officers don't want to make a fuss where it ain't needed. 'Sides, I wanted to talk with you."

Making a show of stacking the planking he had brought to the forecastle, Bryant raised his eyebrows in question, and Jessop stooped quickly to help, lest an over curious officer wonder just what task could be found for four sailors who stood about chatting near the prow.

"Me an' some of the lads 'ave been talkin'," he said and Bryant inwardly groaned, guessing what was coming next. "That last floggin' was unfair. The Cap'n has sailed us into God knows what, and 'e is lookin' for someone to blame. That means us."

"Jessop, I told you before, I'm not interested in any of this."

"Ah, you say that now. You goin' to be playin' the same tune when more dead Frogs come swinging over the side? You goin' to be sayin' that when Brooks 'ere gets 'is throat slit by a walkin' corpse?"

"It won't come to that. The Captain's too good. He has too many years at sea to be put on the back foot for long."

"Maybe you're right," said Jessop, throwing his hands up in mock surrender. "Maybe e'll win all 'is battles, then sail us straight for 'ome, with a couple of nice prizes. 'E does that, an' I'll be the first to admit I was wrong."

That admission drew sceptical glances from Bryant, Brooks and Murphy.

"Then again, maybe it doesn't go the way the Cap'n expects. Maybe the curse catches up with 'im. Maybe 'e isn't thinkin' too straight right now. What then?"

Bryant exhaled heavily. "I can't see it," he said. "Look, we faced the worst possible enemy under the worst possible circumstances. And we are all still here."

"Plenty o' the crew ain't," said Jessop flatly.

"Well, I don't want to seem callous, but men die at sea. The ship is still here though, as are you and I. The Captain saw us through."

"Some might say the Cap'n led us into that battle without thinkin' things through, and the rest of us paid for it."

Beginning to lose patience, Bryant turned to face Jessop squarely. "Look, you've spoken to me about this before and I made my position clear. What is it you are after? This talk is dangerous and I have no intention of being flogged or hung for your loose mouth."

"Well, we 'ave to be careful, sure, if there is a free floggin' for every jack on this ship," Jessop said candidly. "An' if we have to face that Frog frigate an' fight, you won't see me complainin'. It seems to me that a frigate is somethin' worth fightin' for. Plenty o' prize money to go round there."

"Your patriotism overwhelms me," said Bryant. "It has, presumably, occurred to you that your share has gone up now there are less crew to claim it."

Bryant was sickened to see Jessop give half a smile as he rolled this thought around for a few seconds. "That's besides the point," he said. "What concerns me and some of the other lads is that ship 'o the dead. We can't be facin' that again. We got lucky last time. Won't 'appen twice."

"I know where you are going, Jessop, but you won't drag me into it."

"I ain't askin' for nothin'," said Jessop. "All I'm sayin' is that you should keep your eyes open, that's all. If that ship appears again, me an' some of the lads are goin' to make a move."

Holding up a hand to halt Jessop, Bryant looked squarely across to the other members of his crew. "Murphy, Brooks, get below for the rest of the supplies."

"Oh, come on, Bryant," said Murphy. "We're just listenin'... "

"Now, Murphy – before one of the officers sees you lazing around." It was Bryant's tone, as much as his words, that caused Murphy and Brooks to reluctantly walk away from the forecastle and disappear below deck. He turned back to Jessop.

"I swear, if any of my men get caught up in what you are planning... "

"Consider them out of it," said Jessop. "I'm just sayin', if that ship appears again, somethin' is goin' to 'appen. We'll be goin' for the Cap'n and Lieutenants first, the Bosun too. An' anyone else who disagrees. But it would 'elp if you were with us. You'll bring a lot of the lads round to our way of thinkin'."

Bryant knew that Jessop was right, at least in part. He had no illusions about his overall popularity on the *Whirlwind*, indeed, he would be surprised if many sailors on board knew him as anything other than the leader of his gun crew. However, he also knew that it might take only a few voices acting in concert to win an entire ship over to the idea of mutiny.

"You haven't thought this through. Have you even begun to plan what happens after that?" He inwardly cursed as he saw Jessop's triumphant smile. Of course the man had a plan, however half-baked. He was far too opportunistic for anything else.

"We will 'ave a fightin' ship an' the entire ocean to hide in. We'll roam the coast and grow rich on merchant pickin's. We'll even just grab Froggie ships if you like," Jessop said. "Look, I ain't askin' for your support and if there's ever a trial, you can rightly say you were against the idea. But if that death ship comes at us again, somethin' will 'appen – that's all I'm sayin'. What you decide to do then is up to you."

"Don't you get it?" Bryant said. "I don't want to know this. I don't want to know what you are planning and I don't want to know when you are planning to do it. The Captain still has my support. As far as I see it, he has

done nothing wrong and will see us through the next
battle, and the one after that, and even the one after that,
whoever it may be against. We got a tough fight ahead
of us, Jessop, I agree on that. But we'll get through it. For
the love of God and all that's holy, don't throw your life
away by going against the Captain. It ain't worth it."

Jessop smiled. "Well, I don't plan on throwin' my life
away, you got that right. Anyway, I told you what's goin'
to 'appen. What you do then is up to you." He stood
and walked away, passing Brooks and Murphy who had
returned with more supplies from the carpenter's list.

"So, what did 'e say?" Murphy asked, ever eager for
shipboard gossip.

"Never you mind," Bryant said. "What ever that man
says is not worth listening to, remember that – both of
you."

Murphy seemed a bit subdued at Bryant's hard words
but his ears soon pricked up at a cry from the lookout
high above on the mainmast.

"Sail to starboard!"

All three strained their eyes to the horizon but they saw
nothing through the far haze.

"Now what?" Bryant said quietly.

Once again, Havelock trained his telescope on the
horizon, aware that Corbin stood at his shoulder, anxious
to hear what ship was in their vicinity. Though it took
him a moment to focus properly, a familiar shape soon
coalesced through the lens and he smiled.

"It is our old friend, the *Elita*!"

"Can you spy her condition, Captain," Corbin asked.

"I see three masts, all with sail," said Havelock after
a moment's pause. "However, that may mean little. Her
condition will become apparent in the next few minutes.

She is currently heading towards us and her captain will now be aware of our presence. Thus... ah, there you see. She has turned! She runs!" Havelock lowered his telescope and slid it into his belt. "Mr Corbin, we pursue! Change course to match her and raise the stuns'ls. Our girl will give us all the speed she can!"

Corbin grinned. "Aye, Sir! Raise the stuns'ls and pursue!"

Sailors across the deck leapt to the Lieutenant's commands and soon the *Whirlwind* was sailing with its full deployment, a mass of canvas that captured every breath of wind, causing the frigate to skit across the sea as though it were glass. Already, Havelock could sense the change in the crew's demeanour. It happened every time a ship was about to go into battle but it was all the more poignant now, after his men had faced the supernatural. Here was an enemy that was flesh and blood. One they had defeated before and were confident of doing so again. Nothing could rally morale better than the chance of a captured prize and Havelock intended to pursue the *Elita* until she could be engaged and forced to surrender.

For all the pace the *Whirlwind* could muster, the *Elita* was still some distance away and, it turned out, had a good turn of speed herself. The English ship was clearly the faster of the two but it was also evident that the French crew had managed to make good repair. Havelock began to fear they might not make much progress in the chase before night fell which would allow the *Elita* to escape without battle. However, he was also heartened by the French captain's decision to run rather than fight, for it suggested that his ship was still hurting from their last encounter. Perhaps they had sustained greater casualties than Havelock had supposed or they had many guns out of action.

Members of the *Whirlwind's* crew occasionally whooped and cheered, clearly enjoying the speed. It was quite rare for a frigate's true speed to be unleashed in this manner and even Havelock openly smiled as he felt the motion of the ship under his feet, rising with each wave and dropping slightly after their crest.

He could not shake a growing mood of foreboding though and, every now and again, cast a look over his shoulder at the *Whirlwind's* long wake. The *Elita* could be feigning weakness, of course and if it truly were in league with the *Deja*, then a trap was possible. He kept expecting to see the massive dark form of the death hulk streaming over the sea behind them, but the ocean remained clear.

They remained on a course of south-south-east, as the *Elita* continued to run in an arrow straight line, and Havelock began to wonder if she were not heading somewhere specific. Though her sails were now clearly visible to the naked eye, there was still more than a mile between the two ships and the yards ticked away with agonising slowness. The sun was plummeting fast to the western horizon and Havelock's fears of his prey escaping began to resurface. If night fell while they were still out of range, the *Elita* could easily change course and retreat without his lookouts noticing. However, the lookouts were to surprise him with their next cry.

"Land! Dead ahead!"

"Mr Corbin, with me," Havelock called as he quickly marched to the prow of the *Whirlwind* to get a view unobstructed by acres of sail. The Lieutenant joined him and together they peered forward, soon seeing the small but growing land mass, standing proud but alone in the vast ocean.

"That is where she is heading, Sir," said Corbin.

"Aye, Mr Corbin, I believe we have found her harbour. This is where she made repairs – no doubt they have created their own little piece of France on that island. Not on the charts, of course."

"We won't lose her now!"

"Caution, Lieutenant," said Havelock. "We have little more than three hours before the sun sets. Plenty of time for her to swing round the island and strike out on a new course without us seeing. Still, I think you are right. I would wager she plans to anchor there in some cove that will make an approach difficult, if not impossible."

"Orders, Sir?"

"Continue the pursuit for now, Mr Corbin. Let us see what she is up to first."

The sight of land and, with it, the prospect of landfall, further galvanised the crew as they began to dream of fresh water, fruits and, probably, meat. The island was small, perhaps no more than three miles across, and it looked like paradise. Beaches of white sand gave way to thick jungle which stretched up to a line of tall grey cliffs in its centre. It looked like a land of verdant promise, rich enough to support the sailors of a warship indefinitely.

Sailing past the island, the *Elita* changed course to swing behind the landmass, quickly disappearing from view. The *Whirlwind* now appeared to be very much alone on the ocean but every man on board still tensed for battle.

Now, let us see what play you make, thought Havelock. He ordered Corbin to maintain their course, but to keep a greater distance from the island than the French ship. It seemed unlikely to him that the *Elita* would reverse its course with the intention of bearing down on them with all guns blazing but he had not come this far to fall to so simple a trap. A little extra distance as they circumnavigated the island would not unduly delay their pursuit and caution was the watchword of any good captain, he believed.

As the *Whirlwind* skirted the island, all eyes were locked on the beach. Flocks of dark-feathered birds rose from the trees, though none crossed the water to investigate the frigate. No other life made itself apparent on the shore but the whole island appeared inviting, seeming to tempt the sailors onto its sands.

Maintaining a distance of no less than a half mile from the shore, the *Whirlwind* slowed slightly as Havelock ordered the studding sails to be furled, the extra canvas sheets serving no function in the expected battle. Like a hawk, he watched the coastline, keen to see if the French frigate had sailed on or anchored. It was not long before he spied an inlet that marked the entrance to a natural cove, carved from the island by the sea's constant motion. As they sailed past the inlet, Havelock cried out in triumph.

"There she is! Do you see, Mr Corbin? There she is!"

Crewmen rushed to the starboard side of the *Whirlwind* as the ship passed by the mouth of the cove. Lying before them was the *Elita*, already anchored close to the shore, its French ensign flying defiantly in the late afternoon breeze.

"She has trapped herself, Captain," said Corbin but Havelock shook his head.

"Do not be deceived, Lieutenant. Her guns face to sea and she will be a far steadier platform than we. If we try to negotiate the entrance to the cove, she will punish us for it, heavily. Once inside, if we are still afloat, we will find there is little room to manoeuvre. The advantage would be hers. We would be outmatched by both her guns and number of crew." He took another long look at the *Elita* before his ship sailed past the cove and out of sight of the French ship. "We must try another tactic."

"A land attack?" asked Corbin.

"You read my mind. Yes, Mr Corbin, we will find somewhere safe to anchor ourselves, a little further on, then make landfall. The jungle will mask our approach. I doubt we will have the luxury of complete surprise but if we co-ordinate our efforts, the advantage will turn to us, as their crew will be split between ship and shore. If we can deal with those on land without warning to the *Elita*, we may just be able to snatch her before an effective defence can be mounted."

"A bold move!"

"Fortune favours those who make such moves. We'll sail two miles onwards and then anchor. Get the men to prepare the boats."

"Aye, Sir!"

Though no more coves presented themselves to Havelock, he was nonetheless happy to anchor a little way beyond a protrusion of land that snaked a short distance from the rest of the island. The heavy vegetation would serve to shield the position of the *Whirlwind* from curious eyes either on land or the sea, should the *Elita* raise anchor and sail in pursuit of them. Either way, Havelock felt confident enough that a skeleton crew left on board would be able to keep the ship out of the reach of the French should the tables be turned and the attack repulsed.

As the crew heaved the three landing boats to the side of the *Whirlwind*, Havelock called for their attention. He could tell immediately from their anxious expressions that few feared for their lives in this venture. Their captain had presented to them an enemy that was not supernatural in nature and a plan of attack that stood a reasonable chance of success.

"Mr Hague," he said, loud enough to be heard by the whole crew. "The ship is yours. You will take command of the skeleton crew and keep the home fires burning until we return!"

"Yes, Captain!"

"Mr Wynton, Mr Corbin, you will both join me ashore to lead the attack. Mr Wynton, you will land first, taking your men into the jungle to deal with any sentries the French may have stationed. Do so quickly and quietly. Mr Corbin and I will be right behind you with the main body of men. We will join our forces before launching an attack on their beach shelters."

"As you say, Captain," said Lieutenant Wynton.

Satisfied that his officers would act as he had previously briefed them, Havelock turned his attention to the rest of the crew. "Men of the *Whirlwind*, we near our mission's end. The *Elita* lies in yonder cove, stationary and inert, her crew tired and battered. They will have no fight in them! As we march through the jungle to battle, remember you are part of the greatest Navy the world has yet seen. Whether we fight on sea or on land, you have no equal and, indeed, it would take ten French sailors to match any one of you!"

Wry grins began to spread through the crew and Havelock smiled in return. A reminder of the innate superiority of the British sailor never failed to instil courage, it seemed.

"I promise you, in perhaps just two hours, we will be sailing out of that cove on board a captured French frigate. Then, together, we will set sail for home – and our just rewards! Men of the *Whirlwind*, can you find it within yourselves to boot the French off this island and take their ship?"

The roar that answered his words was nearly as loud as that which had greeted his speech at the beginning of the voyage, and Havelock nodded his appreciation. He began to dare hope that their encounter with the death hulk would turn into nothing more than a memory, a tale to be told in taverns that no one listening would seriously believe. If this next battle was won, perhaps everything would be set right.

"Mr Wynton, lower your boat and set away. You have your orders!"

Sailors strained on ropes as the first landing boat was hoisted over the side. Crewmen soon clambered down the ropes to take their place in the small boat, raising the oars before pulling away with strong, confident strokes. Immediately, another boat was swung over the side of the *Whirlwind* and Havelock marched down to the main deck, determined to be the first on board in order to lead his men onto the shore.

Standing at the prow of the boat, feeling it surge forward with each stroke of the oars, Havelock fixed his eyes intently on the approaching shore. Wynton and his men had already landed and, after pulling their boat onto the shore, began to fan out and disperse into the trees as they sought out French sentries. Havelock felt a wave of confidence wash over him. This battle would be his finest moment yet.

CHAPTER NINE

Quietly cursing to himself, Murphy picked his way through the jungle, unhappy to be in an environment so similar to his last landfall. The images of crewmen torn apart by some unknown beast constantly ran through his head and he twitched at the sound of every rustle in the undergrowth and snapping of branches. He and Brooks trailed behind Bryant, who moved slowly, trying to keep the men to his right in view at all times so they did not get lost.

The British sailors formed a thin line of three guns crews, with Bryant's team on the right flank next to another crew who were led by Lieutenant Wynton. They moved with care through the vegetation, anxious to stay silent, yet conscious of the main body of sailors who would not be far behind them. So far, there had been no sign of any French pickets but they were expected to be placed far closer to the *Elita's* natural harbour.

Tripping over a vine Murphy reached out to a branch to steady himself, only to snatch his hand back as a sharp pain shot up his arm. He muffled a cry as he looked to the offending plant which, he now saw, was covered in thorns. It seemed to him that every living thing in jungles, plant or animal, were out to ensure human life did not venture too far in. As Bryant raised an arm for them to stop, Murphy found himself eying the Lieutenant, who had briefly halted to check his pistol.

"So 'ow comes we never gets the guns then?" he hissed.

"Officers only, mate," said Brooks, equally quietly, though their conversation had already caused Bryant to look back with a frown.

"And I just gets me knives," Murphy complained, reaching down to his belt to check that both blades were where they should be.

"Yeah, but you're pretty handy with them."

"I 'ave's me moments."

"Will you two be silent?" said Bryant, so quietly they barely heard him. In any case, Murphy considered the absence of French sentries to mean Bryant's statement was a guideline more than an order.

"Just be glad to fight somethin' that will die when you stab it," he said.

"Well, the Captain didn't seem to think there would be any walking dead on this island – or he would have told us, right?"

"Yeah, that's probably right," said Murphy. "As I always say, you can trust the Cap'n."

Even Bryant turned round to give Murphy an incredulous look.

"Anyways, them zombies won't matter any more," Murphy said, completely unabashed. "As the Cap'n said, we deal with the Frogs, grab their ship, and then it's back to Blighty! No more hangin' around these God-forsaken parts. And that means no more dead Frenchmen to fight."

"Yeah, that would be good," said Brooks, a look of concern crossing his face as he remembered the night they fought the dead.

"Still, I wouldn't mind 'aving Jessop round 'ere right now."

"God lord, why?" said Brooks.

"Well, you can say what you like about Jessop. An' I can say a bit, mind. But 'e ain't 'alf good in a fight. You should've seen 'im fight those zombies. Took three on without blinkin' an eye. I swear, saw it me self. A Frog or ten wouldn't stand a chance against 'im."

Bryant turned back round to confront Murphy. "The Lieutenant made sure Jessop was far behind us which, incidentally, is where I wish you were right now. Jessop has a big mouth that would alert any Frenchies for miles around – just like you are doing now. For the love of God, man, shut up!"

Cowering a little under his friend's words, Murphy shrugged slightly. "No need to be nasty about it," he muttered.

Wynton's group had started to move forwards and Bryant waved for them to match the pace. The jungle was noticeably thinner than that they had experienced on the African coast, so the going was a little easier. Conversely, they could see a lot further, sometimes as much as twenty or thirty yards. Acutely aware that they were on French ground, trying to locate sentries who would be watching for invaders, every sailor crouched low as he moved, taking care to avoid brushing through too much undergrowth. Where necessary, Bryant, along with others who wielded cutlasses or heavy knives, cut through vines and other denser patches of vegetation but only if there was no obvious way around it without losing eye contact with the other groups of sailors. This caused their path to meander somewhat but cutting through even a thin branch created a great deal of noise in a jungle that had grown quiet with the onset of twilight. There was enough light remaining for them to pick out details but all had been warned that night would descend extremely rapidly when on the island.

A flash of movement ahead caught Bryant's eyes and he crouched down, raising his arm in warning. Murphy was about to complain about another false alarm when he too saw something move behind the trunk of a tree, a light blue shade that seemed out of place in the jungle. All three of them stayed low as they peered into the gloom and were rewarded by the sight of a man in French army uniform leaning his musket against the tree as he fiddled with the top button of his jacket – no doubt taking advantage of the absence of officers to loosen it.

Bryant looked at his two comrades, putting his finger to his lips, but they were both alert and prepared for action. He motioned to Murphy to suggest that the small man sneak in an arc to their left, while he and Brooks took a more direct route. Their plans dissipated when sounds of rapid movement through undergrowth were followed by a cry echoed through the trees to their left. Clearly, some of their allies had also located a sentry.

Their man had also heard the sounds of the fight and he grabbed his musket, setting the bayonet as he stared hard into the jungle, trying to decide whether he should run or stay. Bryant decided to make the decision for him.

"Come on, now!" he said to Murphy and Brooks, before jumping up and running at full tilt towards the Frenchman.

The soldier spun around in alarm as Bryant thundered through the undergrowth towards him, leaping over fallen branches and raising his cutlass. A loud shot rang out as the sentry panicked and discharged his rifle, its shot flying well wide of Bryant.

Recovering his wits, the sentry raised his musket to block Bryant's downward swing, then lunged forward, forcing the big man to sidestep as the wickedly sharp point of the bayonet lanced past his ribs. He aimed a side swing at the sentry's head in return, but the man ducked under the blow, thrusting forward with his weapon once more. Bryant was forced to give ground or be skewered and he backed away, crouching on the balls of his feet, ready to dodge another attack.

Waving his cutlass dangerously in a false attack, Bryant caused the sentry to flinch and he took advantage of the opening as the man raised his musket, moving forward with a series of wide, confident sweeps of his blade. Several loud cracks rang out as the sentry desperately parried each blow with his musket, retreating several footsteps as he did so. Then he stopped. Arms dropping to his side, his musket fell to the floor as his eyes glazed over. Bryant was puzzled as the man keeled over, until he saw Murphy behind the body of the sentry, smiling triumphantly as he reached down to wipe his knife clean on the man's jacket.

"Nice work."

"I 'aves me moments."

Brooks trotted up to Bryant's side. "Think anyone heard that?" he asked.

"No doubt of it. This place will be crawling with the French," said Bryant. "Come on, let's find the Lieutenant and see what he wants us to do now."

They trotted in the direction of the first fight they had heard, though the jungle was silent now. Brushing through the branches of a tree whose limbs hung low to the ground, they were confronted by several clubs, blades and a single pistol pointed unerringly at Bryant's head. Lieutenant Wynton sighed as he recognised the men under his command and lowered his gun.

"You found one too?" he asked.

"Yes, Sir," said Bryant, curling a finger to his forehead. "He won't be troubling us."

"Good show. Craggs' crew found two more just aways from us."

"Begging your pardon, Sir, but what are we to do now? Surely the French heard the shots."

"I agree," said Wynton. "We hold here, wait for the Captain to bring the rest of the men up to us. By my reckoning, night is about to fall and we don't want to be stumbling around the jungle while the French are looking for us. We have dealt with the picket line in this area. With luck, the Captain will be with us before the French start a serious sweep of the jungle."

Movement ahead of them brought their conversation to a sudden halt and they all ducked low. Peering through the trees, they spied another two French soldiers. They held their muskets across their chests, scanning the surrounding area as they walked slowly towards the British sailors.

"Unless, of course, they force our hand," said Wynton as he stood up straight. Taking quick aim with his pistol, he fired, the weapon discharging smoke that carried the thick stench of black powder. One of the soldiers fell to the ground but his companion was already raising his musket.

Bryant ran forward, galvanising several other sailors to follow him. The sight of a half dozen maddened British sailors caused the soldier to falter as he tried to decide which target to point his musket at. Before they reached him, he fired and a man staggered but the rest swept onward to batter and slice the soldier as he desperately tried to fix his bayonet to the end of his weapon. He fell quickly and silently to a heavy blow from a club.

Slower to react than most of the others, Brooks went to the wounded sailor who had received shot from the discharged musket. The man was leaning heavily against a tree, clutching his shoulder. He was obviously in a great deal of pain and Brooks helped him sink to the ground before tearing a strip from his own shirt to help bind the wound. Blood covered the man's body to the extent that Brooks could not see whether the bullet had exited through his back or remained lodged among the bones of the shoulder.

Bryant leaned forward to gauge the man's wound. "You should help him back to the ship, Brooks."

"Belay that," said Wynton, who had also moved forward to join them. "There will be plenty more wounded soon and, besides, the lad'll likely get lost at night. Make the man comfortable, then we move on. The Captain and his men will find him and make arrangements. Besides, we need every hand for the fight ahead."

"Aye, Sir," Bryant said, trying hard to keep the reluctance out of his voice. As well as compassion to the wounded man, he had been hoping to find a reason to keep Brooks out of the coming battle. The boy was not only young, he was also inexperienced when it came to life and death fights with the French. He resolved to keep Brooks close by at all times during the next few hours. It might well be the making or breaking of the lad.

Cries and shouts in a foreign, yet familiar, tongue echoed in the jungle ahead of them, growing steadily closer. Loading his pistol, Wynton gave orders for them to spread out and take cover. They would meet any French patrols here until they were joined by the Captain.

The fall of night in the jungle caught Havelock momentarily off guard. He had been aware of the sinking sun, though it was hidden by the tall trees, and the slowly dimming light that forced him to stare hard through the undergrowth to find his footing. Night itself came almost instantly. One moment he was peering through the gloomy wild, then he was calling for men to bring forward torches. The sputtering fire provided enough illumination to proceed with the venture but it cast eerie shadows that moved and jumped at the corner of men's eyes, causing more than one false alarm.

At his side, Corbin monitored the disposition of sailors around them, allowing Havelock to concentrate on the task of reaching Wynton's forward party and then engage the French. Moving as a ragged column, they hoped to ensure none would become lost during the trek, though there was no accounting for a sailor's curiosity at times.

Orders had been given for absolute silence during the march but with nearly a couple of hundred men behind him, Havelock began to fear that the sounds of their approach would alert the French long before they emerged from the jungle, and that was assuming Wynton had been successful in silencing any sentries. If any escaped to get word back to the main French camp, this fight would grow harder still. His only hope then would be that the French crew would be split between those on shore and those still on board the *Elita*. He felt confident that the French captain would maintain a heavy watch on his ship, however, as they had plainly spotted the *Whirlwind* approaching their island and would thus take steps to secure a strong position against attack, either from land or sea. It was Havelock's hopes that in trying to cover all possibilities, the French captain would leave himself weaker overall, permitting the British sailors to fight them piecemeal.

A loud crack resounded through the jungle and Havelock stopped in his tracks, the sailors closest to him following suit. It was quickly followed by several more shots and, straining his ears, Havelock made out the unmistakable cries of men in battle.

"Lieutenant! It seems as though Mr Wynton has found the measure of the enemy," he said to Corbin. "I'll take a dozen men and relieve him. Bring the men up in good order. We'll wait for you to begin the main attack!"

"Aye, Captain," said Corbin, turning round to pick a group of sailors to follow the Captain as he ran forward into the darkness. They had to sprint to catch up with him.

The uneven ground forced Havelock to quickly moderate his pace and he chafed at his own slowness as the sounds of battle grew ever closer. Somewhere ahead, he knew, Wynton was fighting, wondering just when his Captain would bring reinforcements. Two of the men who had joined him bore torches and their light was noticeably less illuminating than the score of torches the rest of his force had carried. He drew his sword, using it to hack down any plant life that threatened to impede his progress, while he carried his pistol in his left.

Several cries from ahead warned Havelock that not only was he close to the fight, but the light from his torches had warned the participants of his arrival. Sparing a thought only for those of his men who had, until now, been fighting a terrifying battle in darkness, Havelock began to run. A bright flash ahead followed by a heavy crack betrayed the position of a musket and he shouted his men forward as he pointed his sword ahead. He was briefly aware of Wynton and a few sailors crouched down behind a fallen tree on his right as he tore past. Leaping over a dense fern, he confronted a surprised French soldier who had his back half-turned as he reloaded his musket. Not giving the man time to recover, Havelock swung down with his sword, embedding it deep in the man's back. Screaming in agony, the soldier fell trying in vain to reach behind with an arm to staunch the flow of blood.

Suddenly aware of several other uniformed soldiers and

raggedly clothed sailors around him, Havelock realised he had charged straight into the middle of the French line. His men rapidly fanned out and found enemies to engage and suddenly the jungle erupted with the sounds of an intense, desperate melee. Trees and ferns shook as men rolled or crashed through them, the air was filled with the sounds of wood and metal connecting with one another and, through it all, the cries of mortally wounded men. A sailor, his face stained with grime, leapt out of the darkness with a cleaver, clearly fancying his chances of killing an English officer. Havelock calmly sidestepped the rush, batting the cleaver away with his sword, before reversing his stroke and running the man through the stomach.

As he wrenched his weapon clear in a spray of blood, he stalked towards two French soldiers who were pressing their advantage home against one of his sailors. The Englishman desperately swung with a cutlass, trying to keep the bayoneted muskets at bay but he was giving ground with every stroke. Calling out a challenge, Havelock marched forward, slashing at the nearest and sinking his sword deep into the man's arm. His companion, suddenly finding himself the outnumbered one, backed away. The Englishman's strength renewed at the sight of his Captain entering battle, the sailor yelled as he sprang forward with two clumsy but powerful chops. The soldier parried the first with the barrel of his musket but the second found its target in his skull. Panting, the sailor put a crooked finger to forehead in salute to his Captain. Havelock smiled and clapped the man's shoulder before moving off to look for Wynton. By the sounds filling the jungle, Havelock could tell the fight was reaching its conclusion and by the number of dead Frenchmen lying on the ground, he was confident of its outcome.

"Captain!"

Havelock saw his Second Lieutenant trotting out from behind the trees, sword as red as his own.

"Mr Wynton, report."

Breathless, Wynton did his best. "Met their first line of sentries, Sir. Dealt with them, but the French got a shot off. Alerted the others. We dug in and met them..."

"Down!" A quick movement caught Havelock's eye and he roughly pushed Wynton to one side, even as he crouched himself. Raising his pistol, he fired near blindly. A French soldier dropped to the ground, clutching his stomach.

Picking himself off the ground, Wynton dusted himself off. "Damn close," he muttered. Then, a little clearer, he gave a half bow. "My thanks, Captain."

"Need to keep your eyes open in this damnable jungle," said Havelock. The familiar sounds of English sailors on the march reached his ears and he smiled. "Ah, here comes Mr Corbin with the rest of our men. Now perhaps we can push on out of this jungle and into more civilised terrain."

"No arguments from me, Sir."

The darkness of the jungle began to yield more British sailors. Havelock was just glad to see them and he waved to get Corbin's attention. The Lieutenant marched briskly towards the two of them.

"Had some excitement already, I see," he said.

"Mr Wynton accredited himself most admirably, I would say," said Havelock. "Just left us a few to mop up."

Wynton smiled as he greeted Corbin. "Let's just say that the Captain's arrival was most timely."

"Form the men up as best you can, Mr Corbin," said Havelock. "They have the taste of a fight in them now but do the best you can. I want to march on within the minute."

"Right you are, Sir," said Corbin, immediately turning to bark orders that gathered sailors together. Havelock reached into a pouch at his belt and began to reload his pistol. Though the weapon could only realistically be used once during a battle, the last French soldier had reminded Havelock that, sometimes, that was enough.

"You have another fight in you, Mr Wynton?"

"Ready and able, Captain."

"Good. That was the easy part. Now we march against an enemy who, by now, certainly know we are coming."

"Did you hope to come this far unnoticed, Captain?"

"Not really. Our sailors are not trained for this sort of battle. However, we can hope that the French are still unaware of our true numbers or even, perhaps, of our true intentions. Still, it will be a hard fight."

"Not to worry, Sir," said Wynton cheerfully. "You said it yourself. Each of our men is worth ten of theirs!"

Havelock returned the smile. "Indeed I did, Mr Wynton. Now come, let us prove it!"

Men crowded close, filling the surrounding jungle in the flickering light of their torches. Checking that officer and sailor alike were ready, Havelock raised his sword so all could see, then marched determinedly onwards towards the beach and the waiting Frenchmen.

It took nearly twenty minutes before the trees and vegetation started to noticeably thin out and, straining his ears, Havelock could hear the sound of the sea, the waves lapping against the shoreline subdued by their passage through the narrow inlet of the cove. He held up a hand to halt the progress of the march and called Corbin and Wynton to his side as he crept forward, instinctively keeping low. The three men, using the trees as cover, padded forward until they reached the end of the treeline.

Before them, a sandy shore extended some thirty yards to the water, its waves glittering with the combined light of a quarter moon and dozens of French torches and lanterns. On the beach itself, they were somewhat surprised to see several hastily erected wooden shacks, no doubt placed by the French as part of their temporary base. They did not seem sturdy enough to resist a brisk wind but, Havelock reflected, in this climate they served their purpose merely by keeping the sun away from sleeping men. Men ran too and fro within the little village but, before the buildings, a clump of men had arranged themselves in a ragged unit. An officer marched up and down their uneven line, shouting out orders to individuals, making them move forward or back in an attempt to make the unit a little neater.

"Must be a couple hundred of them," said Corbin. "And more among the huts."

"Not many more I would guess," said Wynton.

Havelock rubbed his chin as he thought. "Still a formidable force," he said. "They match our numbers, and they are ready for us. We will have to cross forty yards from this position to reach them."

"I don't see any uniforms," said Corbin as he squinted at the French unit. "If they deployed all their soldiers on picket duty, they may not have many guns. What are your orders, Captain?"

Slowly exhaling before he answered, Havelock considered his options before reaching a decision. "Mr Wynton, take a couple of men and scout out our left flank. I don't want to rush these men and then suddenly find the rest of their crew waiting for us in the trees a little further along. That won't do at all."

"Right you are, Captain," said Wynton, as he scuttled

off back into the darkness.

"Mr Corbin, how many marines do we have with us?"

"Seven. Not enough to make a difference."

"It will be enough. They will move up first and position themselves on our right. Order them to hold position. They will act as sharpshooters throughout the fight. No sense in risking our only guns in open battle."

"And the rest of us?"

"We charge," said Havelock flatly. "Tell the marines to open fire as we leave the trees. It will force the French to keep their heads down and buy us a few more seconds of surprise. Then we'll be in amongst them and it will be up to God who wins."

As Corbin ran off to gather their men, Havelock was left alone for a few minutes to study his enemy further. In the pale moonlight, he could see the *Elita*, moored in the middle of the cove, the target of this whole enterprise. She was a fine ship and he was surprised to find himself eager to see how she handled at sea. A skilled captain could do a lot with a frigate like that. He noted the three masts were tall and straight, showing no signs of damage or hasty repair. The Captain guessed this natural harbour had been discovered long ago by the French captain, who had prepared in advance for disaster.

Turning his attention back to the shore, he saw four boats pulled up onto the beach and could even make out the oars piled on the sand next to them. Looking towards the huts, Havelock could not help but smile as the French officer continued to cajole his men into a regular unit. Sailors never made for the best land troops but he fancied the men of the *Whirlwind* would have made a far better representation of themselves. Truly, discipline was the foundation of an effective fighting unit, be it on land or sea, and it was something these French sailors sorely lacked. There was a kernel of truth in the idea that a British sailor was worth ten Frenchmen. The odds were not that great, certainly, but given equal numbers, Havelock would put his money on his men in any fight. Still, the French were not to be underestimated, and their leaders had a habit of rising above the failings of their military to perform some truly remarkable actions. He resolved to not let over-confidence blind him to any surprises the French might have in store. On their home ground, they could be a truly dreadful enemy.

The sounds of breaking branches and hissed curses announced the arrival of his men and Corbin duly appeared.

"Complements of Mr Wynton," he said. "The flank is clear. No surprises there."

"The marines?"

"In position and ready to open fire as soon as we move. We await only your order."

Steeling himself, Havelock took a deep breath. "The best of luck to you, Mr Corbin. Let us be off."

Giving his pistol just one last check, Havelock drew its lock back with a solid click and then, raising his sword, sprang forward at a dead run towards the French. He was aware of the sound of two hundred men behind him surging forward and then the multiple cracks of the marines' muskets sang out to his right. Ahead, he saw a couple of French sailors fall to the fire as others instinctively flinched or ducked. He was gratified to see two more in the rear of the line turn and run, scuttling away to hide in one of the wooden huts.

The indecision of the French line was momentary and, as their officer screamed at the sailors for a response, they started to shamble forward, gradually picking up speed. The distance between the two forces closed rapidly and Havelock found himself being overtaken by some of his faster men. Cries and challenges sprang from the lips of men on both sides while weapons were held aloft, ready to deal a killing blow. The twin masses of French and British hit one another with a dull thud that was audible to everyone. Almost immediately, the cries and screams started as men were gutted, brained and battered senseless.

A few metres in front of him, a French sailor leered at Havelock before reaching to his belt to pull out a knife. With a practised flick, the knife flew through the air, forcing Havelock to check his charge and duck as the blade sailed past his head, whistling as it split the air. The sailor was upon him immediately, brandishing a club that he swung at Havelock's skull. On one knee and at a disadvantage, Havelock rolled to his left before sweeping out with his sword. The blade bit deep into the sailor's ankle, causing him to howl in pain. Standing up straight, Havelock dispatched then man with one slice to the neck but immediately found himself giving ground and parrying wildly as another sailor, a large man with broad shoulders, swung a cutlass at him with broad, powerful strokes. Recovering from the assault, Havelock quickly found the measure of the man. Though the Frenchman was not unskilled in the blade, he was no match for a British officer instructed in the art of duelling. Turning side on to the man, Havelock raised himself on the balls of his feet and matched every stroke, gradually gaining the initiative as he launched his own attacks. A quick feint to the man's face caused him to stumble, leaving an opening for Havelock to give a savage downwards hack that sliced the man open across his chest.

The momentum of the British assault had already pushed the French unit backwards and Havelock found himself having to run forward a few steps to keep with the front line of battle. Dead littered the beach and, in his quick estimation, most seemed to belong to the enemy. Havelock realised that this might indeed be an easy victory and he suddenly grew uneasy. He felt the hairs on the back of his neck begin to prickle and he wondered if something was not very wrong. Had the French captain prepared a surprise that would suddenly swing the battle against Havelock? Was he even now watching, biding his time for the perfect counterattack? Havelock could not shake the feeling that someone was watching his movements very carefully. He cast an anxious glance across the battle rolling all around him.

He saw Corbin a few yards away, fighting a thin man wearing the uniform of a French lieutenant. His own officer had half a smile as he fought, seeming to relish the chance to match himself against his counterpart. The two duelled with no little skill, the sailors around them not intruding, seeming to sense this was a fight of honour that none should interrupt.

His attention was distracted by the sight of a young red-headed British sailor yelling in alarm as two men rushed him, each thrashing with a large cudgel. There was a loud crack as the boy swung wildly with the belaying pin he carried, knocking aside the weapons of the two French sailors, more by luck than expertise. Giving ground wildly, the boy looked as if he would stumble and be killed at any moment.

Havelock rushed forward but was beaten to it by a burly man he felt he had spoken to before. The man chopped with his cutlass, snapping one of the cudgels with the blow, before thrusting with his weapon to sink it deep into the sailor's stomach. Shouting a warning to the other sailor before he struck, Havelock landed a solid blow to the man's shoulder, forcing him to drop his club. Another blow dispatched him just as quickly, leaving Havelock to confront the two British sailors. The larger man was clapping the boy on the back, trying to inspire confidence in the obviously shaken lad.

"Good work, seaman..." Havelock prompted.

"Seaman Bryant, Captain," said the large man, crooking a finger in a hasty salute. "This here is Brooks."

"Watch over him," said Havelock. "We have the advantage over the French and it would not do to lose someone now."

"Right you are, Captain."

Turning back to the battle, Havelock tried to make his way to Corbin, who was still fighting the French Lieutenant. Another sailor tried to claim Havelock's life with a cutlass, forcing him to raise his sword high in a parry. A second Frenchman rushed forward from his right, a wicked looking pike aimed right at his heart. Still straining with his sword to stay the path of the cutlass, Havelock reached across his chest with his left hand and fired his pistol. The shot seemed to catch the pikeman completely off guard and his expression was one of utter surprise as he fell to his knees, then collapsed onto the sand. Striking out with his boot, Havelock connected with the knee of the other sailor, forcing him to back off. He immediately followed up with a well-aimed thrust to the chest that the sailor had no time to parry.

Glancing up, Havelock saw Corbin advance on his enemy with a series of quick cuts that forced the French officer to give ground. A quick flick of the Frenchman's sword missed Corbin's forehead by mere inches as he reeled backwards to avoid the blow but, recovering quickly, he slashed across the Lieutenant's forearm. Blood welled up immediately and the Frenchman was forced to swap his sword to his off hand. His movements became noticeably slower and it took Corbin scant seconds to finish the duel. Bowing slightly as the French Lieutenant hit the sand, Corbin turned to find another enemy but his eyes locked onto Havelock's and he smiled.

"A fine fight, Mr Corbin!"

"Thank you, Captain," said Corbin graciously in return. "It seems we have them beaten. Shall we now finish it?"

"Indeed," said Havelock. As Corbin turned to face battle once more, he caught the Lieutenant's arm. "Have a care, Mr Corbin. We have not won yet. I have a feeling things are not all they seem."

"You think there is a hidden force?" he said. "Mr Wynton reported the trees were clear and those huts cannot hide many men."

"I don't know," said Havelock, suddenly unsure of himself. "It is just... a feeling."

Corbin looked as if he did not know how to properly respond. "Well, we can keep our eyes open, Captain..."

"You are right, of course. Come, our men need us."

Leading the way, Havelock pushed through the body of British sailors that surrounded them. The French had suffered during the course of the battle to the extent that men were having to search for an enemy to fight. The fight had spilled from the open beach to the rickety huts and pockets of French sailors were now on the defensive as they were surrounded by an enemy who could sense victory. A large number of them had formed a loose clump in front of one hut and a number of dead or dying British sailors at their feet proved testament to their ferocity.

Pointing out the French defenders to Corbin, Havelock made his way to the fight, finding himself jostled by his own crewmen as he tried to force his way past them, until they saw just who it was they were trying to push back. Once at the front of the British sailors, he fought alongside Corbin, their blades flicking in and out as much as the light press of men would allow, catching weapons brought down in overhead blows and darting outwards to catch a man's arm, head or heart.

One French sailor confronted Havelock with nothing more than a knife, its short blade coming nowhere near the length needed to reach past his sword. Havelock almost pitied the man as he finished the sailor with one quick slice across the face. It was then Havelock felt the cold hand of fear grip his stomach. He glanced wildly around, trying to identify the source of his unease but nothing was apparent. Corbin continued to fight next to him and though the Frenchmen were fighting like trapped rats, he saw nothing immediately life-threatening in their attacks.

Feeling something pulling his attention, he risked a quick glance over his shoulder. About a hundred yards further down the beach, he saw the sand begin to rise far more steeply than it did around the huts, creating a small rise before the trees of the jungle. Atop this ground, Havelock saw a single dark figure, standing motionless as it surveyed the battle on the beach. The cold hand of fear gripped his stomach harder as Havelock began to realise – how, he did not know – that the figure was looking directly at him.

Returning his attention back to the fight, Havelock half-heartedly parried a few blows aimed in his direction, wondering if this was what it was like to go mad. He glanced over his shoulder again, expecting his vision to be clear but the figure was still there, faintly malevolent in its inaction.

With no conscious decision on his part, Havelock simply turned and left the fight, his place immediately filled by sailors who had been impatiently waiting their turn to battle the French. It took Corbin several seconds to realise his Captain had gone and he glanced about wildly before catching sight of Havelock's retreating back.

"Captain?" He tried to pull away but the defending French chose that moment to redouble their efforts in an attempt to break free of the battle and head to the boats. Havelock did not hear the call of his Lieutenant as he walked, slowly, from the battle. Moving away from the huts, he kept his eyes fixed solidly on the lone figure, still standing proud and unmoving on the small rise. Though not in a daze, Havelock felt as if his actions now were not completely his own. If he had to put a term to it, he would have said it was the hand of destiny that now moved him and he began to dread the coming encounter, though nothing could have prepared him for what he faced once he climbed the rise.

Feet slipping in the sand as he scrambled up the shallow slope, Havelock kept his eyes locked on the motionless figure that waited impassively for him. He could already tell it was a tall man, with a long sword that gleamed dully. When he closed within a few yards of the figure, a familiar stench hit him with a shock, as if a door had just been opened to an ancient tomb. The rotting stink of the death hulk washed over Havelock, and though gagging, he refused to take his eyes off the dead man. Stumbling up the last few feet of the rise, Havelock stood, confronting the nightmare that had appeared on the eve of his mission's completion.

"Captain Havelock," the thing rasped through a lipless mouth, its exposed and decaying teeth grinning manically. Shocked to hear one of the walking dead actually speak, he could see it wore a ragged and mouldering French officer's uniform of antique design, its braid fraying at the shoulders and chest. The skin of its face and hands was sunken and stretched across bone, though it still seemed to possess an unholy strength.

"Captain James Havelock," the thing said slowly, seeming to relish his name. "I am Captain Dubois. I believe you know who I am..."

"Yes," said Havelock, fighting back his revulsion and fear. "You were... are... the captain of the *Deja*. A warship sunk by my grandfather."

"Ah, that is true," Dubois crooned. "'I was killed, you see, by Captain Edward Havelock as I defended men, women and children who sought nothing more than a better life. Innocents, Captain! But that mattered not to your grandfather. Against all the rules of conduct, morality and common decency, he sent many of them to their deaths and, had it not been for the sacrifice of my ship and crew, would have killed them all."

"I know the story, Dubois."

"Then you also know what I want."

Havelock hesitated before answering. "Yes."

The face of the creature wrinkled in what Havelock guessed might have been a grim smile. "Death has taken your grandfather far beyond my reach but now fate has delivered you, and your crew, into my hands."

Though the stink of the French captain continued to assault Havelock's nostrils, his confidence grew as he confronted the talking zombie. He realised what might have to be done, even if he intended to make it as difficult for Dubois as possible. "What my grandfather did *was* wrong – and I am willing to answer for his crimes, here and now if you wish. But you will allow my crew to return home unharmed."

"I will do no such thing! One life will not balance the debt, Captain! The souls of my own crew must be satiated and that thirst can only be satisfied by the lives of your men. Justice demands like for like! I only pity that you have so few men with you."

"I cannot permit you to do this," said Havelock, holding his head high. "I have offered satisfaction. If that is not sufficient, you leave me with no choice."

"Satisfaction!" Dubois spat, the spray causing Havelock to flinch in disgust. "You English believe you have the moral right to do as you wish throughout the world. But you are nothing more than dogs who have no understanding of the true meaning of honour. You know of your grandfather's crime and yet fail to comprehend what it was he did. Your grandfather is now dead, after having enjoyed a life of privilege, luxury and high rank bought, in part, with our deaths. Now you are here, within our power. Your life and the lives of your crew will not balance the deaths of my crew or the murder of those we swore to protect. But it is a start, and I'll take that!"

"Then I will stop you. If you mean to claim my life, I challenge you to do it here, and now!" Havelock calmly stated as he raised his sword.

"You miss my meaning, Captain Havelock," said Dubois. "You will die, and soon, be sure of that. But not before I take your ship, your crew and even your humanity. You will *suffer*, Captain. No less is required of you."

"I will not permit this."

"It is inevitable, Captain." Again, the features of Dubois twisted in a hideous smile. "Here, in this place, it is I who have the power. You cannot kill me. You cannot stop me. Your fate was written when your grandfather killed us all!"

There was something in the creature's arrogance and certainty that angered Havelock. "I will see you in Hell first, Dubois!"

He struck forward with his sword, a powerful thrust aimed at the creature's heart. Dubois did not move as the blade sank into his chest, his dead flesh giving little resistance as the weapon burst out between his shoulder blades.

"Do you see?" he mocked.

Havelock cried out as he withdrew his sword and aimed a vicious swing at the zombie's neck. Dubois moved now, with a supple litheness that seemed at odds with his decaying physique or the lumbering movements Havelock had seen in the walking dead on the *Deja*. In a fluid motion, Dubois raised his sword up in the path of Havelock's, halting the blow immediately with a metallic clang that knocked rust and dirt from the creature's weapon. Havelock's arm ached at the sudden stop and he withdrew his sword, pacing to the left as he sought another opening.

Standing motionless again, Dubois merely held his sword outwards, its point towards his opponent. Havelock took a step forward and he chopped and swung in a rapid series of attacks, but each was met with Dubois' own blade, who blocked and parried the assault without moving from his place on the sand.

Sweating now, Havelock tried again, feinting at the creature's neck before diverting his swing downwards, intending to cut Dubois down at the knee. Again, his enemy's sword unerringly met the stroke but Havelock was prepared for this and slid his sword upwards to Dubois' face, hoping to skewer its dead features. This time, Dubois did move, a single step backwards that gave him room enough to raise his sword and once again hold Havelock's blade still.

Havelock strained against the parry, trying to force his sword forward just a few inches so it would at least mark Dubois' face but it was like trying to push against a mountain. He realised his enemy's strength was formidable, and likely sprang from a source deeper and more mysterious than mere flesh, bone and muscle. His stare of hatred was returned by Dubois as the two stood, straining against each other's weapon. Their faces just a few inches apart, Havelock glared into the colourless eyes of the zombie, the long ovals that marked Dubois' missing nose exhaled no breath. Havelock panted hard with effort but though he was still aware of the rotting stink of the creature, he forced it from his mind.

They stood like this, Havelock trying to force his weapon forward, for several long seconds before Dubois seemed to tire of the game and made his own move. A knee shot up into Havelock's stomach, winding him instantly and forcing him to take a few steps back. Dubois was immediately upon him, hacking downwards in an overhead swing that Havelock barely knocked to one side, before thrusting forward. The sword grazed past Havelock's ribs and he felt a sharp sting of pain before twisting out of the way.

Following up on the ground Havelock had given, Dubois chopped and hacked, each blow numbing Havelock's arm as he caught the blade on his own weapon, sometimes just inches from his face or chest. The sandy rise dropped behind him and, concentrating on Dubois' attacks, Havelock missed his footing. With a cry of alarm, he tumbled backwards, landing heavily on the ground.

Shaking his head to clear his vision, Havelock looked up to see Dubois standing over him. He swung wildly with his sword but the blow was met by the French captain's weapon. With a twist of his wrist, Dubois ripped Havelock's sword from his hand, causing it to fly through the air before landing in the sand a couple of yards from them. Stepping forward, Dubois placed the point of his sword on Havelock's chest, the blade pushing down painfully. Havelock looked up defiantly, determined not to show a trace of fear.

"You have your revenge, Sir," he said, his voice steady but laden with anger.

"I have already told you," said Dubois. "You will die last. First your ship, then your crew. Then, at the last, I will come for you."

Fury filled Havelock. He was well aware of the sins in his family's history but he refused to be mocked or played with. With a strangled cry, he rolled to one side, ignoring the pain of Dubois' blade as it pressed into his chest. He stretched for his own sword, spying its hilt in the sand just a short distance away. Grasping it clumsily, he kicked out while swinging the sword in a wicked blow aimed at Dubois' ankle. Both foot and blade met empty air.

Confused, Havelock cast about desperately, fearing a trick or surprise attack of some kind. He jumped to his feet and began to realise that he was alone on the sandy rise. Believing his enemy to have retreated into the jungle, he sprinted for the trees, their branches whipping his face as he tried to hack past them with his sword. After getting his foot snagged in a creeping vine and angrily cutting downwards, Havelock vented his frustration into the darkness.

"Why are you waiting?" he shouted. "I am here! Come and take me if you will! Coward! Villain! When we meet again, I'll send you back to the bottom of the ocean!"

The trees had no answer for him.

CHAPTER TEN

The beach was strewn with the dead and dying, the cries of the latter a piteous lament in the night. Wounded British sailors were guaranteed of at least a little comfort from their comrades but their French counterparts could only hope to raise enough pity for a little water if they spoke English. Stumbling back to the shore, Havelock observed all this in a daze. He saw that his men had gained a good victory but he took no pleasure in it, his previous encounter weighed heavily on his mind.

Already, Corbin had organised parties to ready the French landing boats to make an assault on the *Elita* who, even now, remained motionless, moored in the bay. Havelock observed a few of his sailors lounging among the makeshift huts, already retelling their part in the fight with suitable embellishments. More than a few swigged from bottles as they spoke and Havelock marvelled at the capacity of British sailors to locate drink wherever they may be. This tiny reminder of a normal sea life served to raise his spirits a little, though his mind still whirled with the memory of Dubois' face, the duel they had fought, and the rotting Frenchman's deadly promise.

As he approached the water, Corbin noticed his Captain and trotted over, his face full of concern.

"Sir?"

"Report, Mr Corbin," said Havelock.

The Lieutenant paused, clearly wanting to ask Havelock where he had disappeared to, but duty and discipline overcame his desire. "We have the beach, Captain. We have perhaps a dozen dead, twice that wounded and Mr Rawlinson is badly hurt, but the French came off worse. Some of them fled into the trees when it became clear their cause was lost, and the men say they saw a few run into the water. I have already started preparing the boats for the attack on the frigate. We await only your word."

"Very good, Mr Corbin, the word is given. Pass my compliments to the men."

"Very good, Sir. Err, Sir, if I may be so bold?"

Havelock cleared this throat. "My mistake, Mr Corbin. I thought Mr Wynton had missed a French party in the trees. Probably just a few animals."

"Sir!" Corbin appeared amazed. "If there had been a French party there, you going alone would have been tantamount to suicide!"

"The men were otherwise engaged. As it happens, there were no French, so don't fuss, Lieutenant. Now, these boats – they are ready, you say?"

"Yes, Sir. We have four of them. Orders?"

"You, Mr Wynton and myself will take a boat each, Mr Kennedy can take the last. You go for the bow, I'll take the stern, and the other two boats will support us in the centre. If we time our attacks more or less simultaneously, we have a chance at outmatching the French crew."

"And if the *Elitu* weighs anchor and sets sail while we row towards her?"

Havelock shook his head. "She would have left already, the moment it became clear the beach was lost. No, I believe her Captain still fancies his chances. Remember, he likely still outnumbers us and we are about to launch an attack on his home ground. Tell the men to keep their heads down as they row. We *will* come under fire."

Though the drink had already started to flow, it took mere minutes to assemble the *Whirlwind's* crew to heave the landing boats into the water and start the short voyage to the French frigate. Havelock stood proud at the prow of his craft, one foot on its hull, as he checked his pistol. He could hear some of the crew muttering behind him, wondering whether their Captain was brave or foolhardy in presenting a French rifleman with such a good target. For his part, Havelock did not know whether he would live or die that night but after his encounter with Dubois, he doubted he would fall to a shot from a French sailor. Not one whose heart still beat in his chest, at any rate.

"Row!" Havelock said to his men. "Put your backs into it!"

As the pace of the small boat quickened under sweating curses, it veered off larboard, heading towards the prow of the *Elita*. Staring into the darkness, Havelock could make out French crewmen on its deck under the light of lanterns hung on the masts and other fixtures. At this range, he could not see evidence of massed ranks of riflemen, and Havelock found himself hoping that the main body of French soldiers had indeed been deployed on the beach. Even so, his heart fell when several gun ports opened on the side of the ship, their cannon pointing ominously towards his tiny fleet.

He heard a faint cry from the frigate, the order to fire, before a series of massive explosions rent the quiet night, bright flashes quickly subdued by thick, cloying smoke. Huge plumes of water straddled the boats of Kennedy and Wynton who, by approaching abeam to the *Elita*, had placed themselves directly in its line of fire. A quick glance showed that they had survived the initial salvo.

Looking back to see how quickly the crew of the *Elita* could reload, Havelock began to smile. The smoke from the attack hung in front of the frigate, effectively obscuring it from view. He heard some of the crew from the other boats give a short cheer as they too realised that if they could not see the *Elita*, then it could certainly not see them. The soft night breeze did little to disperse the smoke and Havelock began to dare hope they could reach the ship before the French had another chance to fire. He counted off the seconds as his boat made its painfully slow progress forward.

Another roar, accompanied by a yellow-orange flash behind the smoke signalled the French Captain's intention to fire blind if need be. Havelock winced at the deafening noise as the guns discharged just a few dozen yards away. Instinctively he glanced to his right but was this time dismayed to see water, bodies and shards of wood flying upwards. Which of the boats had been lost, he could not tell but he cursed. This attack had been a gamble but he had hoped not to lose a quarter of his strength before the fight had even begun.

"Lord have mercy on them," said one of his rowers, and Havelock could not help but agree. He fervently hoped there would be survivors that could swim to the *Elita* once it was in their hands but, given how the men had packed themselves into the boats, he did not rate their chances.

Seconds after the blast, Havelock's boat entered the rolling smoke, thick enough to force him to raise a sleeve to his nose and mouth to filter out the worst of its choking effects. For a moment, he could feel the presence of the *Elita* rather than see it, the ship's great mass seeming to press down on his small craft. Then, it materialised out of the smoke, its great hull rising high above the water. His eyes following the natural sweep of the hull, Havelock shuddered as he saw the gun ports, mounted one above the other on two decks, imagining the raw weight of fire they would be capable of under a crew as well trained as his.

A sailor poked his head over the side of the hull above, and Havelock swung his pistol upwards and fired as the man cried out a warning. The head disappeared, though Havelock could not tell whether this was because of his marksmanship or if the sailor had simply ducked in time. Two sailors stood up behind Havelock as the boat bumped against the side of the frigate with a dull thud. Swinging ropes, they quickly sent two grapples skywards, expertly hooking them over the railings.

Havelock tucked his pistol into his belt and then leapt forward onto one of the ropes, straining as he hoisted himself up, hand over hand. As he ascended the side of the ship, the French sailor reappeared above him. Instead of crying out for help again, he grinned at Havelock as he produced a knife and proceeded to make a great show of slowly cutting the rope. Swearing, Havelock redoubled his efforts, the muscles of his arms groaning in agony as they protested the exertion. As he shot up the rope, the expression of the French sailor slowly turned from glee to anxiety as he realised that the Englishman might actually reach him. Havelock felt the vibrations in his hands as each strand was cut. Realising he would not reach the railings of the *Elita's* forecastle in time, he waited until he felt the rope start to sag then, with one fluid motion, reached out to the second rope alongside and swung across to a safer perch.

The first rope fell away into the sea before the French sailor realised that there was no longer an English Captain hanging on to it and his expression fell. Havelock had cleared the last few feet of his ascent, and holding onto the rope with one hand, drew his sword and swung it in an elaborate slice that cut through the sailor's throat. Shaking the spray of blood from his eyes, Havelock heaved himself over the railings as the dull clunk of another grapple embedding itself close by signalled that his crew had already thrown a replacement rope upwards. Already, one of his sailors was clambering over the railings to join him and they both looked down the length of the ship as they realised that sounds of battle now filled the air.

Sharp notes of metal on metal, wood on skull and the occasional pistol shot announced the arrival of at least one of his other boats, in the centre of the ship, he guessed, from the press of French crew on the main deck. The forecastle was clear of defenders but it did not take long for someone to shout out a warning that drew a rush of sailors towards him. Moving to the centre of the forecastle to give his men enough room to climb on board, Havelock brandished his sword, daring the first man to attack. Despite his bravado, several French sailors deemed their chances good against an English officer and a gang rushed him, forcing Havelock on the back foot immediately as he twisted and parried their blows.

Feeling himself shaking, from fear or excitement he could no longer tell, Brooks hefted his belaying pin as he searched for an enemy, mindful to stay behind Bryant as instructed. He had followed Bryant up a rope at the stern of the *Elita*, with Murphy close below. The Irishman's quips about the size of Bryant's backside as they climbed had raised a smile but all mirth was forgotten as they heaved themselves onto the deck of the enemy ship. Though the French had concentrated their numbers at the centre of the ship, presumably because they expected an attack where the hull was lowest to the water, they quickly swarmed up to the quarterdeck to meet the assault.

Leading the English assault, Lieutenant Corbin had been

the first to set foot on the *Elita* and, skilfully brandishing his sword, immediately set about carving a clear area around the grapples his crew were using to join him. Brooks saw that four corpses already lay at his feet.

Edging forward in Bryant's footsteps, Brooks glanced nervously from side-to-side, wary of a sudden attack from some filthy French sailor. He did not have long to wait, as a man with thick greasy black hair ducked under Bryant's cutlass, skipped to one side and then rushed forward. Brooks felt his heart quicken as he raised his club to meet the man's own and they crashed together with a wooden thud just inches from Brooks' head. Already fired with adrenaline from the fight on the beach, not to mention the nerve-wracking crossing of the cove, Brooks cried out as he tried to hold back the club with his own. Taking a step forward, he kneed the man in the groin, causing him to double up. His weapon now free, Brooks swung with all his strength at the man's skull, the soft crunch causing him to blanch with nausea.

The man sank to the deck and Brooks dashed forward to aid Bryant who, though making good account of himself, was swinging his blade as he tried to keep two more enemy sailors at bay. Brooks swung his club downwards, connecting with the arm of one of them. The man snarled in pain and turned to face the boy, thrusting forward with his cutlass. The sword punched through empty air as Brooks turned back and the man advanced to keep pace.

Seeing the sailor raise his cutlass for a vicious swing, Brooks held up his club to block the blow but icy cold terror began to pump through his veins as the sword sliced cleanly through his weapon. Now defenceless, Brooks stumbled backwards as the sailor leered at him, keen to snatch a quick victory before returning to more competent foes.

Fighting to keep his eyes open while he met his fate, Brooks was as equally surprised as the sailor when a whistle of metal flew through the air between them and a knife planted itself squarely in the man's chest. Before any more thoughts registered in Brooks' mind, he saw Murphy step inside the sailor's guard, pinning his sword arm with an elbow while grabbing his hair and forcing his head backwards. A blade was in Murphy's other hand and he repeatedly stabbed the man in the stomach, blood soon flowing freely as the strength ebbed from the Frenchman. Murphy let him sink to the deck before putting a foot on his chest to pull out his knife. Grabbing the dying sailor's cutlass, he tossed it to Brooks with a wink.

"There you go, lad," he said. "You'll do better with a proper weapon, I fancy!"

Casting a doubtful look at the long metal blade he now held, Brooks tried to remember if Bryant had taught him anything about swordplay. Eying the mayhem around him, he shrugged, figuring he could use it as a sharp club, and let finesse be damned.

The English now had their full weight of numbers on the quarterdeck and commanded about half its area. The Lieutenant still led the attack, though even Brooks could see that he favoured his left leg and was beginning to slow down under the exertion. Ever mindful of the young lad in their keeping, Bryant and Murphy stood either side of Brooks and the three friends fought together, forming a tight wedge that the French found impossible to break. Pushing forward, they began to take ground.

Swinging the unfamiliar cutlass, Brooks soon found it much better suited for blocking attacks and though his parries were clumsy, the presence of two competent fighters to his flanks served to keep him free from harm.

He also appreciated the weapon's reach and more than once he found himself able to thrust forwards to skewer an enemy who was concentrating his attention on one of his friends. Even if he did not score a fatal wound, the distraction usually proved enough for Murphy or Bryant to finish off the attack. One step at a time, they moved forward across the quarterdeck, aware that the other English sailors were making similarly good progress.

Making their way past the *Elita's* double wheel, they fought, leaving a trail of dead or dying sailors on the deck behind them, until they faced just three Frenchmen who had been driven back against the railing of the quarterdeck. A cry went up behind them as the English sailors realised they had all but taken this part of the ship. One of the French spat at them and redoubled his efforts, forcibly pulling his comrade forward to meet blades with Bryant and Murphy. The third, doubting his chances, put one hand on the railings and threw himself over to drop onto the main deck below.

Brooks tried thrusting forward at the man fighting Murphy, hoping to give his friend a little advantage but the sailor twisted away and knocked his blade sideways, the clash numbing Brooks' arm. Murphy stabbed forward but quickly withdrew his hand as the Frenchman's sword cut downwards, missing his arm by a fraction of an inch. The sailor twirled his cutlass with some expertise, creating a singing web of metal as his blade sliced through the air, forcing Murphy to give ground until the Irishman, refusing to back away further, tossed a knife in the air, caught it by its blade and then threw it directly at the man's head. The cutlass whipped round, knocking the knife aside but the man was too slow for Murphy's second throw, which caught him in the stomach. Grunting, the sailor looked down at the blade, giving Brooks all the opportunity he needed to drive his cutlass into the man's side.

Bobbing his head in thanks, Murphy clapped Brooks on the shoulder, who smiled nervously in return.

"I declare, lad, you are getting the 'ang of this," Murphy said.

Having heard many tales from his fellow crew throughout the *Whirlwind's* voyage, Brooks had heard of the fire that instilled itself in the hearts of men during battle. This was the first time he had truly felt it. He had faced too many close scrapes to be anything other than aware of his own mortality but Brooks could feel something changing inside of him. It dawned on him that, if he could survive this battle, he would no longer be a boy amongst men, but an equal to the rest of the crew. That, he felt, was something worth fighting for.

Bryant still battled his opponent, who had learned enough tricks with the sword to keep the large man off balance enough to halt any finishing blow, and they turned to aid their friend. A cry to his left caused Brooks to glance away for a split second and he saw his Lieutenant near the stairs leading down to the main deck, crouched as he faced a French soldier who wielded a long chain that he swung above his head. Corbin's left arm hung limply at his side and he was in obvious pain. He watched as the chain swung quickly in a tight circle, before it snaked out to connect with Corbin's arm once more. The force of the blow sent him flying to the deck, where he landed heavily. Looking up at his attacker, Corbin vainly raised his sword to ward off the next blow.

Without knowing quite what he was doing, Brooks leapt forward, skipping past Murphy who had already engaged Bryant's opponent, trying to keep the man occupied until his friend could land a telling blow.

Running the few yards between himself and the prone

Lieutenant, Brooks found himself standing over Corbin, the French sailor looked at his new foe in some surprise. That did not halt his attack, however, and the chain whistled through the air at head height. Instinctively, Brooks raised his cutlass to block the attack but was perturbed to see the chain wrap itself round the blade and only his adrenaline-fuelled reflexes saved him as the metal links whipped across his face, drawing a line of blood across the bridge of his nose.

Blinking back tears, Brooks tried to wrench his sword free but his strength proved no match for the larger sailor's, who pulled hard, nearly throwing Brooks off his feet. Deciding not to fight on equal terms, Brooks gave up trying to free his weapon, satisfied that the Frenchman could not use his chain either. Lowering a shoulder, he threw himself forward, catching the sailor completely off guard. He ran into the man, who tripped as he back pedalled, trying to keep his ground. They both experienced a brief second of weightlessness as they fell over the stairs behind them, before landing with a heavy crash on the wood of the main deck.

The French sailor was obviously winded by the fall and Brooks felt giddy from the impact but he recovered quickly. Straddling the man to pin him in place, Brooks rained down punch after punch into his face, smashing his nose and lips until blood began to flow freely. Gathering his wits, the man snarled and grasped one of Brooks' wrists but his own blood made the grip slippery. Wresting his arm away, Brooks spied the man's chain to one side and reached for it, taking a hammer-like punch to the chest for his effort.

Fighting back the pain, Brooks grabbed the man by the hair and wrapped the chain round his throat, quickly tightening the loop before the man could force his fingers under the metal links. Pulling with all his strength, Brooks forced the chain to dig into the man's neck, cutting off his windpipe. Turning red, then purple, the man lashed out at Brooks, who ignored the steadily weakening blows. The last strike was more of a slap across his bloody cheeks as the man finally gave his last.

Panting, Brooks stared into the dead man's face, barely aware of the battle that raged across the entire length of the main deck. He started as he felt someone grab his shoulder, and he fumbled for his cutlass, trying to free it from the chain.

"Whoa there, lad!"

It took Brooks a second to recognise the voice as that of his Lieutenant, and he looked up into the man's face which beamed with delight.

"I owe you my thanks. You are a credit to his Majesty's Navy!"

His heart still racing from the fight, Brooks could do no better than mumble his thanks, but Corbin seemed to understand as he ruffled his hair.

"Now, lad, you think you have it in you to kick the rest of these Frenchies off this ship?"

Brooks finally found his voice. "I'll be right behind you, Sir!"

"Come then!"

His arm still hanging wounded at his side, Corbin rushed into the melee of the main deck with a challenging cry, his sword rising and falling with a new found energy. Brooks stood to follow him and caught sight of Murphy and Bryant rushing to descend the stairs from the quarterdeck. Murphy had an odd twinkle in his eye.

"Saw that, we did!" he said. "You done well there, Brooks. Saved Corbin 'imself from certain death! Only thing better than that would be savin' the Cap'n!"

Bryant smiled widely. "That's right – I'm thinking there will be some favours coming your way when we set sail later, lad!"

Standing, Brooks shook his cutlass free, letting the chain drop to the deck. He tried to shrug off the complements but a smile forced itself onto his face. He knew he had done well.

"Still," said Bryant. "That will be enough heroics for one day. Don't tempt fate. Stick with me and Murphy from now on, and we'll get through this fight alive." He looked into the press of sailors battling one another mere yards away. "Come, let's make an end of this. We can't let the Lieutenant have all the fun to himself."

"Aye, t'would be a shame 'im dyin' now," said Murphy. "Before 'e 'as a chance to properly thank Brooks!"

Unlike the smaller *Whirlwind*, the forecastle of the *Elita* was raised above the main deck, in the same manner as the quarterdeck at the stern. This worked in Havelock's favour, as it allowed him to lead his men in a bloody fight that eventually saw them victorious on the forecastle, having swept it clear of all resistance. A half dozen of the crew that had rowed with him lay on the deck but this part of the French frigate now belonged to them.

Standing at the top of the stairs that led down to the main deck, Havelock quickly judged the state of the battle. Across from him, he saw that Corbin was already leading his men down from the quarterdeck, having successfully taken that ground too. However, in the centre of the main deck, the English were taking a dreadful beating. The French had massed in number there and, with one boat missing from the frontal assault, they had obviously found it easy to attack his sailors as they tried to clamber up their boarding ropes. A few had made it and managed to create a small perimeter that permitted their remaining shipmates to climb on board as well. Once on the deck, they immediately found themselves surrounded by more than a hundred angry Frenchmen eager to exact justice for the slaughter on the beach.

A loud voice called out in French, ordering the enemy sailors balance the defence, from what Havelock could make out. He quickly found the source of the shout, a tall Frenchmen dressed in the fine braided uniform of a Captain. The man had not yet entered battle directly but was directing men with his sword to meet Corbin's flank attack. Seeing another of his sailors fall to a French cleaver, Havelock spied his only chance to gain victory and take the *Elita*.

"Come on!" he cried to the men still on the forecastle as he jumped down the stairs, sword high in the air. They quickly fanned out to engage the French from a new direction, but Havelock made a bee line for the opposing Captain. Just a few yards from the man, Havelock stopped and, saluting with his sword, called out.

"Monsieur."

The French officer turned round to face Havelock, who was struck by how young he appeared. No scars graced his face and his skin appeared to have survived the rigours of sea life without blemish. Havelock might have presumed he was a junior officer, were it not for the uniform and something in his eyes that spoke of both experience and wisdom.

"Captain," the Frenchman said, acknowledging Havelock with a slight nod of the head. He placed his off-hand on his hip in the traditional French duelling pose and raised his sword point forward. Around them the battle seethed, with the British gaining a new vigour now that more of them had entered the fray.

"I have the pleasure of addressing Captain Guillot?" said Havelock.

"Indeed, Sir. You have me at a disadvantage."

"Captain Havelock, of his Majesty's Navy."

"I will accept your surrender now, Captain Havelock. Your men are outnumbered."

Havelock smiled. "You will find it takes more than a good thrashing to beat an English crew, Monsieur."

"So be it."

With a grace Havelock found admirable, the Frenchman lunged forward with his blade, its shining edge glittering in the light of the *Elita's* lanterns. With a flick of his wrist, Havelock brushed the point of the sword past him, then reversed the stroke to slash across his opponent's chest. Seeing the strike, Guillot stepped backwards and once again gave Havelock a slight nod.

"You have some skill in the sword, Captain Havelock."

"You will find English officers to be quite well trained," said Havelock, closing the distance between them to lunge himself. Guillot accepted the attack and their blades met with a loud metallic ring again and again, as they made stroke and counterstroke, each sensing in the other an enemy to be respected.

Guillot feinted to the right and, drawing Havelock's guard as he intended, struck suddenly with an upward swing. Havelock jerked his body from the sudden blow but, off balance, he failed to parry Guillot's next attack, which sliced his left thigh. Grunting, he felt the blood start to flow, staining his leggings. Though painful, he did not feel he had been crippled by the blow and he matched the Frenchman's strike with several hard swings that forced Guillot backwards. Each was checked by a skilful block or dodge, but Havelock allowed his rage to guide him for a brief moment, using his anger to give him strength.

He paused in the assault for a brief instant to avoid a coil of rope snaking across the deck but Guillot was waiting for a respite. Again, he lunged with perfect skill, the point of his blade driving for the centre of Havelock's face. Havelock sensed the oncoming blade rather than saw it and tilted his head to one side. Though he avoided having his skull skewered, the point still dug painfully into his cheek, drawing a deep line of blood that quickly drenched the side of his face. This time, it was Havelock's turn to back off a couple of steps.

Still keeping his off-hand at his hip, Guillot started to circle Havelock, looking for an opportunity to finish the Englishman off. For his part, Havelock started balefully at his opponent, not blinking as he waited for the next attack, determined to force Guillot's hand.

Guillot obliged and stepped forward to launch a series of blows aimed at Havelock's head, shoulders and chest. Had Havelock been observing the Frenchman in a gentlemanly duel, perhaps in London, he might have described those swings as an almost beautiful display of swordsmanship. Here, on board an enemy ship in the South Atlantic, that skill could prove deadly. Purely on the defensive, Havelock parried each attack in turn, not seeking to riposte and turn the tables until Guillot relented.

After a few seconds that stretched into eternity for Havelock, Guillot finally stopped and, once again, stepped back. No longer caring about the conduct of gentlemen in duels, Havelock did not allow him to retreat and instead took two steps up to the man, grabbing his sword arm with one hand. He struck forward with his other hand, smashing his sword's gold-laden hilt into Guillot's face.

Crying out loud in both pain and surprise, Guillot staggered backwards, before tripping over the coiled rope, his sword clattering to the deck. He looked up with an expression that Havelock thought was somewhat disapproving, a line of blood trailing down from a smashed lip. Havelock stood over the man, the point of his sword on Guillot's chest.

"I will accept your parole now," he said.

Guillot sighed and then nodded, slowly reaching for his sword, then offering it to Havelock, hilt first. "D'accord."

"Order your men to stand down."

Rattling out a series of instructions in his own language Guillot commanded his men to drop their weapons and surrender. The British crew cheered mightily as soon as they realised their Captain had been victorious in his duel. Just a few seconds ago, many had been convinced they had been about to die and their elation was genuine and heartfelt.

"Mr Corbin!" Havelock shouted, and the Lieutenant quickly ran to his Captain's side. Aware of blood trickling down his neck and into his tunic, Havelock withdrew a handkerchief from a pocket and held it to the side of his face, trying to stem the flow.

"The ship is ours, Sir," he said. "Congratulations!"

"Save the celebration, Lieutenant, we still have work ahead of us. Make sure the French crew are disarmed and then have them escorted to the shore."

"You are marooning my men?" said Guillot as he stood to face Havelock. "What kind of man are you?"

"Monsieur, I fear your men were too successful in their defence of both shore and ship," said Havelock. "I do not have enough crew to guard them and I fear there would be some among them eager to turn the tables against us while at sea."

Guillot seemed set to protest but Havelock raised his hand before continuing. "However, it is not my intention to doom anyone. You have many wounded on the beach that we could not take with us anyway – your men will be able to look after them. We will supply them with food and water from your own hold and I believe they will be able to forage for anything else on this island. You will return to England with us and, once there, I will ensure the French Navy hears of your crew's location. That is the best I can do for you."

"In light of the wounded on the beach, I find this acceptable, Captain Havelock."

"Good. Mr Corbin, get the French on the boats but make sure they are escorted. We have our own wounded to bring back from the beach, remember."

"Right you are, Sir," said Corbin as he ran off to fulfil his Captain's wishes.

"Mr Wynton!" Havelock called out but this time he was met with silence. Instead, Kennedy approached him.

"Beggin' your pardon, Captain."

"What is it, Mr Kennedy?" said Havelock, though given the Bosun's presence on the *Elita*, he had already guessed the news.

"I saw Mr Wynton's boat sink under fire as we rowed. I've already told some men to keep an eye out for survivors as they take the Froggies back to the beach, but I didn't see any survivors."

Havelock sighed. He had lost men and officers before but this enterprise was starting to demand too high a price. "Very good, Mr Kennedy. Gather a few men and make a quick search of this ship. Watch out for any remaining crew below decks and report to me of her condition."

As men, both French and British, began to scatter across the deck to their duties or off ship to the boats waiting below, Havelock and Guillot were left alone. It was the French Captain who broke the silence between them.

"A fine series of attacks, Captain Havelock," he said. "You will no doubt be commended upon your return to Portsmouth. Or do we go to London?"

"You know I will not tell you that yet. And this mission has had a heavy price."

"C'est la guerre," said Guillot simply. He paused, thinking, and then continued. "The name Havelock. Have I heard it before?"

"Perhaps. My grandfather..."

"Ah, yes, Admiral Havelock. The scourge of the Southern Seas, the Terror of the French."

"I am familiar with my own family's history, Monsieur."

"And brave butcher of colonists..."

Havelock gave Guillot a sour look but the Frenchman pretended not to notice.

"Yes, the name Havelock is well known to the French Navy. And now his grandson sails the same seas where those tortured souls met their end. I wonder if you will survive to be feted in England?"

Something about Guillot's tone made Havelock's expression change to one of curiosity.

"Is there something you want to tell me?"

Guillot shrugged. "A man must live with his own conscience, and maybe his family's as well. As I said, we are at war. Then as much as we are now. In any event, it is no longer my place to avenge the deaths of my countrymen."

"I am not sure I understand."

"Perhaps there is nothing to understand. You are the victor and I am but your prisoner."

Havelock was not sure if the man was mocking him. A

little frustrated, he pushed on. "Is there anything about the state of this ship you will tell me?"

"I have nothing to hide from you now, Captain. I am a French officer alone on an English ship."

"And?"

"Your first attack against us was most impressive," Guillot said. "A fine de-masting shot. I presume that was deliberate. Still, as you now know, we had the advantage of this island which we used to make repairs. You'll find she still sails well, as we had prepared new masts sometime earlier. There are still gun carriages to replace or repair and some regions of the hull are not all they should be. Still, the *Elita* will get you to England, and with good speed. Just don't think of taking her into battle, though I presume that is not your plan, given how few men you have."

"I guessed as much. Most efficient, Monsieur, you are to be commended for your efforts."

"All wasted now, with the *Elita* in English hands."

"As you say, it is war."

Havelock continued to watch the French crew depart the frigate with their escorts, the landing boats slowly travelling to the beach to offload their prisoners and take on British wounded. Seeing his wounds, one crewman offered to bind his leg, and Havelock gratefully accepted. After a few minutes, Kennedy emerged from below decks and, saluting Havelock with a crooked finger, he made his report.

"It's a pig sty, Sir. In fact, I wouldn't keep me pigs in these conditions."

Havelock cast a sideways look at Guillot, but the Frenchman seemed unapologetic.

"We can make her proud during the voyage home," Havelock said.

"It will take the whole trip and then some, and that ain't me grumbling, Captain. It really is that bad. The great cabin is in good shape though and the galley is well-stocked. You'll be eating fine, if you can live with the stink, Sir."

"My least concern right now, Mr Kennedy. Any surprises?"

"Both gun decks are a mess. At a push, we can put up a fight, but I wouldn't want to meet anything more than an armed merchantman on the way back. Didn't see any stragglers but I would want to do a more thorough search later."

"Granted."

"And the hold is a pit of foulness, Sir. Not sure what we can do about that until we put into port. Still, it seems fairly full – should make the lads happy, with prize money and all."

"Then it seems like we have been successful in our mission. Start organising the watches, Mr Kennedy, and then... what is going on there?"

The first boat had returned to the *Elita* and its crew, including Lieutenant Corbin, were just clambering onto the main deck. One of them was drenched in blood and seemed to be raving. Though his shipmates tried to calm him down and attend to his wounds, he refused to be placated.

"The Cap'n, I gotta see the Cap'n!"

Frowning, Havelock spoke quietly to Kennedy. "Bosun, bring that man to me."

The man seemed exhausted and though he had collapsed to the deck, he kept repeating his need to talk to his Captain. Kennedy tried to quieten him down but gave up as the man's protests grew in volume. Instead, Kennedy hooked an arm under his shoulder and, supporting the man's weight, walked him across the deck to face Havelock.

The man's eyes opened wide in relief when he saw his Captain. His face was a wash of blood and Havelock could see he had many more wounds across his body. He was amazed the man still had any strength left within him.

"Cap'n, thank the Lord! They slaughtered all of us, even chasin' us through the jungle!"

"Calm down, sailor," said Havelock, trying to quieten the man down with a steady, even tone. "Go slowly, you are not making sense. Are you saying there are still French crew from the beach who can fight?"

"No Sir, I wasn't fightin' on the beach. I was one of them that was left behind on the *Whirlwind*."

Even before the man's next words left his lips, a now familiar cold hand gripped the pit of Havelock's stomach.

"The *Whirlwind*, Sir. She's gone. Sunk,' he said, beginning to grow hysterical again. "That death hulk, the *Deja*, came speedin' out o' nowhere. It was on us before we could do nuffin'."

Seeing the few crewmen on deck look up sharply at this, Havelock grabbed the man's collar and jerked him hard. "For God's sake, man, keep your voice down!" Thinking hard, he man-handled the wounded sailor towards the quarterdeck and, dragging him up the stairs, faced him directly. He was aware that Kennedy, Corbin and Guillot had followed them.

"Now, calmly – and quietly – tell me what happened."

"Sir, it was dreadful, ain't never seen nuffin' like it. That death ship, it moved so fast. Its guns started blazin' and we felt the *Whirlwind* holed almost straight away. Then it smashed into us and the dead swept over us. We were too few! They just tore us apart, in minutes! Mr

Hague was killed first, 'e was tryin' to hold 'em back!"

"There were survivors though?"

"A few of us jumped overboard and swam for the island – the ship was already lost and sinkin', Cap'n, I swear! But the damned zombies followed us!" The sailor panted for breath and swallowed before continuing. "We ran through the trees, tryin' to reach you but they took us, one by one. I 'eard the screams of me mates as they fell. One came at me, but I fought it off. Took its 'ead off, I did."

The man began coughing and Havelock motioned to Kennedy to take him below decks for care. Judging by the state of his wounds, Havelock guessed that he would not last the night. He looked at Corbin and Guillot. The Lieutenant seemed pale as he tried to make sense of the news. The Frenchman raised an eyebrow.

"The *Deja*? That name is also well known in the French Navy, Captain Havelock. Just what is it you have awoken?"

For once, Havelock had no answer.

"It seems as though the sins of the father will face justice after all," said Guillot. "I fear you have doomed every man on this ship."

"Captain Guillot, you will go below deck! I will instruct my Bosun to make you comfortable."

"A man of honour might offer himself in order to save his crew."

"That offer has already been made. It was deemed insufficient."

"Ah, then you already have some measure of the enemy you now face?" said Guillot.

"More than you can imagine."

"I think this is something you cannot defeat."

Havelock was grim. "We'll see."

Guillot seemed ready to argue the point but instead, he shrugged then descended the stairs to the main deck to seek new quarters. Corbin was still silent and Havelock had to shake him by the shoulder to get his attention.

"Lieutenant, assemble the men," said Havelock.

"Sir, the *Whirlwind*..."

"Get a grip of yourself, man! We still have the *Elita*, a larger and more powerful ship. The mission will still be deemed a success by the Admiralty, but we have to leave now! Thanks to that man's ravings on deck, the crew will already know the fate of the *Whirlwind* and what pursues us. I must get them on side, and quickly. Call them to assemble. Now!"

Corbin started to move slowly away but he soon picked up pace and, after having found his voice, called for Kennedy to gather the crew on the main deck. Havelock impatiently waited for them to appear below him and noted that more than a few threw surly looks in his direction. He could not entirely blame them, for the night's expedition had already cost them many friends and comrades and now they had lost their ship. Corbin returned to his side on the quarterdeck as he began to speak, and some crew were still climbing on board from one of the landing boats, the cries of the wounded punctuated his words.

"Brave sailors of the King's Navy," he said, deliberately avoiding addressing them as the men of the *Elita*. "We have suffered many losses tonight but look at what you have achieved! This fine frigate had a crew that outnumbered us by more than two to one, and yet it is now in our hands. I swear to you, there are perhaps just two or three other crews in the entire fleet that could have done what we have. You are all heroes, the best of what is British and a credit to the nation!"

He paused and a deathly silence hung in the air, broken only by the occasional cry or whimper from a wounded sailor. Most of the faces that looked up at him were expressionless, their owners thoroughly exhausted. Others glared with outright hatred.

"You have heard the... regrettable news of the *Whirlwind* and its demise. I, myself, am saddened by its loss. However, our mission is now complete, and we set sail for England! I have been informed that this ship's hold is full and so the prize money will flow like water when we return home. You will all be wealthy! Now, steel yourselves for one final journey as we make the trip home."

A few weary nods met his words, but otherwise the crew remained silent. Havelock inwardly cursed, knowing he would have trouble with discipline on the voyage home. Even the thought of great riches did little to raise the morale of his crew, and that meant more than one sailor was considering mutiny. The only consolation was that things would get easier the closer they sailed to England and the prize money they were all now due. Of course, he would have to face a court martial for the loss of the *Whirlwind* before any money would be paid, but that was something he would gladly face if he could just make it home safely.

"Mr Corbin, prepare to set sail."

The Lieutenant looked at him quizzically, leaning across to speak quietly.

"Sir, we still have wounded on the beach. We need just a little more..."

"Now, Mr Corbin," said Havelock, looking at him meaningfully. "We have no more time!"

Corbin opened his mouth to say something, then closed it as it dawned upon him just what Havelock meant. He glanced through the night towards the entrance of the cove, half-expecting to see the dark mass of the *Deja* lurking at its edge, waiting to send the *Elita* to the bottom of the sea. Reluctantly, he nodded.

"I understand, Captain." He turned to face the crew. "Prepare to set sail!"

CHAPTER ELEVEN

Together, Bryant, Murphy and Brooks stared at the wreckage of the lower gun deck, gazing at the smashed gun carriages, dislodged cannon and broken fittings. Their elation at having been given one of the heavy 24 pounders to work had quickly crumbled when they saw their working environment. Murphy had made a great show of clasping a rag to his nose and mouth as they went below decks but they were all staggered to see just how much damage had been done to the *Elita* during its duel with the *Whirlwind*.

"You can see now why the Frogs ran from us," said Brooks.

"Aye, lad," said Bryant. "Only a few of their big guns are still serviceable starboard. One quick turn from the Captain, and they would have been defenceless. And now we have to clean up the mess."

Murphy removed the cloth from his face but gagged and quickly replaced it. "Of all the foulness," he said, his voice muffled. "When did they last clean this ship?"

"It is entirely possible that it has never been properly cleaned," said Bryant, shaking his head in mutual disbelief. "They'll get some ventilation going once we set sail. Until then, you'll just have to get used to it."

"I ain't never gettin' used to this."

Brooks cast a look around the deck, eying up the huge guns that dwarfed those he was used to on the *Whirlwind*. He could already imagine the back-breaking work of resetting the heavy weapons back onto their carriages, and further down the deck, he could see two other gun crews debating the task as well. "So, where do we start?" he asked.

Bryant sighed. "Might as well take the nearest," he said. "Look, this one is only dislodged from its mountings. The carriage itself looks fine. Murphy, see if you can find us a good bit of rope. It will be easier winching the gun from the rafters than lifting it with our bare hands."

Murphy scuttled off into the shadowy recesses of the lower gun deck as Bryant bent low over the gun carriage to see if the wood had been split by the weight of its cannon. He became aware of a presence behind him and guessed a member of one of the other gun crews was looking for advice or a favour. He was about to stand up when an all too familiar voice floated down to him.

"Bryant, been lookin' for you, man," said Jessop. "We need to talk."

"I'm busy."

"You 'eard what 'appened to the *Whirlwind*. Too fine a ship to be lost to them dead Froggies. But that is exactly what the Cap'n 'as gone and done!"

Knowing he would regret it, Bryant stood up and faced Jessop, sitting himself on the gun carriage.

"I told you before, Jessop. I know what you are after, and I ain't interested "

"The Cap'n is leadin' us straight to our deaths," said Jessop insistently. "You know it and I know it. We've already lost a good two-thirds of our crew."

"At least." Murphy's voice rang out from somewhere in the shadows.

"At least! You see, even the little Irishman knows it!"

"Jessop, I am serious," said Bryant, pointing a finger towards the burly man. "This is hanging talk."

In return, Jessop rolled his eyes. "An' tell me this, Bryant. Just what is the difference between *possibly* 'anging from a yard arm and definitely gettin' a rusty sword in the gut from a Frog who just don't know when to lie down an' die, eh?"

"I know what you are saying..."

"You want your old mate Murphy to die this day? Or Brooks? What about Brooks, eh, does the young lad deserve to meet 'is end?"

Uncomfortable at having been brought into the conversation, Brooks looked from Jessop back to Bryant, but stayed silent.

"You don't 'ave to do anythin'," said Jessop. "Just a word or two 'ere and there. I got me lads on side but the crew likes you. You'll pull the rest round."

"And then?"

"We'll take 'em by surprise!"

Bryant could not help himself from giving a short laugh. "Jessop, do you really think the Captain ain't expecting something? He has had too much sea beneath him to know something ain't up with the crew."

"Well, maybe," said Jessop. "But it makes no difference anyway. The officers 'ave been dyin' alongside us, an' there's just a few of 'em left. We'll take care of the Captain, and that Froggie officer too. Corbin'll 'ave to go – shame, as I sort of liked 'im. But it 'as to be done clean. All officers 'ave to go."

By now, the other two gun crews had heard what was being discussed and they moved up the deck to lend their weight to the argument. All Jessop's men, Bryant could sense the mood turn dark quickly.

"It's them or us, plain an' simple," said one.

"Come on, Bryant," said another. "The *Whirlwind* 'as gone, an' that death 'ulk is in the area, we know. It's comin' for us right now."

"That's right," said Jessop, bolstered by his support. "We ain't got no choice. We act now, or die today!"

Taking a deep breath, Bryant stood up to stare Jessop

squarely in the eyes. "My answer has not changed," he said. "I will not aid a mutiny in any way. But hear me well, Jessop – you are on a fool's errand with your plan. The Captain is smarter than you and, whether you believe it or not, he is tougher than you. If you attack him, he will cut you down. And then make mincemeat of your friends. We all saw how he fought against the French." He cast a meaningful look at Jessop's co-conspirators and was a little gratified that at least a couple of them began to look doubtful.

"Can I at least rely on your silence?" said Jessop, and Bryant saw the man begin to clench his fists, as if he were readying himself for a fight if he heard the wrong answer. Though he was not swayed by the implied threat, Bryant understood well the code upheld among shipmates.

"You are going to regret what you do, Jessop, but I ain't no tell-tattle. Go seek death at the Captain's hands if you must. I won't interfere."

"But I will." The new voice from the near end of the gun deck caused them all to whirl round in surprise. Jessop groaned softly when he saw the lithe form of the Bosun step into the lantern light.

"Ah, I ain't got no argument with you, Mr Kennedy," he said.

Kennedy did not miss a beat as he stepped up to Jessop and prodded him in the chest with a finger. "If you 'ave a problem with the Cap'n, you see me about it first. Get past me an' the Cap'n will hear your complaints."

Bryant moved back slightly as he saw Kennedy was poised on the balls of his feet, ready to react to any move Jessop made. He grabbed Brooks' sleeve and pulled him back as well.

Jessop grinned at Kennedy. "Ah, it don't 'ave to be like this," he said. "You can see what is goin' on, surely?"

"Jessop, you're an ignorant bully, which is a shame, as you 'ave guts and the makins of a good sailor about you. Right now we need every man we got, so get back to your guns and make us ready for battle should that damned ship make another appearance."

"An' if I refuse, Bosun?"

"Then I told you before. You want some o' the Cap'n, you got to get through me first. An' don't you think I won't be enjoyin' it!"

Letting the challenge hang between them for a few seconds, Jessop smirked then half-turned away from Kennedy. He sprang round like a coiled spring, aiming a meaty fist squarely at Kennedy's nose but the Bosun had been ready for the ploy. He ducked under the punch and then exploded into action, launching a series of heavy blows into Jessop's body, the thump of each hit echoing across the gun deck. Jessop exhaled noisily but forced himself to stand up straight, just in time to take a blow to the chin which sent him reeling.

One of Jessop's crew mates took a step to join the fight but was arrested by Bryant's firm grip on his shoulder.

"This is between Jessop and the Bosun," he said.

"Aye, that's right," said Kennedy. "What about it, Jessop? You 'ad enough? You wantin' to be droppin' this matter and getting' back to work?"

As a reply, Jessop roared and charged Kennedy, ignoring another blow to the face as he crashed into the man. They fell, arms and legs flailing as each sought to get a quick advantage. Jessop's crewmates surrounded them, shouting out words of encouragement. Curiosity getting the better of them, Bryant, Brooks and Murphy joined them, but remained silent.

On the wooden floor, Jessop had hooked a leg across Kennedy's body, trying to pin him down while he started to rain punches downwards. Kennedy took a few blows to the face and chest before catching Jessop's fist in his hand. Raising his head, he bit down on Jessop's hand, getting a howl of pain for his efforts. Distracted by the blood that now flowed, Jessop relaxed his hold on Kennedy slightly, giving the Bosun the opportunity he had been looking for. Jabbing with a knee, he caught Jessop in the side of the head and knocked him sideways before standing up, fists at the ready for another assault.

Jessop rolled across the deck, panting. Too late, Bryant saw a flash of metal on the floor nearby, a short blade that he guessed one of Jessop's friends had dropped. As he cried a warning to the Bosun, Jessop grabbed the knife and stood, turning to face Kennedy with a look of triumph.

Spitting in disgust at the low tactic, Kennedy remained impassive, merely beckoning Jessop on. All too keen to oblige, Jessop charged forward again, stabbing down at Kennedy's chest. Freed from any excuse to restrain himself, Kennedy watched Jessop's movements closely before springing into action again. He caught the descending knife hand, then twisted his body, forcing his back into Jessop's chest. With his free arm, he hooked his elbow backwards into Jessop's face but instead of letting him stagger backwards, he brought the hand still holding the knife down onto his raised knee.

Again, Jessop cried out in pain and the knife fell from his nerveless fingers. Releasing his grip, Kennedy stooped to pick up the weapon but twisted round as Jessop grabbed him from behind. They struggled for an instant before Jessop managed to curl a foot behind Kennedy's leg and, heaving forward with all his strength, threw the Bosun to the floor again with a solid crash.

Back-swinging with his free hand, Kennedy caught

Jessop across the side of the head, throwing him on his back. In a sudden lunging motion, Kennedy planted the knife firmly in his opponent's chest. Jessop, exhaled one bubbling breath and then fell still.

Leaving the knife in Jessop's chest, Kennedy stood and cast a withering glance at the ring of sailors who had now all fallen silent.

"Anybody else 'ave a problem with 'ow the Cap'n is doin' things?" he said, demanding a response from Jessop's crew. To a man, they avoided his grim stare.

"Thought not," said Kennedy. "Clean that mess up. Then get back to work."

Reluctantly, Jessop's crew started heaving their fallen friend towards an open gun port as Kennedy gave them one last glance and then turned to check on the repair details on the upper gun deck. Bryant's crew slowly drifted back to their own gun carriage, Murphy smiling as he produced a length of stout rope. Brooks was wide-eyed.

"That was incredible," he said. "The Bosun knows how to fight!"

"You don't get to be a Bosun unless you can give as well as you take," said Bryant. "Just you remember that in later years. You never, ever cross the Bosun."

Using the light of the breaking dawn pouring through the windows of the Elita's great cabin, Havelock poured over Guillot's navigational charts. He had to admit, they were most complete. Havelock had heard rumours of French explorers and their accuracy in producing maps of the southern seas, but this was the first time he had seen a set first hand. It was little wonder that a French commerce raider could retain an advantage in these waters.

His impressions of the rest of the ship during his brief tour were less than complimentary, and the frigate had pretty much lived up to every stereotype due a French vessel of war. The cabins used by the officers, including the lodgings of the former Captain in which he stood, were luxurious and well-equipped, and he had already heard reports of the contents of the galley which was stocked with preserved foodstuffs that made the *Whirlwind* seem primitive. There was little doubt that his voyage back to England would be one of the most comfortable journeys he had ever made by sea.

Take one step out of the officers' cabins, however, and Havelock was all too aware of the ship's deficiencies. Leaving aside the damage the *Whirlwind* had done to the frigate in its duel, which his crew would have to work hard to repair while sailing, the *Elita* had not been maintained in a manner befitting a ship of the King's Navy.

Structurally, it was sound and the hull had weathered his earlier attacks well, even if the fixtures and fittings had not. The living conditions, however, were terrible and he did not envy his crew who would have to make the best of them until the *Elita* pulled into port and could be stripped down, from stem to stern. The decks had not been regularly scrubbed, refuse had not been disposed of properly, if at all, and the air had been allowed to linger. Havelock knew that more than a few of his crew would succumb to various maladies over the next few weeks

The one consolation would be that, with so few crew on board, they would have a great deal of individual space, a luxury in itself on board a ship of war. They simply had to live with the dreadful stench that seemed to permeate the very wood of the entire vessel.

The disastrous casualties his men had sustained weighed heavily on Havelock's mind as he turned his attention away from Guillot's charts and back through the large windows of the great cabin. The *Elita* had already raised anchor and was now sailing towards the entrance of the cove, leaving the wounded on the beach behind. So many men were being left behind but far more were already dead, shipmates that had looked to him for wise command and reasonable assurance that they would see the green fields of England once more, whether they were volunteers or pressed. Once on board his ship, it made little difference to Havelock how a man came to be there.

The loss of the *Whirlwind* was a savage blow too and, in some ways, it pained him more than the deaths of British sailors. His claims to the prowess of the frigate had not all been bluster by any stretch, for she had truly been a fine ship, quick across the waves and nimble of turn. The speeches to the crew of prize money and great wealth might also turn to dust, for the loss of any ship in the King's Navy inevitably resulted in a court martial for its Captain, with a board ascertaining the circumstances of its loss. Quite what he could tell them about the *Whirlwind*, he did not know. He began to fervently hope that the tales heard in the Admiralty of Napoleon using the walking dead within his armies in Europe might actually be true. It might lend his own story some credence.

As a replacement ship, the *Elita* could do well, he knew. With a thorough strip down and refitting, along with a new crew, the two gun deck frigate would be both fast and powerful, with few equals in her class. Right now, she was a pale shadow of what she could be. He could feel it in her movements beneath his feet, there was something in the way she rode the waves and made sharp turns that just did not *feel* quite right. It would be hard, sailing on board a ship of such unrealised potential for so long.

Thoughts of returning to England might quickly become academic, of course. The jungle-covered island, now beginning to recede behind the *Elita*, seemed idyllic in the growing rays of the morning sun, but Havelock was not deceived. An evil lurked in these waters and he could feel in his heart that a reckoning was coming. The *Whirlwind* had already been claimed, along with most of his crew, and Dubois would no doubt seek to finish his vengeance. Havelock had not been completely unsympathetic to the plight of the old mariners, their souls doomed by the actions of his own blood.

There would have been some honour in a Captain's sacrifice for the good of his crew but Havelock had come too far now to simply roll over and die, and the encounter with Dubois had ended any possibility of making recompense with the dead. He had already resolved to fight the dead captain and sink his ship in return for what had been done to the *Whirlwind*. History be damned, it was time to live in the here and now. Havelock vowed to ensure his crew and the *Elita* made it back to England safely, death hulk or no.

His military mind began to turn over, considering feints and countermoves that may work against the supernatural horror that pursued him across these waters. He still had an agile ship that could keep the lumbering death hulk off balance, though it was no match for the *Whirlwind* in that area. The *Elita* did have potentially greater armament but the big guns on the lower deck especially would take some time to restore to full working order and, in any case, he did not have the crew to man them all. Initiating or receiving a boarding action was completely out of the question. His crew had only escaped with their lives by the skin of their teeth the last time they had met the hulk and with so few of them left now, the battle would be a foregone conclusion. Havelock had few illusions that the hulk still held hundreds of zombies that had not yet been committed to battle.

He knew he could simply hope that the death hulk and its unholy captain would not notice their departure from these waters but Dubois had so far seemed to know exactly where he was at all times. In any case, he had witnessed the *Deja's* straight-line speed and knew there was not a ship afloat that could outrun it, though he was painfully aware that he was still entirely ignorant as to how long the hulk could sustain such speeds. It had not appeared to be entirely dependant on the wind for motion.

The cannon fire of the *Deja* had been notably sporadic in their last battle, which gave Havelock a little hope, as he knew his return fire might be no better. However the report given by the wounded man who escaped from the *Whirlwind* had seemed to indicate that the hulk was at least capable of co-ordinated fire, and this was a very real concern. He might be happy to chance trading broadsides, fancying the accuracy and speed of his own gun crews to be far superior to those of walking corpses, and French ones at that. The balance would lie somewhere between the skill of his gun crews and the heavy 32-pounders that lined the triple gun decks of the *Deja*, which were far larger than the cannon of this frigate. If they could indeed be fired in unison by Dubois, the *Elita* would be shredded into matchwood in minutes.

It all seemed to come down to ifs and buts, leaving Havelock with few real options. Perhaps he could score a series of lucky hits that would hole the hulk and sink it, or dismast it – if it even needed sails to manoeuvre at the sea, which he was beginning to doubt. Maybe he could outwit Dubois and force his ship to ground on a reef or sand bank. However, the waters around this island seemed clear and deep, typical of a land mass thrust up to the surface by volcanic activity. With Guillot's charts he might be able to find a suitable area off the coast of Africa or further afield but he doubted he would be given enough time to sail that far.

Whatever the outcome of their next encounter, Havelock made himself a solemn promise. He would not make it easy for Dubois to find victory and, if possible, he would save as many of his crew as he could. As a gentleman and officer of the King's Navy, he could do no less.

Footsteps outside the great cabin diverted his attention from the panorama outside and he turned before a sharp rap at the door resounded in the small room.

"Enter!" he said, feeling resolve come back into his voice. Thrusting the door open, Corbin appeared.

"Captain. Sail sighted to larboard," he said.

"Is it our old friend?"

"Yes Sir. Looks like the death hulk has come for us."

Clearing the steps two at a time, Havelock ran up to the quarterdeck, telescope already in hand as he scanned the horizon behind the *Elita*. The jungle island was to their rear larboard quarter but no hulk was in sight. Kennedy waited for both the Captain and Lieutenant, pointing towards the island.

"Saw 'er as we left the cove, Cap'n," he said. "Disappeared as we rounded the island but she'll be back."

Havelock raised his telescope to view the shoreline but saw nothing but sand and trees. Making a decision, he turned to Corbin.

"Full sail, Lieutenant. Let us put some water between us, and that island. At sea, we have options – here, none."

"Aye, Sir. Mr Kennedy?" The Bosun scrambled down the stairs to the main deck, bellowing orders that unfurled canvas and filled the sheets with wind. The *Elita* soon picked up speed noticeably and, despite his sense of foreboding from the impending battle, Havelock began to feel the old thrill of a fast frigate skimming across the waves.

Damn the hulk, he thought. This would be a fine and well-fought battle, whatever the outcome.

A dark shadow appeared to pass over the island, arresting Havelock's attention. Raising his telescope once more, he saw his enemy. Sweeping from behind the curve of the island's shore, the black hull of the *Deja* surged forward, already turning to face the *Elita*. The arrival of the ship seemed to suck energy from the climbing sun and every man on board the frigate felt a blackness descend upon him, chilling his bones.

Now in broad daylight, Havelock had his first clear look at the ship of the line that had chased him all this way. The sails were ragged and though they looked as if they were filled with the wind, their angle appeared all wrong to him, as if Dubois had not cared how his lines were set. The speed the ship drew from the sails, however, could not be denied and an impressive wake extended from its stern, the water churning from the quick passage of something so large. Casting his eyes forward, Havelock studied the hull, trying not to feel intimidated by the triple line of gun decks that could amass a truly terrible weight of firepower. The painted wood was flaking all down its length, with barnacles and sea plants gracing every square yard. More than a few planks along the hull had popped free of their fixtures, robbing the vessel of any atheistic grace – though they seemed to do little to hurt its performance.

Lining the deck and grasping at vantage points on its masts and rigging were the crew. Havelock thought of them more as a horde, a ragged and decaying mass of zombies that soundlessly gesticulated, seeming to jeer and mock the ship they pursued. Adjusting the focus of his telescope, Havelock studied the *Deja's* quarterdeck, searching for his counterpart and took a sharp intake of breath when he realised that Dubois was indeed standing there. Rigid, the zombie Captain's attention fixed on the telescope he held in his mouldering hands, Dubois looked straight back at Havelock. As the two stared at one another, Havelock thought he could make out a chilling grin on the face of his opponent. He lowered his telescope before turning to Corbin.

"Are the crew steady?" he asked.

"They will follow your orders, Captain," said Corbin, not quite evading the question.

"Good. We'll let her follow us a little longer, gauging her speed. I imagine she will close range in good order but let us test the theory first. If we can outrun her, we should."

"I heartily agree with you, Sir."

Havelock cast a glance back at Corbin. "Be prepared to fight, Lieutenant," he said. "I fully expect she will overhaul us and that battle will be inevitable."

"As you say, Sir."

"Good." Havelock rubbed his chin, ignoring the stubble he found there as he watched the hulk sailing towards them. Though it had moved with great speed as it sailed round the island, the *Deja* had now seemed to settle in its pace, matching that of the *Elita's*.

That gave Havelock cause to wonder. He had already

guessed that the warship did not draw on the same winds as he for its sails. Could it be that whatever supernatural source drove it on was limited in some way? Perhaps it was daylight that robbed the ship and its crew of power, or maybe the remaining crew of the *Whirlwind* had damaged it in some way before they fell.

It was equally possible that Dubois was merely toying with him, of course.

Across the deck of the *Elita*, Havelock saw that his crew went about their tasks with a certain mechanical detachment, and he noted that more than one took strenuous pains to avoid casting a look back at their pursuer. He winced involuntarily as it was suddenly made apparent that the main deck and rigging were conspicuously empty of able bodies. The *Elita* was a larger vessel than the *Whirlwind*, true, but the casualties he had sustained would be a major factor in the fight ahead, and one he would have to contend with if victory was to be secured. The first step, he decided, was to instil some backbone into his shaken crew.

"Mr Corbin, gather all men that can be spared," he said. "I wish to address them."

Corbin, called for order and those on the wooden deck looked up at the quarterdeck, while others still working high in the rigging of the sails dutifully relaxed in their efforts to give the Captain their attention. Havelock stepped forward to the railings of the quarterdeck and looked down at them, hesitating for a moment as he marshalled his thoughts.

"I have met Lord Nelson just once," he said, his statement catching the crew off-guard. Expecting to hear another platitude appealing to their own bravery, they leaned forward to hear a tale of the Navy's greatest hero, one who had constantly met and confounded England's enemies. Private stories of the man from officers who met him were rare and always eagerly received by a ship's crew.

"It was perhaps six years ago, while I was First Lieutenant on the *Heracles*." He noticed a couple of nods at this, and recognised two crewmen who had also served on that ship.

"Our ship was part of a squadron that sailed in the Mediterranean, tasked with guarding Nelson's flank as he began his now infamous Battle of the Nile. The night before he sailed to engage the French, Nelson gathered his captains for a fine meal on board his ship, the *Vanguard*, to discuss tactics and stratagems. As commander of the flanking squadron, my Captain, one Thomas Maccalsson, was invited too, and I was lucky enough to be brought along as his escort."

Havelock gave a brief smile as he remembered the evening, the heady company of so many competent Captains, each of them senior enough to command a ship of the line. And then, of course, there was Lord Nelson himself.

"What a place for a First Lieutenant to be!" said Havelock, noting his crew were fixed on his tale. "I kept quiet, as you might imagine, while I listened to the captains talk over a fine roast beef. Ploy and counter ploy was raised and discarded as they argued the best way to achieve victory over the French. Through it all, I watched Nelson. While some tempers frayed, he remained calm, allowing each man to say his piece before moving on.

"Whether it was my fortune or not, he soon spied the quiet Lieutenant at the other end of the table, sipping wine and trying not to be noticed. 'Sir!' he called out to me, silencing the entire company. 'Be you an officer in the King's Navy or not?' I don't mind telling you, as all those experienced eyes turned to me, I was mortified." Havelock noticed a few of his crew chuckling at this image and he nodded candidly. "Aye, there was a time as a young officer when I did all I could not to be the centre of attention." This drew some outright laughs, which Havelock stalled with a raised hand.

"I tripped over my words, amazed that this man, already a legend in the service, was sparing the time to talk to a Lieutenant who would not even be involved in the battle. 'Speak up, Sir!' he said to me. 'Every other man here has told me how he would fight the French and yet you sit there and say nothing! Explain yourself!' Well, how does one respond to that? I tried...

"I started to say that I was but a Lieutenant while every other man present was a post-captain but Nelson dismissed that with a wave. 'Nonsense!' he cried. 'You are a First Lieutenant and hope, I presume, to make Captain one day, with a command of your own, yes? Then explain yourself. How would you fight the French tomorrow?'

"Well, I studied the charts Nelson had laid out in front of us and started to make some noise about drawing up our ships into a line and moving in close to pound the French ships. No doubt I failed on some details and this brought some sniggers from the assembled Captains. I faltered, red-faced, but Nelson rapped a cup on the table to silence them.

"He stood and faced me. 'You need another year or so at sea, lad, but you may show some promise, I'll warrant you that!' Then he said something that, I swear, I will never forget so long as I live. 'Gentlemen,' he said, though he looked at me. 'If you do nothing more tomorrow than place your ship alongside an enemy vessel, you will not go far wrong in my book!'"

Havelock paused as each sailor weighed this in his

mind. "As you know," he went on to say, "Nelson won the battle, setting the tone for our Navy's war against the French right up until this day. I won't lie to you men, you all know something of the terrible nature of the enemy that chases us now. And we have all lost friends and comrades. We will soon be in battle against that dark ship and whether we die or are victorious will be down to what each one of us does. But I say this to you; if you do nothing more than carry on firing your gun or stabbing with your blade, you will not go far wrong in my book!"

The crew cheered, a ragged cry that was borne by their small numbers, as Havelock cast a glance back at the *Deja*, still matching their speed behind them.

"Mr Corbin," he said. "A hard starboard turn on my mark, and get the men to run out what starboard guns we have. I tire of being chased. It is time we made an end of this, one way or another."

Taking a deep breath, Corbin steeled himself and saluted. "Aye Sir, a hard turn it is. On your word."

Corbin quickly got the men working again, and as they prepared to adjust the tack of the sails, he looked back at his Captain, brow raised in anticipation. Taking one more look at the hulk, Havelock turned to Corbin and nodded.

"Now, Lieutenant."

Orders rang out as sailors scuttled throughout the rigging and across the deck as they heaved and tied the sails to new positions while the helmsman spun his wheel. The *Elita* lurched for an instant under the strain of the manoeuvre, then her prow lifted from the waves and swung round to face the direction she had just come from, the whole ship tilting as it turned.

"Two points to larboard, helmsman!" Havelock called out, setting a course that would keep the *Deja* on their starboard side.

Now they sailed towards the hulk that had chased them, few crew could avoid looking up from their work to see their enemy as the two ships rapidly closed. However, Havelock fancied that the feeling of certain doom had gone from them. There were perhaps few who expected to win the coming battle, but he thought they might at least trust him not to send them to their deaths unnecessarily.

For several minutes, Havelock and Corbin watched the distance between the two ships slowly shrink. On the main deck, Kennedy nodded up to Corbin, who turned to his Captain.

"Crew reports the guns are ready, Sir."

"Very good, Mr Corbin. Now we will see what this ship is capable of, though she be only half fighting fit."

The *Deja* continued to close until there was little more than a couple of hundred yards between the two ships. The hulk then seemed to rear out of the water, its deck canting backwards as jets of spray were thrown upwards past the prow. It surged forward with unnatural speed, appearing to make a lunge for the *Elita*. Seeing this, Havelock smiled.

"She'll never turn on to us in time, not at that speed," he said. "Mr Corbin, on my word, fire our guns."

Though the hulk had cleared the remaining distance to the frigate, Havelock was right. It was now going far too fast to make any reasonable turn and the *Elita*, travelling slightly off angle to the vessel, would be carried by the wind straight down its flank. As the ships passed within just a few yards of one another, the British sailors got an all too close look at their enemy, the chilling cries of zombies screaming through broken throats made an eerie sound. All made crude gestures at the crew of the *Elita*, seeming to perform a macabre dance as they clawed the air and bared rotting teeth. Havelock eyed the *Deja* carefully, noting the stinking seaweed dressing the masts, the crumbling railings and various forms of sea life littering the decks. He also watched the gun ports lining the hull of the hulk begin to open but he could already see the cannon would not be run out until his ship had passed them by. Keen to strike the first blow, Havelock gave the order to attack.

"Fire!"

The order was relayed down to the gun decks several times before a massive blast and billowing smoke erupted from the *Elita* as the whole ship shuddered with the recoil. Large holes were blasted into the decaying wood of the *Deja*, and more than a few zombie crew spilled out into the sea. The cheers of the crew on the main deck were quickly overwhelmed by a staccato series of more gun fire, the sporadic shots smashing into the other warship one by one, this time aimed at the upper part of the hull and masts. The dirty sails rippled as shot passed through them and several zombies were annihilated in an instant as a combined quarter ton of metal tore through their massed ranks. Havelock looked quizzically at Corbin.

"What happened there? Why the delayed shot?"

It took Corbin just a second to guess. "Limited crews to man the guns, Sir. Someone must have readied the crewless cannon to fire, running down the deck to touch off the fuses after they had fired the main guns."

Havelock smiled at the ingenuity of his crew. "A pint of rum after the battle to the man who thought of that!" he said. "Still, we won't have enough time to do that again. We'll have to rely on the crewed guns alone."

"Aye, Sir." Corbin stared at the *Deja* as it passed them by. "Did we do any significant damage?"

"The fight is just beginning, Mr Corbin, there will be no

miracle shots here. Bring us about behind her stern and tell the crew to fire when ready."

The *Elita* dipped its prow into the water again before turning, a trait that was beginning to irritate Havelock, as it robbed the ship of a few seconds of manoeuvring. Then it swung round beautifully, presenting a broadside to the rear of the hulk, the rotting wood still sporting the marks of their previous duel in the *Whirlwind*. Once again, the *Elita's* few manned guns roared, and this time Havelock was glad to see large chunks of blackened wood blown clear of the *Deja*, one large section of the upper hull spinning gracefully through the air before it landed in the sea with a large splash.

"Reload, Mr Corbin," said Havelock. "Tell the crews to aim at the waterline. We'll try holing her. If nothing else, it should slow her down on the turns."

As the frigate turned starboard once more to this time race alongside the *Deja*, Havelock could hear orders to reload and aim being relayed to the lower decks. It was with some alarm that he saw the gun ports down this side of the hulk begin to open, one by one. However, they did not fire as the cannon were rolled out and instead seemed to be waiting for an order. Havelock gritted his teeth, knowing a full broadside from a ship of the line could be telling, even to an outsized frigate such as the *Elita*.

He was gladdened to hear his own guns were ready to fire and he nodded at Corbin to proceed. Yet again, explosions and smoke poured from the frigate's broadside and the shots found their mark below the triple line of gun decks on the hulk. Spouts of water were thrown up across its length as some of the fire thudded into the hull below the waterline and elsewhere, massive holes were gouged into the side of the *Deja*. Undismayed by this damage, a few zombies leered from their gun ports until an order silent to those on the *Elita* instructed them to fire.

The titanic roar that belched from the hulk deafened Havelock briefly, and he staggered from the concussion while wreathed in filthy smoke. Men screamed as they were rendered limbless or blasted overboard, while wood splinters flew through the air with equally lethal results. Beneath his feet, Havelock could feel the frigate groan under the battering, its wood shifting in ways it had never been designed to accommodate.

Gasping, Havelock staggered to the helmsman who, thankfully, was still on his feet. "Hard to larboard!" he said. "Take us back around!"

The Elita seemed sluggish in the turn and reluctant to pull away but once the deck crew saw what their Captain was trying to do, they rushed to the rigging to reposition the sails. Havelock watched their efforts but his eye was quickly drawn to the main mast in the centre of the ship. Likely nicked by a shot from the *Deja*, it had an inch wide crack running vertically up its length. Though it seemed to hold, he knew it would not last long under the strain of the sails as they filled with wind.

"Mr Corbin, furl the top'sal and topgallant. Just keep the main'sal flying."

"Aye Sir, but that will rob us of any advantage of speed."

"Regrettable but if the main mast gives, we may be dead in the water. Literally. And run out the larboard guns!"

Continuing its turn, the *Elita* came about as the crew on the gun decks ran from one side of the ship to the other to run out cannon that now faced the hulk. Havelock knew that constant switching of broadsides could not be kept up during battle without exhausting his men but he had dared not risk trading shot with the *Deja* after its initial attack. His first instinct was to get out of its line of fire, then to swing back behind it for another attack on the hulk's wounded stern. If he could throw enough metal into that part of the ship, he would not be able to avoid dealing some serious damage. While the last exchange had dealt his ship a grievous blow in terms of men and guns, his more carefully planned attack would hurt the *Deja* in its mobility. At the end of the day, if he could reduce its ability to make sharp turns, he could pound it at a safe distance until the hulk sank to the bottom of the ocean once more.

The hulk continued to sail away from the *Elita*, and Havelock guessed that Dubois was trying to put some distance between them in order to protect his stern. *You have not reckoned on the accuracy of British gunners*, he thought.

Once more the frigate found itself passing astern of the *Deja*, though at greater range this time and in the opposite direction. The larboard guns kicked the *Elita* as they sent more burning metal through the air, and though some shot missed its mark, creating great geysers of water just behind the hulk, others were aimed to perfection. More debris spun off the back of the *Deja* and Havelock eagerly raised his telescope to inspect the damage.

He barked a short laugh in delight as he looked on to see what his crew had accomplished. The stern of the *Deja* was a complete mess now. Though this insult to its Captain cheered Havelock a great deal he was far more interested in the rudder, which had been shot away with the last volley.

Smiling, he waved Corbin over to his side. "We have her, Mr Corbin," he said, passing the telescope. "Rudderless, she is no longer a match for us. We'll stay in her rear quarter and sink her at our leisure. Pass the word to the crew – we'll take no prisoners for what they have done to us!"

"Shall I get more crew to the gun decks? We can increase the weight of fire with more guns being manned,"

"Yes. But make sure the wounded are tended to first. We now have time on our hands."

"Aye Sir." Corbin turned to enact Havelock's instructions but then stopped, standing absolutely rigid.

Havelock noticed the strange posture in his Lieutenant and frowned. "Something, Mr Corbin?"

At first, Havelock could not hear Corbin's whispered reply. The man then cleared his throat and spoke again.

"Sir... She's *turning*... "

"Impossible," said Havelock, though he sounded less than certain. He took the telescope back from Corbin and raised it to the hulk but he could already see the ship was indeed beginning to come about, for the first time seeming almost graceful in its movements.

"How can she do that?" said Corbin but Havelock had no good explanation. Instead, he thought furiously.

"Lieutenant," he said but Corbin continued to stare at the hulk, now bringing its prow to bear on the *Elita*. "Lieutenant!"

The shout stirred Corbin and he spun round, eyes wide. "Sorry Sir!"

"Make sure the larboard guns are ready. We'll give her a blast at point blank range."

"But then she'll be on us!" said Corbin and Havelock could hear a thin strain of hysteria begin to edge into his voice.

"And then we'll fight! We have beaten her once in an attempted boarding, we'll do it again! Only this time, we have been pounding her steadily. Who knows how many of her accursed crew we have destroyed already?"

"Not enough. It will never be enough!"

Havelock began to notice that more than one sailor was looking up from the main deck and he gave them a meaningful glare that encouraged them to get back to work, before he returned his attention to Corbin. He had fought too long and too hard on this voyage to be scuttled by a shaken officer. Taking a step to put Corbin in-between himself and the rest of the crew so no one else would see what he was about to do, Havelock grabbed the Lieutenant by the collar and pulled him within inches of his own face.

"Pull yourself together, man," he said, voice low but laced with an unmistakable undercurrent of threat. "Remember where you are." He held onto Corbin in this fashion until sanity began to return to the younger man's eyes.

"Now, prepare the larboard guns and ready the men for boarding," Havelock said, slowly and carefully as he released Corbin.

"With respect, Captain," Corbin said as he straightened his jacket. "We hole her and she will not sink. We attack her crew and nothing short of placing them in front of a cannon will kill them. We cannot fight this enemy!"

"And what would you suggest we do, Lieutenant?" said Havelock angrily. "That ship will overhaul us if we try to run. What does that leave? Are we to just lay down here and die?"

Corbin opened his mouth but found he had nothing to say in reply.

"No!" said Havelock. "We will stand and we will fight, and if this battle is ever remembered, history will be our judge! I, for one, refuse to go down without my sword in my hand and a pile of enemies at my feet!"

"This is the doom of us all," said Corbin mournfully.

Havelock bit back his immediate response and took a deep breath before speaking. "Lieutenant, I do not require your consent or your hope. All I require is that you obey my orders and fight!"

Slowly, mechanically, Corbin drew his sword and, after a brief pause, raised it in salute to Havelock. His voice was quiet, almost inaudible as he spoke. "I'll fight, Sir."

"Good. Now make the preparations." Havelock spun away and walked to the railings of the quarterdeck overlooking the sea between the *Elita* and the rapidly oncoming *Deja*. He thumped a fist on the wood in frustration, partly at Corbin's loss of nerve but, most of all, because he cursed the fate that had brought both him and his crew to ruin.

He knew Corbin had been right, in his facts if not in attitude. They faced an enemy ship that could not be sunk, crewed by sailors that were all but impossible to kill. What captain had ever been matched against such an enemy before? All he knew was that if they were to die, what mattered was the manner of their departure, whether they died as brave heroes or craven cowards. If only there were some other means beyond fighting or running, neither of which promised success against the *Deja*.

Havelock blinked. Of course there was a third way, an answer to the horror that could vanquish his enemy, sending Dubois and his nightmare crew back to the bottom of the ocean. It was an unthinkable course of action but that, in itself, gave him an advantage. Dubois could not see it coming, for it bordered on the suicidal. He turned back to Corbin who was just descending the stairs to the quarterdeck, a twinkle in his eye as he started to smile.

"Mr Corbin!" he said. "A moment more of your time, I think."

There was something in Havelock's tone that made Corbin frown with curiosity, and he marched briefly back to learn what the Captain had now concocted.

"A slight change in plans, Mr Corbin, a little addition, if you will permit me," said Havelock, beginning to relish his new thought.

"Sir?"

"Ready the boats, prepare to drop them over starboard. Make sure there are enough ropes to get men to board them quickly when I give the word. Then assemble everyone. The guns will fire once, then their crews will join us. I don't want anyone below decks after the volley."

"I understand, Sir, but what are you saying? We should abandon ship? The hulk will just chase us down in our boats."

"Ah, but therein is the beauty of it," said Havelock, smiling broadly now. "There is one more task I would like you to perform. See to it personally, I don't want any of the crew to see what we are doing until there are zombies swarming all over us. You see, I have had an idea..."

CHAPTER TWELVE

Havelock gave the oncoming hulk one last, disparaging look before he turned to the main deck to set his plan in motion. Corbin had already retreated below to fulfil his duty, though the Lieutenant had looked at Havelock with incredulity as he explained what was required. Corbin had looked set to argue but seemed, at last, to realise that they had few choices left and the unthinkable might be their only salvation, even if it could claim the life of every man on board in the process. Some of the crew, at least, might have a chance of survival.

"Mr Kennedy, my side, if you please."

The Bosun threw the ropes he had been wrestling with to a nearby sailor as they began hoisting one of the boats up into the air in preparation to lower it into the sea. He bounded up to the quarterdeck at Havelock's call, eager to hear the full extent of his Captain's plans. He was to be disappointed.

"Mr Kennedy, I would like you to remain here on the quarterdeck until the Lieutenant returns. He is... completing a special task for me."

"Aye Sir, as you say," said Kennedy. He cast a glance at the hulk, now just a hundred yards away. "Might I be enquirin' as to your intentions, Cap'n?"

Havelock smiled evasively. "Why, Mr Kennedy, I mean to give that unholy ship a damned good thrashing! Now, quick to it, she closes. Give me full sail, Mr Kennedy, I want every ounce of speed we can wring from this fine vessel."

"Full sail? Cap'n, the mainmast is cracked, she won't take much."

"She won't have to, Mr Kennedy, I assure you. But right

now, I need speed!"

Without further comment, Kennedy nodded and shouted down to the main deck, where sailors scuttled to do his bidding, racing up the masts to unfurl canvas while others pulled hard at the rigging. Sails dropped down rapidly, the mainmast creaking ominously above the ship as the wind caught the *Elita* and the sheets billowed forwards. The frigate increased in speed noticeably and Havelock walked to the side of the helmsman as he turned his attention back to the *Deja*, now barely forty yards away. Again, its crew seemed to swarm over the hulk's deck, brandishing rusting weapons or vicious claws as they mimed what they intended to do to each and every crewman on board the *Elita*.

"She's goin' to run us down," said the helmsman under his breath.

"Steady, man," said Havelock in reply. "We will snatch the initiative here. Hold her steady for just a moment more, make them think we are ready to meet our fate... "

The *Deja* ploughed through the waves then, with just thirty yards to go, her prow picked up in its characteristic way as the massive ship laid on its unnatural burst of speed. It was what Havelock had been waiting for.

"Now, helmsman," he said. "Hard to larboard! Cut across her path!"

Nearly caught off guard, Kennedy bawled instructions down to the sailors working the rigging, getting them to adjust the sails to the new course as the *Elita* lurched round. Its speed and sudden movement carried it past the prow of the hulk, and a collective howl erupted from the zombies on board, the sound chilling the hearts of even veteran sailors, as they realised their quarry was escaping. Watching his broadside line up on the *Deja*, Havelock grinned as he gave his next order.

"Mr Kennedy, fire!"

A few critical seconds passed as the order was passed down to the gun decks and then the cannon roared, chugging out both smoke and metal as the hulk was pounded. The *Elita*, leaning hard away from the hulk in its turn, fired its cannon at an inclined angle, discharging its anger directly across the deck and masts of the *Deja*, just as Havelock had planned. Corpses, now finally having the life blasted out of them, were hurled clear of the ship in pieces, their limbs and heads scattering across the sea. The *Deja's* foremast lost a yardarm but Havelock now had few illusions that it actually required sails to move across the ocean. His intention was to do anything he could to end the existence of as many of its crew as possible before the next stage of his plan.

As the *Elita* passed abeam of the *Deja* on its larboard flank, Havelock smiled grimly as he saw none of its gun ports were open, and he felt a little gratified that Dubois did not have all the answers, that he could be surprised by a sudden and unexpected move. This would prove to be vital if Havelock were to triumph over the undead Captain.

The *Deja*, its prey running, began to slow down to more normal speeds and began to turn towards the frigate, intending to follow it. However, it still carried a great deal of momentum, and the turn was shallow, making Havelock think that, perhaps, the loss of its rudder *did* have an effect after all.

"Helmsman, hard to starboard," he said. "Bring us right around – reverse our course!"

Though the expression of the man at the giant wheel seemed to flicker between desperation and despair, he followed his Captain's orders with automatic obedience. The sails reset for this manoeuvre, the *Elita* began to turn in the opposite direction, again leaning hard over.

A mighty crack, like thunder, resounded across the *Elita's* deck and Havelock looked up in alarm to see the top length of mainmast begin to sag under the weight of its sails. The fracture running up its height had widened to four or five inches in places and he could see the two pieces begin to move against one another. The mast began to lean forwards noticeably but then checked its movement, and Havelock realised it was being held in place by the rigging and little else.

"Lord, spare me that mast for just one more minute," he said under his breath.

Sailors still working high on the mainmast looked at one another uncertainly for a brief moment and then began scuttling down to the perceived safety of the deck. Others gave it nervous glances as they worked, fearful that the mast would topple at any second on to them.

Emerging from the lower decks, Corbin reappeared, his face grim, followed by the gun crews. He cast an appraising look at the damaged mainmast as he marched to the quarterdeck to join Havelock, shuddering at the damage the frigate was taking.

"You could really feel that break below decks," he said, nodding to the mast. "Will she hold?"

"I pray to God she will – for just a little further," said Havelock. "Is everything set below?"

Corbin gave him a meaningful look. "Aye Sir. It is alight now, four minutes by my reckoning."

"Very good, Mr Corbin."

"Sir, if there could be another way... "

Havelock shook his head. "You said it yourself. We cannot kill her crew; this is all that remains." He slapped Corbin on the shoulder. "Be of good cheer, Mr Corbin! We may yet escape this and send that damned hulk to the bottom of the sea!"

The mainmast once again groaned ominously, but Havelock ignored its underlining of his words. The *Elita* carried through its tight turn and every sailor on board watched the *Deja* as they circled round until, finally, it was dead ahead of them.

"Straighten her up helmsman, steady as she goes," said Havelock. "Then lash the wheel and join your shipmates on the main deck."

The sailor gave Havelock a fearful glance as he began to realise what the Captain intended to do but obeyed without argument. Kennedy frowned as he looked to the helmsman, the *Deja* and then back at Havelock, it slowly dawning on him too what was going to happen. Corbin just looked sick.

"Mr Kennedy, prepare the men to receive boarders, but keep them away from the forecastle. It won't be safe up there."

"Cap'n," said Kennedy in protest. "This is..."

"You have your orders, Mr Kennedy. I would be obliged if you follow them."

The Bosun gave a quick look at Corbin, who refused to meet his eye. Finding no support, he had little choice but to do as Havelock had instructed.

"Aye, Sir."

The *Deja*, going too fast to turn quickly and being too large to slow down in time, had been out-manoeuvred by the nimbler frigate. After passing broadsides, the *Elita* had managed to turn a complete half-circle inside the hulk's own turning radius so that the frigate was now thundering over the gentle waves at full speed straight towards the *Deja's* side, a reversal of what Dubois had planned for Havelock earlier.

"Come, Mr Corbin," said Havelock, unbuckling his

sword belt and letting it drop to the deck as he drew his blade. "It is time to join our crew."

Leading the way, Havelock descended the stairs to the main deck. He began to focus his attention on the fast approaching hulk, not seeing the salutes of his crew or their well wishes. He no longer thought of duty, or his career, or the court martial he would face for losing two ships on this mission. All that mattered now was the final confrontation with Dubois, and being able to look into those cold, dead eyes as the French Captain realised the tables had been turned and that it was he who was doomed.

The *Elita* sped towards the hulk and several sailors cried in dismay as they saw its gun ports open and cannon rolled out. On the hulk's deck, zombies gathered in a throng at the railings, waiting for the chance to leap onto the frigate's deck and begin rending its crew. For their part, the British crew dove for the deck, trying to find any scrap of cover behind the mainmast or coils of thick rope as the *Deja* unleashed the full weight of its broadside into the *Elita's* prow. Only Havelock and Corbin remained upright, the latter out of an officer's duty, the former more from a belief that fate would not snuff his life out just yet.

The upper half of the prow was turned into matchwood in a second, though this did little to slow the metal shot as it blasted the *Elita's* forecastle apart and then sped onwards across the main deck. All around, the air was filled with a deafening howl, flying splinters and the cries of men who lost limbs to the speeding metal. Wails of pain soon gave way to those of terror as sailors saw shipmates decapitated or torn in half by the attack, drenching the living in hot blood.

Corbin was one of the first to die, a heavy 36 pound

shot moving at terrible speed catching him in the chest. Mercifully, he felt no pain as his life was snatched away, his body thrown backwards to be pulped by the wooden structure of the quarterdeck in the blink of an eye. To anyone watching, he seemed to simply disappear, leaving a thin red mist of blood which quickly fell to the deck.

Another shot found its mark squarely at the base of the mainmast, severing it in two instantly. No longer having any support within the wooden shaft itself, the rigging gave way and the mast toppled forward, hitting the foremast with a terrible crack. This too snapped like a twig, dragging canvas and rope onto the deck. Lucky sailors found themselves having to fight their way clear of the entangling sails and rigging, while others were crushed by the masts themselves.

His attention so rigidly fixed on the *Deja*, Havelock did not notice any of this, missing even the disappearance of his Lieutenant. He had the presence of mind only to grab a railing as the *Elita* closed the remaining yards to the hulk and smashed into it with an horrendous splintering of wood that seemed louder than even the *Deja's* guns.

Every man on the frigate was hurled forward by the impact as their ship came to a sudden and abrupt halt. The *Elita* had carved its way through the hull of the *Deja* so that what remained of its prow was rooted deep within the lower decks of the hulk. The two ships were locked firmly together, with only the *Deja* holding the frigate upright instead of listing to one side after the terrible pounding it had received. For a few seconds, everything was quiet, with only the lapping of the sea and the grinding of wood upon wood filling the air. Then, a dreadful, inhuman cry came from the hulk as swarms of zombies, hundreds of them, began to throw themselves onto the deck of the frigate in search of the living.

The *Elita's* crew, stunned by cannon and the sudden ram, were slow to respond at first and those furthest forward died cruelly with no chance to retaliate. Others, galvanised by the sight of their shipmates being torn apart, quickly stirred to action. Several, fearing for their lives and believing all was lost, threw themselves overboard, even as Kennedy began shouting at a small group to lower the boats over the side. The rest grabbed whatever weapon lay closest to hand and prepared to fight for their lives.

Canvas shredded and men screamed as they died as the horde of the walking dead poured onto the *Elita* in a seemingly never-ending stream. The sailors were soon driven back into a tightly packed mass around the ruined stump of the mainmast, huddling together for mutual protection as zombies threw themselves into the fray, sweeping round the sides of the main deck to begin encircling the living. Now cornered, a palpable change began to stir in the hearts of the British. Trapped, with nowhere to run, they developed a terrible vengeance, beginning to fight like demons, almost eager to wrench the limbs off one zombie or slice clean through another. Some limbless corpses, still twitching with unnatural life, were hurled high into the air to land in the centre of the sailor's group, where they were torn apart by those not yet pushed to the front line of battle.

"Dubois!" Havelock shouted as he strode forward, separate from the rest of his men. He hacked to all sides with his sword, laying zombies low with each strike, the dead no longer holding any fear for him. He searched for his counterpart, the rotting French Captain whom he had sworn to lay to rest. One zombie, its legs torn free by an enraged sailor, crawled along the deck and grabbed for his ankle. Havelock spat at it and brought his heel down hard on its skull, splitting it open with ease. Grey pulp sprayed across the deck, but Havelock had already moved on to send another zombie's head spinning with one strong swing of his sword. The blade quickly became sheathed in grey skin and flesh, tattered remains of the enemies he had dispatched.

"Dubois!"

One immensely tall zombie, close to seven feet, bellowed as it charged the sailors, determined to force their tight unit open, leaving them vulnerable. Heaving a massive wooden plank, perhaps torn from the ruined prow of the *Elita* herself, the creature smacked aside a cutlass raised to parry the blow, sending the weapon spinning across the deck. The now defenceless sailor tried to back away but could take no more than a step before being pushed forward again by the men behind him. He raised his hands in a desperate attempt to ward off the coming blow that would crush him like an insect.

Havelock cut downwards into the knee of the zombie and it buckled instantly, falling to its hands. Another blow severed its head but before the sailor could stammer his thanks and grab another weapon from a shipmate, Havelock had already turned and once again resumed cutting his way through the mass of zombies.

"Dubois!"

More zombies clawed at his face, losing limbs to his sword in the process, before they parted at some unspoken command, intentionally stepping aside before continuing onwards to slaughter his men. Looking forward towards the hulk, Havelock caught a glimpse of the dirty French Captain's jacket as he jumped down to the deck of the Elita. He grinned wolfishly. Casting a quick glance back at his men, Havelock, for the first time, saw how precarious their position was and also realised that Corbin was no longer with him.

"Mr Kennedy!" he called to the Bosun, who was at the forefront of the British sailor's mob, keeping zombies at bay with broad sweeps of his cutlass. Already a small mound of still corpses lay at his feet, causing those behind to stumble on the uneven pile and then fall prey to his attacks. Briefly, their eyes met.

"Get what men you can to the boats!" Havelock said, straining to be heard above the noise of battle. "Your duty here is done."

Without waiting for a reply, Havelock stalked forward, sword at the ready, as he marched to confront Dubois. No zombies made a move to harm him. Behind Havelock, a few men bolted as soon as they heard their Captain's order but, once alone, they were quickly surrounded and torn apart by the zombies.

Seeing Havelock disappear into the fray, Kennedy took command of the sailors, organising them to move, slowly but with determination, towards one of the boats. Taking the lead in guarding the backs of the retreating crew, Kennedy shouted for those nearest to start lowering the boat to the water while he fought to drive the pursuing zombies back, anxious to give his men as much space and time as he could. He heard the distant splash as the boat was dropped into the sea and was soon aware of men leaving his side to dive overboard, before heaving themselves into the small craft. A quick rush of zombies, perhaps stimulated by the sight of living men escaping, caught Kennedy by surprise and he gave a sharp cry as one got under his guard and sank its remaining teeth into his shoulder. He struggled to force its head back but the distraction was all its fiendish companions needed as they bowled the Bosun over, dragging him to the deck. Once pinned under the weight of several moving corpses,

Kennedy found himself unable to even raise his arms as claws and teeth started to rend his flesh. His cries of agony were quickly silenced by a large axe splitting his skull in two.

Finding an area of the deck relatively clear of debris from the masts or the battle, Havelock waited calmly for his enemy to join him, confident that none of the zombies still climbing down from the hulk would trouble him. They raced past to catch any crewman still remaining on the *Elita*, any who were too slow in abandoning the ship. Dubois then approached with a limping gait Havelock had not noticed before, his appearance all the more hideous in broad daylight. Havelock did not even bother to salute with his sword, merely holding it at a slight angle, ready to either strike or parry any sudden lunge from the creature that had robbed him of two ships.

"Come, Dubois. I no longer fear you." Havelock's voice was calm and even, now certain in what he had to do. There was now nothing left but to play the final part of the act.

"You have doomed your ship by your own actions, Havelock!" the hateful thing spat. "Your crew lies in tatters and those escaping will not get far, I promise you. Now all that remains is for me to claim your own, worthless, pathetic life."

"Claim it then." Havelock's smile seemed to enrage Dubois. The zombie's lipless mouth gaped open as he howled in anger, while his entire body shook with rage.

"Worm!" Dubois exclaimed, as he lunged forward with his blade, straight for Havelock's heart.

Ready for the opening move, Havelock sidestepped the strike, cutting with a back swing aimed at Dubois' skull. The zombie reacted with equal speed, cocking his head to one side to let the blade pass harmlessly above him.

Havelock felt his sword bite for just an instant as it sliced Dubois' ragged ear clean from his head.

White eyes blazing, Dubois advanced, swinging his sword wildly but with great accuracy. Knowing he could not hope to match the zombie Captain's raw strength, Havelock hopped from foot to foot as he dodged most of the blows, attempting to parry only the keenest of attacks, and then just angling his blade so Dubois' weapon would slide away, rather than be held fast. During the assault, Havelock was careful to keep half an eye on any obstructions behind as he was forced to give ground, lest he find his foot caught in a rope or jagged hole punched through the deck. He had little doubt that Dubois was no longer toying with him, that this was, indeed, the end.

Though he seemed to have endless reserves of stamina, Dubois checked his attack for an instant, perhaps wanting to re-examine his opponent to find a point of weakness in the swordplay. Havelock saw his chance and stepped forward to initiate his own series of attacks. Doing his best to avoid meeting Dubois' sword with his own, he made several feints that forced the zombie to manoeuvre in order to avoid being flanked and caught out of position. Their blades clashed twice but Havelock checked his swing each time, knowing that to use his full strength against Dubois would give him nothing more than a numb arm or, worse, a broken blade.

Dubois checked one of Havelock's attacks and then hacked downwards in a powerful blow intended to split him in two. Havelock twisted at the last moment and then lunged with all the skill the dead Frenchmen had shown in the past. Dubois, caught by surprise at the sudden strike, backed off two steps, arching backwards as the point of the sword came close to his desiccated face. He tried to knock the blade away, but Havelock had already withdrawn it and the parry went wide, leaving Dubois open.

With any living opponent, Havelock might have ended the fight right there by delivering another lunge to the heart or stomach, or perhaps sweeping his blade in from the side to dig into Dubois' neck. Knowing such attacks would do little to this creature, Havelock instead cut downwards at Dubois' left hand, which was outstretched and flailing as the zombie tried to keep balance. Using two hands to drive the stroke down with as much speed as he could muster, Havelock again felt his sword bite, a moment of resistance, before it carried on downwards to splinter the deck.

White-clouded eyes looking a little dumb, Dubois watched as his hand, severed at the wrist, flopped to one side before lying still. He hissed as his attention went back to Havelock, their eyes locking, one with loathing, and the other with something approaching amusement. Screaming, Dubois raced forward once more to attack Havelock with three lightning fast lunges aimed at heart, head and stomach. Ready for the maddened zombie, Havelock once again gave ground, staying out of reach of the sword. His smile bubbled over and he began to laugh.

"Why do you laugh, Englishman?" Dubois said, demanding a response. "You think these pinpricks you have dealt mean anything to me, to one who has spent decades on the seabed waiting for a chance of rightful vengeance?"

"You cannot defeat me, Dubois," Havelock said, still chuckling.

"Your crew are already dead men. And I think you will tire before me in this fight!"

Havelock shook his head with a sad smile. "You have

already lost. Victory, today, will be mine."

Stepping forward to renew his attack, Dubois quickly checked himself, stopping as if he were trying to puzzle out just why this enemy, who had already lost his ship and could not possibly win in a straight duel, was so confident. Havelock had no intention of giving him the time to guess and swung loosely with his sword, aiming for Dubois' own weapon. The zombie parried solidly as Havelock had expected and he made a brief show of trying to strain against Dubois' strength. He then took a step forward to place himself under his opponent's guard and, hooking a foot behind Dubois' leg, pushed forward with his shoulder, throwing his whole weight behind the move.

Too late, Dubois saw what Havelock was trying to do and though he back-pedalled to keep balance, his foot locked with Havelock's and he fell to the deck, sword clattering from his deathly grasp. He screamed, a wrenching cry mixing frustration and anger as he hit the deck heavily, clawing upwards with his remaining hand to ward off Havelock's inevitable follow through.

It never came. Dubois hoisted himself on his elbows and looked up at Havelock, his rotting skin wrinkling in surprise.

"Why did you not try to finish me?" he said. "Even if you cannot kill me, you might try to hinder me further. Is this some foolish pretence of honour?"

Havelock took a step back, though he kept the point of his sword towards the prone zombie. "I told you, Dubois. I have already won. Now, pick up your sword and continue, if that is your wish. I am quite ready to play this out to the end."

A bone cracked as Dubois got to his feet, then turned to bend down to retrieve his sword.

"You are foolish, Captain," said Dubois. "Now your soul will be claimed for the deep."

"That may be true, but it will not be at your hand, accursed creature!"

Still side on to Havelock, Dubois bowed his head for a moment, enough to make the Englishman wonder what the creature was doing. Then Dubois whipped round, his sword following the line as it split the air with an audible whistle, its blade sailing true for Havelock's throat with all of his supernatural strength. He raised his own weapon to parry the attack and caught the force of the blow completely, staggering backwards several steps from its momentum. Havelock's sword arm fell to his side limply, numb from having taken much of the blow's force.

Dubois did not relent and he stalked forward, shoulders hunched like some predator poised to strike. Havelock took another step back and tried vainly to raise his sword to ward off another heavy blow. Then his world turned black and deafening as his body was blasted into the sky. Before he faded into unfeeling darkness, Havelock heard Dubois' cry, a long, mournful lament of a man who had striven for decades to complete but a single goal, only to find it snatched away at the last moment. His last thought was one of gratitude, to Corbin, for having followed his orders faithfully in setting a fuse to the ship's magazine. Then he thought no more.

The explosion blasted the bottom out of the *Elita*, shredding its hull, before boiling upwards to throw the deck and masts yards into the air. Fuelled by methane created in the filthy hold, fire incinerated the lower decks, gutting the ship utterly. Zombies and dead sailors alike were catapulted skywards before falling into the sea, some at great distance from the floundering ship, raining down into the sea like clumsy blackened gulls diving for fish.

The remains of the *Elita* began to take on water rapidly and it listed heavily, its stern already beneath the water. Its shattered prow locked into the *Deja*, it dragged the hulk with it, the larger ship pulled heavily to one side. The sea flooded into its open gun ports, racing through the lower decks in an inexorable tide that swept the remaining zombies with it, their arms and legs flailing uselessly as they tried to stop themselves being slammed into bulkheads. As the hulk began to fill with water, it listed even more, rolling almost completely onto its side. The sea, now able to flood through the open main hatch on its exposed deck, soon filled the rest of the ship and the *Deja*, robbed of all buoyancy and still locked in the *Elita's* death grip, sank downwards rapidly, returning to its original grave on the seabed.

Within a minute, all that remained of Havelock's last battle was a mass of bubbles where the ships had been as the last vestiges of air was squeezed out of them by the ocean. For a hundred yards in every direction, debris floated to the surface, a mix of wood, canvas, rope and bodies, those recently killed carried on the gentle waves alongside those long since dead.

The feel of cold water surrounding him, making his clothes sodden and heavy, roused Havelock to a sense of semi-consciousness. His thoughts disjointed and not entirely of this world, he began to dream, of battles at sea in an age before his own, of French armies sweeping across the globe to threaten his beloved British Empire, and a future dominated by Napoleon's imperial court.

He saw legions of zombies decimating a fleet led by Lord Nelson, who fought long and hard against impossible odds as the French invaded England. He saw King George fighting alongside Pitt the Younger in the streets of London, both surrounded by townsfolk as they desperately sought to defend the palace against blue-coated French soldiers. Visions of the old American colonies flashed through his mind, begging for aid from a friendless world as the French swarmed across the Atlantic to claim their territory in recompense for aiding their cause of freedom before everything started fading to blackness once again.

Havelock jerked, violently, as he fought for life. His actions seemed slow and inaccurate, as if he were moving in soup. Fighting for breath, he opened his mouth and found himself swallowing the sea. Panicking, he opened his eyes and discovered himself under water. Dimly aware of light to one side of him, he struck out, limbs flailing as he desperately sought the surface. Throat constricting and lungs bursting, he seemed no closer to open air and, at that point, he almost gave up, ready to let the sea claim his body as he slowly spiralled downwards into the darkness. Then, he heard the echoes of Dubois' mocking voice and he swam with renewed vigour, ignoring the crushing pain in his chest.

Surfacing with a splash, Havelock drew in a huge lungful of air and then started choking. Trying to catch his breath, he cast about the surface of the quiet sea through watering eyes, he saw the dark mass of the *Deja* roll over and quickly disappear between the waves and felt utter relief. Completely drained, he lay on his back, allowing the sea to carry him where it wished as he slowly began to recover.

It took him only a few seconds more to realise that he was not alone in the water, as three of Dubois' remaining crew clawed hungrily through the sea towards him, their

sightless eyes fixed on his living flesh. With no more
fight in him, with no strength left to give, Havelock took
one last look at them and then closed his eyes, beginning
to laugh as he waited for the end.

CHAPTER THIRTEEN

The small boat bobbed gently on the vast expanse of sea, the waves carrying it up and down on the low crests in a continuous rolling motion. Only three men were carried inside, the only survivors of the desperate flight from the doomed *Elita* and, though thoroughly exhausted, they had returned to the scene of the battle in the vain hope of finding more of their shipmates alive and praying for rescue.

At the prow of the boat, Murphy sat, his chin resting on his arms which were folded on the hull. He kept half an eye open for any stranded sailors but, not seriously expecting to find any, he lulled on the border of sleep. Behind him, Bryant pulled weakly at the oars, his shirt in tatters as his torso bled from dozens of scratches from claws and flying wood splinters. Brooks was curled up at the back, nursing a leg injury that was bound with cloth ripped form his trousers. Having been in the frontline against the zombies as they closed in around the mob of sailors on the centre of the main deck, he had fought well but had taken a swipe from a cutlass for his trouble.

"So, where you plannin' on takin' us after this, Bryant?" Murphy said sleepily.

"Back to the island."

Murphy raised his head wearily and scanned the horizon around them, seeing nothing but the endless ocean.

"Can't see no island," he said before sinking back down.

"Think we go southwest from here," said Bryant. "Won't be too long before we see it. We didn't travel far before that ship caught us."

"An' 'ow do you know which way southwest is?"

"It's that way," said Bryant, nodding slightly ahead of them, though Murphy did not bother turning round to see the gesture. However, the Irishman frowned.

"You got a compass tucked away somewhere?"

Bryant sighed. "How did you get to join my gun crew, Murphy? Look at the sun. It is still morning, so take your bearings from that."

"Only morning?" said Brooks. "I feel like I have been fightin' for a year."

"Aye, you fought well, lad," said Bryant. "How's the leg?"

"Still bleedin'. Stopped most of it though. Think I'll get gangrene?"

"Not if we get you to the island quick enough. We'll take a proper look at it then."

"Could still be zombies on the island," said Murphy. "I 'eard they were chasin' our men through the jungle."

"Yeah, but we also got our own men on the beach," said Bryant as he paused in his rowing for a moment. He gave a short laugh. "We even have some of the French to help us there!"

"It was the damn Froggies that got us into this," said Murphy.

"But we'll all be in the same boat on the island." Bryant cast a look about the small craft. "So to speak. I can't see they will be in any mood to fight."

"Then it will just be a case of whose ship turns up first – theirs or ours," said Brooks.

"Aye, possibly, though I imagine some passing merchant has more chance of stumbling across us. Not every vessel at sea is a warship. You see anything up ahead, Murphy?"

"No," he replied, not even bothering to lift his head. Bryant snaked a foot forward and kicked him gently in the back before returning to his oars.

"Oww! Okay, I'm lookin', I'm lookin'!" He made a show of stretching up and looking around the horizon, before sinking back into rest. "That 'ulk went down pretty fast," he eventually said.

"Not surprised with the blast it took," said Brooks. "You see the *Elita* go? Blew men and zombies clear into the heavens!"

"Nice of the Cap'n to warn us about that," Murphy said under his breath but his voice carried in the quiet air. He earned another kick from Bryant for the comment.

"Don't you go talking ill of the Captain," said Bryant. "It's because of him that you, me and Brooks are still alive. And you have to give him credit for staying on board, going down with the ship. Despite the stories, there are not many Captains who would do that."

"No, many of 'em would be the first to push their way onto the boats," said Brooks. After a moment of reflection, he added "He was alright, was the Captain."

"Aye." Bryant continued to row slowly, careful to avoid tangling the oars in any of the debris that had started to float past them. Though fascinated at the amount of wreckage nearby, they all tried hard not to look at the various body parts that were carried on the surface.

Bryant frowned as he squinted into the near distance. "Hey, Murphy. You see that? Over there, movement in the water."

"Umm... " Murphy propped himself up and stared hard. "Ah, Bryant, steer away. Them's zombies, still alive an' kickin'."

"Well, where are they going? Is it one of ours in trouble?"

"Someone in the water. Think they're dead."

"Zombies don't go after the dead, Murphy!" said Bryant.

"Brooks, get up here, help me with the rowing – we need to get there before they do!"

Brooks grunted with pain as he moved forward, relying on his arms for support more than his legs. He lifted his injured leg over the plank Bryant sat upon as he moved into position, before taking an oar.

"Put your back into it, Brooks. I don't want to lose anyone we don't have to."

His interest now caught, Murphy sat up straighter, trying to get a good look at the body floating in the water. "Hey, Bryant. You saw the Lieutenant buy it, right?"

"Blasted by cannon before we rammed the French ship."

"That body's wearin' a uniform – I think it's the Cap'n!"

"Brooks..."

"I know, I know," Brooks said, fighting back the agony of his leg as he pulled back and forth on the oar. He crooked his injured limb to one side, using his good leg to brace against a rib within the boat as he strained to propel the craft as quickly as possible.

Working together, Brooks and Bryant gave the boat a good turn of speed and they closed rapidly on the floating body, trying to steer into a position where they were between it and the zombies clawing their way through the water. As they drew alongside, Murphy cried out aloud that they had indeed found the Captain and he leant over the side to begin dragging him on board.

Bryant stood up and raised his oar as the first zombie lunged out of the water to scramble onto the boat. A loud crack was carried by the gentle breeze as the paddle of the oar connected with the zombie's head and it reeled backwards, stunned or finally dead, Bryant could not tell. He had already reversed the oar and was driving it downwards onto the skull of a second creature, repeatedly battering it until it stopped moving.

Behind him, a third zombie had thrown its arms over the side of the boat and was beginning to clamber on board, its swollen tongue passing over rotting teeth as it leered at the fresh victims on board. Without thinking, Brooks reached forward and plucked a knife from Murphy's belt before turning round to confront the boarder.

The zombie swiped wicked claw at Brooks, opening a shallow wound in his arm. Ignoring the pain from both that injury and his leg, Brooks scrambled into the back of the boat, raising the knife. He stabbed forward, driving the blade deep into one of the zombie's eye sockets. The creature twitched violently, then fell still. With a last mighty effort, Brooks shoved the creature overboard, where it started to sink immediately.

As he sank down into the boat, he heard Murphy cry out. "Hey, Brooks, that was me best knife!"

Murphy had only managed to get Havelock's shoulders out of the water and was clearly struggling. After casting a suspicious eye at the water to make sure no further attacks from the dead were likely, Bryant crouched forward to help him. Together, they pulled the Captain onto their boat, noting that, aside from a few cuts and grazes, he seemed to be more or less intact.

After checking to see if Havelock still breathed, Bryant gently tapped him on the cheek, adding a little more force when he was met with no response.

"Captain?" he said hesitantly. "Captain, we're from the *Whirlwind* – the *Elita*. You're safe now. Captain?"

Looking curiously onwards, Murphy was about to ask if the Captain was dead, when Havelock gave a start, and immediately lapsed into a coughing fit. Bryant placed a hand on his shoulder as he began to look about wildly.

"It's alright Captain, you're safe. We are among the living."

"Dear God," were Havelock's first words and he rubbed his eyes as he sat up and tried to catch his breath. He frowned when he saw the other occupants of the boat. "You are the only survivors?"

"Sorry, Captain, yes."

Havelock leaned heavily against the side of the boat and sighed. "I had hoped for more."

"There is no shame in it, Captain," said Bryant with conviction. "I don't think there is another Captain who could have done what you did today."

"'Tis true," said Murphy. "You are a true blue-blooded hero. Captain Havelock, killer of the unkillable, sinker of the unsinkable!"

"And willing to stay on a doomed ship to the end," said Bryant. "You get yourself another ship, Captain, and we'll be the first to sign on!"

Waving back their praise, Havelock thought back to his duel with Dubois, the rigged explosion of the *Elita's* magazine and, finally, the zombies racing through the water to fulfil their Captain's promise of death. He rubbed his temple in disbelief.

"I was to die, you see," he said, causing Murphy to give a curious and perplexed look. "That was what was meant to be."

"I don't think so, Captain," said Bryant with confidence. "Perhaps you should have been killed several times over. But you were thrown clear of the explosion and we were here to pull you from the water. I would say that God clearly preserves you for another purpose."

"And perhaps honour is now satisfied," said Havelock but he did not explain himself to his remaining crew. Settling down into the boat, he allowed his eyes to close as he thought of Dubois and what the French Captain had sought so fiercely.

He hoped Dubois was finally dead, blown apart in the explosion of the *Elita* and that, perhaps, some peace could be found in that rest. Try as he might though, Havelock could not bring himself to believe Dubois was completely vanquished. Maybe Havelock would receive a visitation of a vengeful spirit in the future. After the events of the past few days, he could now believe almost anything was possible. More likely, Dubois was trapped somewhere in the joint wreckage of the two ships, lurking on the sea floor for another chance to strike at the Havelock family.

The truth remained, however, that Dubois had been bested. It might well be that Havelock would, one day, have to face his nemesis once more to again answer for the actions of his grandfather. Perhaps it would be a later generation of Havelock that would be given that onerous task. For now, at least, he believed he could relax and, finally, sleep.

Watching his Captain rest, Murphy cocked his head as he watched an expression of serenity wash over Havelock's face. Looking over his shoulder, and seeing no sight of land, he turned back to the recumbent Captain.

"Bryant says the island is somewhere southwest. Is that right, Cap'n?"

Murphy received no answer. Havelock was already fast asleep.

THE END

MATTHEW SPRANGE - With a solid history in roleplaying design, Matthew Sprange has written over two dozen gaming books, including the *Babylon 5*, *Judge Dredd* and *Starship Troopers* games, and has won two Origins Awards for his work in miniature wargames. *Death Hulk* is his second novel, with his first being a trip into the *Babylon 5* universe, entitled *Visions of Peace*.

coming
May
2007...

Now read the prologue from the second
gut-wrenching zombie novel in the
Tomes of The Dead collection

TOMES OF THE DEAD

THE WORDS OF THEIR ROARING

Matthew Smith

COMING MAY 2007

ISBN 13: 978-1-905437-13-9

ISBN 10: 1-905437-13-7

£6.99 (UK)/ $7.99 (US)

WWW.ABADDONBOOKS.COM

PROLOGUE

4 November 1917
Ten Miles East of Ypres, Belgium

As the soldier ran, he barely raised his eyes from the battle-scarred earth, intent on watching one foot replace the other, propelling him from danger. The rattle of gunfire had slowly faded the greater the distance he put between himself and the trenches, and the occasional mortar explosion was merely a dull thud behind him. Even so, he dared not slow his pace, despite the growing ache in his limbs. The ground was not easy to traverse; sludge becoming quagmire, plain disappearing into crater, every movement was an effort to stay upright, and to keep his boots on his feet. He had to pick his way carefully through barbed wire, sprawl in the mud if he thought he heard whisper of the enemy (and just who was that, now that he had chosen not to belong to one side or the other?). Exhaustion threatened to overwhelm him; but one notion kept him going, reassuring him as he watched his legs driving him towards that goal: *escape.*

Private William Steadman did not want to die.

He supposed there was a little of the childish logic in the way he kept his head down as he ran, reasoning that what he could not see would not hurt him; and rather than stop to get his bearings, he put all his effort into the act of flight itself, pointing himself in one direction and seeing where it would take him, as if he was a schoolboy released for the summer holidays. It was difficult to deny he felt as lost and scared as if he was twelve years old, shrunken and vulnerable in an adult's uniform. But that was hardly a unique phenomenon; he'd seen his fellow soldiers – men perhaps in a civilian context he would've considered unscrupulous scoundrels and brawlers – reduced to bawling infants. Their faces had been masks of incomprehension and fear; they knew how close they were to death, how their dreams for the future, their desire to see their families again, hinged on an order. To leave the comparative safety of the trench, cross no man's land and embrace the German guns was to strip a man of everything he had and was ever likely to have. And so Steadman, with his own tears icy on his cheeks, had had to listen to one of the most terrifying sounds he'd ever heard, far worse than the shriek of shrapnel cutting through the air: that of grown men crying with regret and loss. It was utterly alien and impossible to forget.

He slid his way down a bank and felt the dirt beneath him crumble. Trying to regain his balance, he increased his pace, but only succeeded in pushing himself forward and tumbling head-first into the mud. He rolled onto his back, a part of his mind yelling at him to be back on his feet instantly, but a curious lethargy came over him, as if the earth were sapping him of strength; as if, once this close to it, it would suck him to its bosom – revenge for the damage that had been wrought on its surface. He imagined lying here, relaxing his grip on life and watching the sun and moon chase each other across the sky, his body slowly sinking into the ground, becoming part of the landscape like so many other corpses had. Every morning for the past sixteen months, he'd woken and looked out on carcasses littering the battlefield, human and animal seeding the soil. What would it be like, he wondered, to join that silent sea of the dead? To succumb to the exhaustion and close his eyes one final time? The idea stayed in his head longer than he anticipated, perversely attractive. In the last letter he'd written home, he'd said how he'd forgotten what it was like to be warm and clean, to eat and sleep in comfort, not to have the tight ball of dread lodged in his gut; those concerns would just fade away if he was to give up now, if he was to relinquish the struggle to survive...

Steadman clutched a handful of mud and brought it to his nose; it smelt rotten, diseased. It served to fuel his anger and clear his mind of any thoughts of surrender. He would not sacrifice himself for this war; it meant nothing to him. As was common with most of his comrades, he knew little of the history behind the conflict, the objectives of taking part in it, or indeed how the world will have changed once everything returned to normal. They had just been shipped over to this godforsaken hole, instructed to stand in a freezing field, point their guns in the direction of the Hun, and wait until they could be told they could go home. It was difficult to picture a more futile image than two sets of opposing forces facing each other down from opposite ends of a muddy stretch of earth, while somewhere – invisible, in another world – generals bluffed and blustered. It would be laughable, were it not for the thousands of men being thrown across the lines. Then, the stalemate became a massacre.

He held his commanders in absolute contempt. Their strategies were idiotic, their disregard for the troops who fought for them breathtaking; many was the time he had seen Allied shells landing on their own attacking battalions because the advance had been planned with so little forethought, or frightened, sobbing young lads barely out of puberty executed for refusing to obey an order to go over the top, obviously incapable of holding a rifle without shaking let alone firing it. The injustice made him want to scream. He wanted to shout at the sky and pummel this sick, stinking earth. He was not some expendable, unthinking automaton they could put in front of the German bullets; as far as he was concerned, it *did* matter whether he lived or died. He thought of his parents raising him as a child, fretting when he was ill, glowing with pride when he returned from his first day at school, taking the time to show him the difference between right and wrong and the good teachings of the Lord, to be the best person he could be, and all that pain, all that effort, all that heartfelt love, blown away in an instant as he charged at the enemy and his brains splattered on the ground.

He clambered to his feet, taking deep breaths, steeling himself for the next stage of his journey. A mist was rolling in, the air chill and damp, and he assumed darkness would begin to fall within the next couple of hours. He had to find shelter if he was to last the night. He wished he'd remembered to get his watch repaired; the sky was sheathed in a thick blanket of cloud and giving nothing away, so he had little idea of the time. He didn't even know for how long he had been running; it seemed like most of the day, but he had a niggling suspicion that he hadn't covered as much ground as he hoped. The area was notoriously easy to get lost in, or to find yourself travelling in circles. He set off at a trot, intent on bedding down in the first shattered town building or abandoned farmhouse he came across.

But what exactly were his plans beyond that? He had no money, no contacts he could enlist to help him out of the country; his chance of escape seemed as slim as if he were back in the trench and awaiting that final whistle. The problem was that his desertion had been spur of the moment, a frantic bubbling of panic that eventually burst into full-blown terror. Although he had fixed bayonets in blank obedience and prepared to engage the enemy in combat, his gaze never straying to anyone on either side of him, the moment the signal came and the first soldiers went over and the shooting started, he had lost his nerve, dropped his rifle and faked injury. In the rush and confusion of men surging forward and then falling back as they were struck, he'd buried his head in his hands and played dead. As he'd willed himself to remain stationary, he could do nothing but listen to the thunderous, ear-splitting roar of the mortars, the high-pitched wail of injured men pleading for help and then cursing venomously when none arrived, and the rapid *thunk-thunk-thunk* of bullets meeting muscle and bone. When he'd opened his eyes, what was left of his regiment was several hundred yards away and he lay beneath a pile of bodies, butchered by machine-gun fire. Extricating himself slowly from the wretched heap, he'd crawled inch by inch in the opposite direction to the battle, praying silently that no one should see him and at the same time asking his Saviour to forgive his cowardice. Occasionally he would glance up, pulling corpses around him if he thought he heard anyone approaching, hating himself for his weakness. It was time-consuming, arduous work, and he calmed himself through concentration, fixing his sight on some distant object, be it blasted tree or wire fence, and driving himself towards it. He was dimly aware that he was humming a hymn under his breath, a thin keening sound that suggested he was teetering on the brink of outright hysteria.

Indeed, this *was* insanity; he knew he had nowhere to go, knew he would be crossing dangerous – more than likely mined – terrain, knew he could give no excuse if he was discovered and was almost certainly facing court martial and the firing squad. But, he had reasoned, he had made his decision, however sudden, and should stick to the matter in hand, putting all his effort into finding a way out of this mess rather than questioning its wisdom. When he came to a secluded spot he vomited copiously, and some of the anxiety seemed to drain away with it; his mind was set, and every minute he stayed alive was a tiny triumph.

With that, he had wiped his mouth and started to run. Onward, Christian soldier, he had thought bitterly.

He had been fortunate, of that there was no doubt, that he had not been picked off by some lone sniper, and he was aware that his luck could not last for much longer. It occurred to him that maybe he *had* been seen by the enemy, but they had discerned in him no threat; they recognized a scared fellow human being fleeing for his life, someone who had opted out of the war, and who was not worth the trouble or the waste of ammunition. The thought gave him hope; he imagined others like him, from all sides of the conflict, congregated to wait out the hostilities. But such a haven amidst this hell, he realized, sounded fantastical.

Darkness was closing in far more quickly than he had guessed. Soon it would be pitch black, and he would be stranded out on the plain; it would be a choice of freezing to death during the night (a fire was out of the question if he was trying to avoid attention, even in the unlikely event of him finding dry tinder), or blundering on through the dark, and risk impaling himself on barbed wire or stumbling on a German gun emplacement. Neither option appealed. He scanned the horizon for any kind of shelter, but saw nothing. He slowed his pace to a walk, his eyes roving the landscape, but the light was faltering with every step; he could barely see his hand in front of his face. Resignation and a little fear was just beginning to worry at him, to gnaw away at his resolve, when something tripped him up.

Despite himself, he yelped in alarm as he flopped to the ground and immediately swore; he knew instantly that it was a body his legs were hooked across, and more often than not where there was a body there were the remnants of an army. He glanced around quickly, certain his cry would've alerted somebody on watch, and sure enough, if he squinted, he could make out the thick seam of shadow that was a trench. But there was no sign of life. Steadman lay motionless for long minutes, waiting for anyone to emerge from the darkness, the razor-sharp wind chilling his skin and raising goose bumps. He resisted the urge to shiver, and breathed slowly, watching the thin, condensed streams dissipating in the air. But from the trench there was no movement.

Gradually, he began to edge forward, kicking his legs away from the corpse and lifting himself up onto his knees. If the trench was occupied, he thought, there had to be some kind of guard. But there was no light, no muted chatter or snores. The only explanation was that it had been overrun, the soldiers inside killed; but which side did it belong to? And could reinforcements be heading this way even as he sat here and deliberated?

Steadman turned back to the body, his hands outstretched in front of him like a blind man, feeling the contours of the uniform, his eyes aching as he concentrated on trying to see through the gloom. The design of the jacket was unfamiliar; the man seemed to have been an officer. Steadman's fingers grazed a holster and he gingerly removed the revolver, running his touch over it. It was of German issue. Clutching the gun in one hand, he lightly brushed the man's face, grimacing when his index finger disappeared into a penny-sized bullet hole in the man's forehead. It came away sticky.

At least they hadn't died by gas, he mused. It meant he wasn't in any immediate danger.

Wiping himself on the corpse's tunic, he looked back at the trench; it would be ideal to see out the night, hopefully providing him with some much-needed supplies, and it was unlikely British troops would be back this way if it had been disabled. The only problem he could foresee was a German regiment answering an injured radio operator's request for help just before he died and arriving here at daybreak. Then again, he could probably make use of one of the slain soldiers' uniforms and disguise himself amongst the dead once more.

He stood and moved to the lip of the trench, peering over cautiously; there was a dribble of light weakly spilling across the duckboards at the bottom. He returned to the German officer's body, took hold of both stiff arms and dragged it back with him, yanking it over the wire that circumscribed the trench's edge with as much strength as he could muster. The weight of the carcass made it bow in the middle, and he stepped across quickly, easing himself down into the earthwork. His eyes sought the light he had seen, and discovered it was buried beneath several corpses; faintly illuminated pale white faces stared up at him, the blood that criss-crossed their features appearing black in the darkness. He pulled them away dismissively, ignoring the lifeless thumps they made as they landed at his feet, and grasped the lamp – little more than a half-melted candle in a glass case – in his left hand before swinging it to either side of him.

"Sweet Jesus," he whispered.

It was an atrocity: the dead lay stacked like timber the length of the trench, one on top of the other. Each new sweep of the lamp brought a fresh horror, a new coupling, as soldier was piled upon soldier; they had been slaughtered like cattle in an abattoir. Steadman had thought he had witnessed every possible obscenity that man could perpetrate on his fellows, but this brought the bile rushing to his throat in an instant; there was something about the sheer scale of devastation here, all contained within the claustrophobic confines of the trench, that made him retch. That, and the noxious smell which seemed to palpably clog the air; it was the sickly stench of matter breaking down and liquefying, yet these corpses looked as if they had only been dead several hours at the most. It wasn't as if the heat of day could have brought about such a change; it had rained steadily the past few weeks, the temperature barely a couple of degrees above zero.

He brought the back of his free right hand to cover his nose and realized he still held the gun. It seemed suddenly paltry and comically unnecessary in the face of such carnage, but he felt loath to let go of it; as he gripped it tighter, he sensed himself drawing strength from it, gaining courage. Slowly, he began to walk down the centre of the trench in search of the supplies centre, the dead pressed high to either side, threatening to topple over onto him at any moment and drown him in a flurry of cold, white flesh. He felt a little of the wariness the Israelites must have experienced as they were led between those high, dark, roiling walls of the Red Sea with nothing but their faith to protect them.

Steadman tried to keep his eyes on the ground, using the lamp to guide himself past outstretched limbs that he would've otherwise stumbled over, but the lure to raise the light and gaze upon the ravaged soldiers' features was too great. A ghoulish curiosity, he supposed. The sight was appalling, but he kept returning to it, testing his endurance the way the tongue endlessly probes a painful tooth; agonizing yet irresistible. Even so, when he did glance up, many of the dead no longer had recognizable features; their faces were indistinct, pulpy masses as if they'd been shot at close range. Others were eviscerated, evidently bayoneted repeatedly. He shook his head, ashamed to call himself human, refusing to align himself with a species that could commit such acts of barbarism.

Why had they been so systematically slaughtered, and with an obviously bloodthirsty callousness, he wondered. If this was the result of some mania, why then take the time to stack the bodies as if for a funeral pyre?

The smell was beginning to make him feel dizzy, and every time he closed his eyes gory images assailed him. His legs cried out for rest, and his throat for water. He was on the verge of collapse when the lamp illuminated ahead the opening to some kind of officers' structure, judging by the map-table standing outside it. He sighed with relief and increased his pace towards it. There was a tarpaulin hanging across the entrance acting as a makeshift door, and Steadman hoped it would provide adequate shelter, not only to shield him from the cold but also remove from view, at least temporarily, the horrors of the trench; out of sight, if not mind. He covered the last few yards at speed and stumbled inside, pulling the sheeting closed behind him.

The first thing that caught his eye was the bed in the corner, half-hidden in shadow; he couldn't remember the last time he'd felt the caress of a pillow. He looked around the dark room quickly, taking in the large table, the surface of which was scattered with the remains of a meal, a couple of chairs, the stove, the walls plastered with maps and directives. He crossed to the table, placed the lamp and the revolver upon it, picked up a jug three quarters full of water, and took a long swig; it tasted rusty, but he drained it to the last drop. Then, he searched for scraps of food on the plates, shovelling hard pieces of bread into his mouth and chewing appreciatively before slumping exhaustedly into a chair.

Steadman sat unmoving for what seemed a very long time, too spent to think cohesively. Finally, he ran his hands over his face, his fingers rasping against his unshaven chin, and realized he was trembling. He felt hollow and scared; he would need a miracle to get out of this situation. He tried to reason through the consequences of today's actions and plan what he should do next, but his mind would not stay still for a moment; it fluttered, startled, from one scenario to another and would not allow him to concentrate. He assumed it was tiredness; his eyelids were beginning to droop as sleep crept up on him, and he was just considering whether to attempt to get the furnace going before burying himself beneath the bedclothes when he heard a soft mewling coming from the far corner.

He froze, unsure whether he had imagined it, deciding it could possibly be a combination of the wind and his fatigued senses. But then it came again, louder, undoubtedly human. It sounded like someone in considerable distress. He inched his hands across to the lamp and pistol and simultaneously rose to his feet, taking cautious steps around the table, shadows dispersing before him. There was a shape on the floor, silhouetted in the blackness. He shuffled closer and crouched down, lifting the lantern to see clearly.

Lying with his back to the wall was a British soldier, his familiar uniform soaked with blood. His eyes, rolling wide in their sockets like a beast aware of its impending death, squinted at the sudden light and tried to turn his head to face it. As he did so, Steadman saw the extent of the man's appalling injuries: a portion of the right side of his skull was missing, a cavernous red hole where his ear should have been, fragments of bone and clumps of hair standing at right angles. There was a vermilion halo sprayed on the wall behind him. Between his legs were three kerosene cans.

The soldier kept attempting to open his mouth to speak, but only made the soft, piteous cry that Steadman had heard. The man's eyes were perpetually moving wildly as if panic-stricken, his head shaking from side to side. Steadman got the impression that he was trying to communicate something, or maybe to warn him, but it wasn't until the man raised his right hand that had otherwise been hidden beneath his body and revealed the gun that was still clutched in it that he realized the horrific truth: the soldier had done this to himself. It had meant to be a suicide, but something had gone wrong, for it had left him mortally wounded and more than likely out of his mind in pain and shock. He pointed at the doorway and pulled the trigger repeatedly, grunting with each effort as the hammer slammed down on empty chambers. Presumably he'd tried to use the last bullet on himself.

"Can you hear me? Can you understand?" Steadman started to say, but faltered, realizing it was pointless.

He muttered an oath under his breath, unable to comprehend. He felt dislocated, as if in his escape he had torn through a veil and discovered madness existing alongside him. He wanted to ask him what had happened here, what had terrified him to the point of trying to take his own life, but the soldier was obviously beyond rational thought; indeed, it was remarkable that he was still alive at all. But it left Steadman with a dilemma; he was loath to leave him in this state and prolong his suffering, but didn't know if he possessed the courage to finish what the man had started. The latter was the merciful option (there was nothing a medic could do for him now), but he wasn't sure he could reconcile that fact with his faith. In all his twenty-five years on the planet, he had never killed anything higher up the food chain than a bluebottle.

Odd, he mused, that with all the mass murder going on around him, thousands of men dying in seconds to capture a few feet of ground, he should balk at one act of kindness.

The soldier started to wail louder, and Steadman thought he caught the semblance of actual words beneath it; surprised, he moved closer, straining to hear.

"... they... they *come*..." he gurgled, waving the gun in front of him. "... they know you're *here*..."

"Who? The Germans?"

If the man heard the question, he gave no indication. "... *burn*... should've *burned*..." His voice descended into a groan.

Steadman was puzzled for a moment, then glanced down at the kerosene cans and flashed back to the corpses piled outside.

...as if for a funeral pyre...

...burn...

"Mother of God," he said quietly. Understanding gradually began to dawn, and with it came a tingle of fear; had this soldier been left here to destroy the remains? But to what end? To cover up a war crime? Or to make absolutely sure they were truly dead? For some reason he hadn't been able to go through with it – what had he seen that suicide was the only way out?

There was a scrabbling from beyond the doorway, a sound that turned Steadman's bowels to water. Both their heads snapped in its direction. The dying soldier suddenly became animated, shaking and crying ever more violently. Steadman stood and backed away, his eyes fixed on the tarpaulin-covered entrance. He tried to reason that it could be rats scurrying amongst the bodies, but couldn't even convince himself. He felt his breaths becoming shorter, his scalp prickle with sweat despite the chill. The revolver was slippery in his hand.

A low moan echoed outside; and then the sheeting bulged as if something was pushing against it, looking for a way in. Steadman attempted to swallow, the inside of his mouth like sandpaper, and raised the gun. He sensed a breeze brush against his face, but had seen nothing come through the doorway; he moved nearer, peering into the gloom.

"Show yourself," he demanded, his voice cracking; then yelled in fright as something grabbed his leg. He staggered, glanced down and recoiled in disgust: the upper half of a German soldier's torso was crawling across the floor, one hand clutched around his ankle. In its wake, like a snail's trail, it left a glistening smear of blood, painted there by the entrails emerging from its rapidly evacuating stomach cavity. Its head was upturned, its eyes glazed, its mouth open and emitting a tiny wail from the back of its throat. Immobilized with shock, Steadman could do nothing but stare as the creature puts its lips to his trouser leg and attempt to bite through it.

Blinking himself out of his paralysis, he roared in revulsion, kicked out at it and managed to loosen its grip; he stepped away and without thinking fired the gun, catching it in the shoulder. The impact knocked it back, but it was clearly still alive; it struggled to right itself like a turtle flipped onto its shell. Steadman moved closer in horrified fascination, raising the revolver for a better shot, then caught himself before he could pull the trigger. He'd never killed anything before, either on two legs or four, and yet here he was prepared to act without pause; this *creature*, as his mind had fixedly called it, was still a man. He had survived horrendous injuries, either through enormous willpower or some quirk of physiology that enabled the heart to still beat even as the veins and arteries spurted into empty air, and like the British soldier could not be long for this world. Did that give him the right to help usher him towards death?

The German was crawling in his direction once more. Clearly, despite the pain he must be in, he was not going to give up on Steadman as his objective. Steadman allowed him to draw closer, and dropped to his haunches.

"I cannot help you," he enunciated, wishing he could recall what little of the language he knew. He shook his head, holding up his hands. "*Nicht... gut...*"

The man didn't seem to understand, or even to hear him. Still he approached, whimpering like a whipped dog, his insides rasping against the wooden floor. He grasped Steadman's boot and started gnawing on it as if it were a bone; Steadman could feel his teeth attempting to penetrate the leather. Tears sprang in his eyes; he knew now that this was not one man desperately clinging onto life despite the ravages of his injuries. This was something else entirely, something beyond any kind of reasoning. He was no longer human, but the product of something... unholy. He shook himself free of the man's clutches, put the revolver to the back of his skull and squeezed his eyes shut at the same time as he squeezed the trigger. He winced at the bang, thinking: *forgive me*.

When he opened his eyes, the man was finally

motionless, the contents of his head spread out in a parabola around him. Steadman shivered uncontrollably, the gun trembling before him. He could not stay in this charnel pit a moment longer; better he took his chances on the battlefield or in a military cell than spend the night amongst this horror.

He moved towards the doorway, glancing back at the British soldier when he heard him cry out. "I'm sorry," he said, turning his head away.

Steadman pulled back the tarpaulin and bit down on a scream: the trench was alive. Where there was once dead stacked upon dead, shadows now shifted and slithered, a familiar wail carrying on the wind. He saw arms and hands clawing themselves free like the freshly buried rising from their graves. Dark figures wobbled as they stood and grew accustomed to their newfound resurrection; some were missing appendages, some emptied viscera at their feet the moment they were upright, but it didn't take them long for their heads to turn in his direction. He could see them sense him, almost as if they were sniffing the air and hearing the beat of a warm, living heart. They began to shuffle forward, tripping over one another, the trench a tangle of grasping limbs.

Steadman did not hesitate. He rushed back to the soldier, grabbed the kerosene cans and began to splash them through the entranceway at the approaching creatures. When all three cans were empty, he flung the lantern into the throng.

Instantly, the dark confines of the trench became an explosion of white and yellow light. The first of the figures were immediately immolated, man-sized candles awkwardly stumbling into those behind, the touch allowing the fire to spread. Thick black smoke began to billow into the air, and soon it was impossible to distinguish between the shapes being devoured by the wall of flame. For a moment, Steadman felt a small spark of hope; the inferno seemed to have halted them. But mere seconds later he saw that they were still coming, implacable and relentless, that ever-present moaning barely rising an octave. The ones at the front were shrivelled husks, turning to ash before his eyes, but they were replaced by others, unconcernedly treading on their fallen comrades as they surged forwards.

Steadman let loose a cry of frustration and fired at the nearest creature, blowing a puff of soot from its arm. There was no way out. He checked the chambers of the revolver and found he had three bullets left. That was at least some comfort.

He walked over to the British soldier and knelt beside him. He knew what Steadman intended and nodded slightly, his eyes pleading. Steadman embraced him and placed the gun barrel under his chin, offering a silent prayer before firing.

He sat down next to the body and surveyed the room, littered with the dead. His faith had instructed him that life was to be preserved at all costs – but that had been shattered. Death was preferable to the parody of life these creatures exhibited.

They were beginning to come through the doorway, shadows dancing on the walls as the flames flickered. They bumped into the table and chairs and bed, trying to find their way around, igniting fires as they did so.

He put the revolver in his mouth, tasting the oil. Funny: he had refused to be sacrificed to the war, made the choice of life over death, and yet here was preparing to offer himself up to Purgatory. This seemed the lesser of two evils; whatever those things were – and the Army was aware of them, that was plainly evident – he guessed that if they took him, he would end up in a far, far worse place. Better this way; better a sinner than a victim of the Devil's works.

Steadman turned his head and looked up at a map of Europe on the wall, which was starting to smoulder and blacken as the creatures brushed past. Maybe this is the Apocalypse, he thought as his finger tightened on the trigger. Maybe this is the beginning of the end.

If they're the future... God help the living.

Dreams of Inan

A KIND OF PEACE

Andy Boot

Price: £6.99 ★ ISBN: 1-905437-02-1

Price: $7.99 ★ ISBN 13: 978-1-905437-02-3

THE AFTERBLIGHT CHRONICLES

The CULLED

Simon Spurrier

Price: £6.99 ★ ISBN: 1-905437-01-3

Price: $7.99 ★ ISBN 13: 978-1-905437-01-6

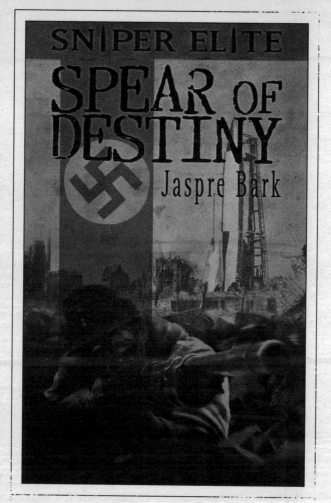

Price: £6.99 ★ ISBN: 1-905437-04-8

Price: $7.99 ★ ISBN 13: 978-1-905437-04-7

Abaddon Books

WWW.ABADDONBOOKS.COM